A SHORT HISTORY OF RICHARD KLINE

AMANDA LOHREY

A SHORT HISTORY OF RICHARD KLINE

Black Inc.

Published by Black Inc.,
an imprint of Schwartz Publishing Pty Ltd
37–39 Langridge Street
Collingwood VIC 3066 Australia
email: enquiries@blackincbooks.com
www.blackincbooks.com

The National Library of Australia Cataloguing-in-Publication entry:

Lohrey, Amanda, author.
A short history of Richard Kline / Amanda Lohrey.
9781863957182 (paperback)
9781925203042 (ebook)
Middle aged men – Fiction.
A823.3

Printed in Australia by Griffin Press. The paper this book is printed on is certified
against the Forest Stewardship Council® Standards. Griffin Press holds FSC chain
of custody certification SGS-COC-005088. FSC promotes environmentally responsible,
socially beneficial and economically viable management of the world's forests.

This project has been assisted by the Australian Government through the
Australia Council for the Arts, its arts funding and advisory body.

All our scientific and philosophic ideals are altars to unknown gods.

WILLIAM JAMES, *Varieties of Religious Experience*

I set down this memoir in order to record a strange event that intervened in my life at the age of forty-two. I say 'intervened' because that's how it seemed at the time, as if it came out of nowhere and without warning, but I see now that the animating spirit of the event had been with me from the very beginning; it was simply that I had not known how to recognise it. It was as if I were an arrow shot out at birth towards a distant target that I could not see, but that I was destined, at the moment of impact, to strike with the full force of my being.

home

Until I met her, I confess that for most of my life I was bored. It's an unattractive word, boredom, and I flinch from it now, but for a long time it was the only word I could summon to describe my condition. Today I would say that for much of my life I suffered from an apprehension of lack, but one that I found difficult to put into words. In essence it consisted of a feeling that nothing was ever quite right; something was always missing.

How many of us have been dismayed by that feeling? And ashamed of it at those very moments when we ought to feel happy? We ask ourselves: what is the flaw in our being that gives rise to this discontent?

In my case the effect of it was to create a sense of detachment, because if something was missing, then all action must ultimately prove to be futile.

And this was not a conclusion reached by my mature self; it was something I experienced even as a boy. There were days when I brooded on it, and if I as a youth had been taken to a therapist I might have been diagnosed as suffering from depression, except that I was neither listless nor withdrawn. I was an energetic child, reckless even, and what I experienced was more like a baffled disappointment.

As I grew older I began to reflect. What *was* this lack, this something missing? And how did I know it was missing if I didn't know what *it* was? Did others feel its absence or was it only me? And if the latter, where had I acquired this pathology? And then it occurred to me that there was a logic at work here: if there was lack, it followed there must somewhere be fullness. But how would this fullness, were I ever to find it, manifest itself? What would it look like? Was there a flaw in creation such that it didn't exist? Or was it at the core of some cruel joke: that it did exist but could never be found?

My parents considered me difficult; I was prickly and wilful. Certainly my mother thought so. One year when I came home after spending the summer at my uncle's farm, less than a day had passed before Ann snapped at me in exasperation, 'I'd forgotten how you always have to have your own way.' And then, with one of her lengthy sighs, 'Why can't you be more like your brother?'

Yes, why couldn't I? For once I agreed with her. Gareth was four years older and the good-natured one. Gareth had a ready smile, along with a gift for taking the world on trust, and I loved him for it. It was Gareth who seemed at ease in any situation, who shone with a casual grace that drew everyone into his orbit. As for my sister, Jane, she too appeared to be uncomplicated. I, on the other hand, was 'picky', and in my mother's eyes the most sullen and self-absorbed of her three children. 'That's Richard for you,' she'd say, 'never satisfied with his lot. Why can't you just be grateful for what you've got?' This as I sulked over or commented acidly on some tedious family outing.

As a consequence, the word 'gratitude' began to take on a detestable colouring. Gratitude said mediocrity, said also complacency

4

and self-deception. Gratitude was a euphemism for conformity and resignation; at least, that was my intellectual position. Emotionally it ate away at me, this idea that I was difficult and ungrateful. It made me feel inadequate, at odds with the world. I was too restless, my parents said, too critical. I, on the other hand, wondered why adults seemed to be so easily pleased.

I could cite many instances here but will give only one, my First Communion. My parents made a great fuss, but for me it was a non-event. The priest droned on, the hymns were solemn, the cathedral intimidating and gloomy. Afterwards we walked in quiet orderly lines to the school and sat down in the boarders' dining room to a communion feast of dry sandwiches and sickly pink cordial. I remember looking up at the big clock on the wall, where the minutes limped on in silence, while behind us the nuns patrolled the aisles, or stood like sentries, their black arms folded across their chests.

Something momentous was supposed to have happened, but what? That night, in bed, I asked myself if I felt any different. I searched for signs but there were none. I was the same, and the world was the same.

My father, Ned, was an engineer and a devotee of the slide-rule. He was a nominal Catholic but wore his religion lightly, like a protective outer garment between him and the metaphysical weather. I suspected he went to church to please my mother; at heart he was a complacent rationalist whose tone and demeanour managed to insinuate that if his children could not reason their way through to sense, then it was simply a question of time before all the mysteries would be solved by science and the riddle of the cosmos unravelled. My mother's response to every dilemma was an arsenal of clichés – 'Tomorrow's another day'; 'You can only do your best'; 'Time will tell' – any one of which could incite me to a savage rudeness.

One thing I did know: at the heart of Nature was a mysterious force, and that force was the ground of any possible perfection, a promise both of fruition and of annihilation. How did I know this? From those moments of clarity that sometimes came to me as a child, days when we camped beside a remote beach and I floated on my back in the ocean, the water a pale, glassy green, the sky a hazy infinity. Or the time when I was nine years old and walking with my father in the vicinity of an old copper mine. We were trekking along the pebbly rim of a barren hill that had been denuded by sulphur waste, and the only growth we could see was a small bush in the distance, sprung to life on a rocky out-crop. The outcrop had no rail and Ned called to me, 'Stay away from the edge.' But I ran to the bush and looked down into its centre, into the thick cluster of its stems, its dense whorls of un-curling leaf. What I saw there was perfect symmetry, and that I was a part of it. For a moment I disappeared, and in that moment I was free.

But there were other, darker times. Some nights, unable to sleep, I sat up in bed and gazed out my attic window at the stars. Then I felt a cold, shivery awe at the great maw of the sky; the stars blinked into a black void and I felt my own inconsequence. I was someone who didn't matter. No-one mattered. It was terrifying and I curled up in my bed and wept from fear and desolation. But then, on the cusp of sleep, I experienced a strange cognition, an uncanny feeling of nostalgia. It felt like homesickness, but for what? I was living at home, had lived in the same house since I was born. Still, I sensed that in the space between sleeping and waking there was another realm of being, and in that surreal country, both strange and familiar, lay my true home. But where *was* that place, and how could I get there? Sometimes when I was alone in the bush behind my uncle's farm I felt that same nostalgia well up in me, a sweet sadness, a desire to merge, to know again what I had been separated out from.

But my most intense experience of it as a boy came after masturbating: first the rush, then the sense of falling away, the fleeting apprehension of a lost Eden.

Wherever that feeling came from, by the time I was twelve it had gone. It was then that death came to me, not as an idea but as a reality. And it wasn't that anyone close to me died, it was just that suddenly I *knew*. I knew that death was one day going to ambush me, and that it might even be just around the corner. Life was both unspeakably precious and at the same time utterly futile. And if that was the case, why was I born? Why did humans have such powerful minds? Why did *I* have a mind if it could not save me?

At the age of thirteen the pain of the death paradox drove me into absurd behaviours. If everything was precious – and it must be because otherwise there was only waste – then even something as mundane as electric light must be precious. I calculated the amount of light needed to illuminate a dark room and the number of light bulbs that could be dispensed with. I remonstrated with my mother over her profligacy and the array of table lamps she would switch on at night to create a 'mood'. Then I would prowl the house, turning off any lights I considered unnecessary.

Today I would be diagnosed as suffering from an obsessive-compulsive disorder and perhaps given a pill, but my earnest attention to light switches proved to be no more than a phase, a brief experiment in my war with death. As abruptly as I had initiated this practice, suddenly one day I abandoned it. And this was more or less the pattern of my early life, staying intently and resentfully within the boundary of the normal, while feeling for most of the time that I lived just outside it.

~

All through my adolescence I saw an inherent darkness in things, layer upon layer, and on some days felt submerged in it. I bled out into the world and the world bled into me. I can recall moments of disassociation from my body when I would be crossing the road at night and suddenly see my own corpse stretched out on the bitumen. But I knew these glimpses were not premonitions, not prophetic of things to come. They were hauntings from some dark world of the psyche where a sense of evil was at times palpable, though this was not, I knew, the Devil (what a joke) but something infinitely more subtle. And it seemed to me that you could read this scientifically as a physics we didn't yet understand, a terrible warp in the field, or a leakage of bile on the surface of things, because sometimes I could feel it, like a coating on the skin or a thin membrane across the eyes.

'Richard thinks too much,' my mother liked to say, and the very tone of her voice infuriated me, though this was, in a way, true. It seemed to me that my brother didn't think much at all, he simply *acted*, with an instinct that appeared never to fail him. When I prolonged an argument with Ann and Ned over the dinner table, Gareth would get up, push his chair back and give me a look of exasperation mixed with affection, a look I would pretend not to notice. But inwardly I felt chastened, though not for long, and certainly not by my mother's verdict, for already I knew from experience that what is a weakness is also a strength, and while there were times when I would think myself into a black hole, I could with some effort think – rationalise – myself out of it, at least in relation to my own discontent. Other people's distress was something else. It was here that logic failed me. It could not answer the simplest of questions: why did people suffer?

I recall one incident that aroused me to an almost animal fury and shame. I attended a party for the sixteenth birthday of a schoolfriend, Glenn. Just after eleven Glenn's mother brought in the cake, and as we gathered around the supper table Glenn's drunken father took exception to a careless remark by Glenn and with methodical rage proceeded to beat his son senseless. The heavy fruit cake slid onto the carpet with a thud, Glenn's blood sprayed across the white tablecloth, his mother screamed and broken glass scattered at our feet. His sister knelt in a pool of sticky liquid and held Glenn's head up from the floor while we, his friends, froze like wooden trolls, stranded in a scene of intimate carnage.

At last there seemed nothing for it but to slouch off down the steep driveway, and though it was cold I did not accept the offer of a lift and chose instead to walk the several kilometres home, breathless with impotent fury.

Never had I witnessed such a criminal humiliation. I had seen boys bash one another, but this was different, and when at last I reached the park opposite my house I stopped and drove my fist repeatedly into a tree until the pain blurred all thought.

When finally I let myself in through the front door, my father was lying on the couch in front of the late movie.

'How was the party?' Ned asked.

I held my hand behind my back to conceal my bloodied knuckles and bounded up the stairs. 'The party was shit.'

I found that while I could bear another's pain, I could not bear their humiliation, and I wondered: did this mean I was weak? Once, driving home with Gareth, I saw the victims of a car smash laid out on the road, and, although this was distressing, there was not the same sense of something sacred having been violated as when one human being abused another. Confronted by cruelty, only my imagination kept me from imploding. In my head I would fantasise a series of righteous murders, night after night, wherein my powerlessness was annulled, and justice, however crude, was done. Who was God that he permitted such injustice? God should be ashamed.

And so if I could not have a just god I would have no god at all. Instead I turned to science. My heroes were J. Robert Oppenheimer and Edward Teller, and in their feats I saw the glamour of true knowing as opposed to blind superstition. My father, I saw, was a mere functionary, a fixer, but the lives of these men were fables of the possible. Teller was the smartest of them all and perhaps, I explained to Gareth, the smartest man ever born. More than that, he was a knight in scientific armour, a man with a mission. The Nazis had killed his parents and his sister, and Teller wanted to build the hydrogen bomb to kill them in return. It was the perfect emotional equation. This was the work of the true superman, solving the problems of the universe while everyone else was asleep.

I read a lot then, read with an urgency that was one part anxiety, one part impatience and two parts will and determination. Since my all-consuming aim was to find the meaning of life, I would take a book and strip it of what its author had to say. I would sit, or lie awkwardly on my bed, pen in hand so that I might underline important or revealing phrases.

Some books spoke directly to my heart: when I was seventeen, one of my teachers, a florid self-dramatising hippie called Tess, gave me a copy of Hermann Hesse's *Siddhartha*. I liked Tess: she had good legs and her eyes sang at me. One morning at the end of a History class she called me back from the door and, after rummaging in her big embroidered shoulder bag, produced a slim paperback.

'It's not homework,' she said. 'Keep it and read it when the mood strikes you.'

I read it at once, flattered by the implied comparison. It was easy enough while reading *Siddhartha* to imagine myself as a young prince, 'strong, handsome, supple-limbed'; a boy with 'fine, ardent thoughts'. Most of all, I identified with Siddhartha's unhappiness: '. . . there was yet no joy in his own heart. Dreams and restless thoughts came flowing to him from the river, from the twinkling stars at night, from the sun's melting rays.' There was ritual, Siddhartha perceived, and there was knowledge, but they did nothing to 'relieve the distressed heart'.

Meanwhile my own teachers, just like Siddhartha's teachers, 'poured the sum total of their knowledge into his waiting vessel; and the vessel was not full . . .'

In that phrase, *the vessel was not full*, I found consolation; found deep reassurance that my own state of discontent was not some mental leprosy that would one day corrode me into madness. If it was good enough for Siddhartha, it was good enough for me. It was irrelevant that he was brown-skinned, of royal blood and spoke in a foreign tongue. These were the superficial trappings of mere embodiment, and at its core my adolescent ego was without race or colour and knew only its own yearning, its hunger for the meeting of like minds, for acknowledgment and validation. Yes, I am not alone in how I feel; *this is how it really is.*

Of course, the body made urgent claims, and there were other distractions, mostly girls, but more often than not the feminine compounded my problem by being elusive and unknowable. There were many silent infatuations, all with a common pattern. I would begin by feeling dizzy and sick at the very sight of Her and six months later would wonder what I had seen in her. My pining would seem pathetic and absurd, but it would not prevent me succumbing again.

So many girls had that delicate beauty that left you speechless in their presence. It made you giddy, so that you wanted to throw yourself at their feet in abject worship. Others were like sleek, pampered pets. One in particular, the daughter of one of my mother's tennis friends, had a molten, animal sensuality, a complacency of being that mesmerised me. I thought of this girl every night for months. It was inconceivable that such a creature could suffer even a moment of self-doubt. And this idea was an affront to me: that she should possess something I lacked; that she should have *unearned* access to a mysterious source of well-being. That she should possess this . . . this essential thing.

It produced many dark fantasies that are better left undocumented here.

~

At nineteen I left home. I told my father I wanted to study theoretical physics.

'Why?' Ned asked.

'Because,' I replied, 'only physics can unravel the riddle of the universe.'

Ned shook his head and stated categorically that I was making a bad decision, that I would not be able to support myself. In this city there were taxi drivers with physics degrees, and he wanted no child of his to embark on such an unreliable profession. 'Look,' he said, 'if you want to study physics, get an engineering degree.'

But I had no desire to be an engineer, a fixer, a manager of the known. Instead, with a defiant sense of chancing my luck, I enrolled in an Arts degree, majoring in pure mathematics and medieval history.

Ned was furious. It was the first time I had seen him not just angry but enraged. There was more than one shouting match, but I had a scholarship and I was prepared to get casual work if I had to. It was time to leave home.

For the first two years of my studies I lived in a run-down student terrace in Newtown with mattresses on the floor and an outside dunny. At night and into the early morning I served watered-down spirits from behind the bar of the Purple Parrot, a louche nightclub in King Street. The licensee of the Parrot was a middle-aged Londoner known as Coop who had served with the British SAS, or at least that's what he told the staff, his 'boys'.

I was fascinated by Coop, for he was the opposite of my father: exotic and venal, a pugnacious man, tall and thickset with a bald head, heavy jowls and a watery, myopic stare. He drank too much and could be extremely rude, but in his good moods he was charming. And he seemed to like me. 'Hello, old dear,' he'd say when I arrived for work, and he would pat me on the shoulder as if I were a favourite nephew. 'I've got you sussed,' he'd say, 'you're smarter than the others.' Sometimes after closing he would go into the kitchen and cook for the staff, and his food was always better than the chef's. It had a delicacy that was surprising. But when roused he could be vicious and would brawl with the lethal economy of the soldier he once was.

As I got to know Coop I saw that he was neither a good man nor a bad one; he could be rude, savage and sadistic, yet he could also be generous and at times sentimental. When sober he treated the club's patrons with elaborate courtesy, but when drunk he would harass them out of the club and shut the doors. Then he would order his 'boys' to open some French reds and we would sit around while he reminisced about his army days. In those early morning hours a certain mood would come over him, an uncanny melancholy threaded through with menace.

Or, if he was in a roistering mood, we would move on to the small apartment he kept in Glebe for his all-night parties, where occasionally he would orchestrate a live sex performance. Here he kept a riding crop mounted on the wall, and it was no mere ornament since what he wanted most was to be beaten and humiliated. More than once I wandered into the lavatory for a leak only to stumble over Coop, down on his knees and pleading with some startled young woman, perched on the bowl with her knickers around her ankles, to urinate on him. Not that he was ever fazed at my intrusion. 'Hello, old dear,' he'd say, and, gazing up at the girl looming above him, he would smile, beatifically. 'All I want is for her to piss on me. It's not much to ask, is it?' Then he would sigh. 'Isn't she beautiful?' They were all beautiful.

After I graduated I looked around and thought: what now? On the recommendation of the father of a friend I joined an oil company as a trainee manager and worked for eighteen months in a state of casual boredom. One of my achievements was to reduce the number of forms used in the personnel section from nineteen to three. For this I was commended as a 'thinker'. Though I liked the men I worked with, the job demanded too little of me. After six months I enrolled in intensive night classes in the new science of computing and found I was a natural. I was one of the first. Within two years I was working for a new start-up company in Chatswood.

By then I had moved on from the Parrot. I couldn't be bothered with its self-conscious wickedness. It was the striving to be wicked, the desperate contrivance of it, that bored me, not sex itself. I do not want to give the wrong impression here, since there was never a time in my youth when I wasn't consumed by the intensity of my sexual cravings. But what I sought was a loss of self that blotted out the critical intellect, not sharpened it – something to switch off the thinking mind.

And it was my experience that this could never be contrived, that it came at you unexpectedly and often from the most unlikely places; could spring out of the mundane like a scarlet flower blooming through a crack in a stone wall. What I wanted was to lose myself in the moment, to be in a place so utterly right that all sense of separation would fall away. I wanted more than sex, I wanted communion, but this 'wanting' was more in the thinking than in the living, and my relationships with women were erratic. I lost ily; needed to be able to do what I liked on impulse without insulting anyone; was not one of those young men who was prepared to settle gratefully into an early marriage, de facto or otherwise. Sometimes the idea of love – love that would hold me captive and abject – was terrifying.

Only sex could blot out my painful awareness of separation, and the more reckless, the better. There was an affair with an older married woman that led to me being king-hit at a party in Bondi. An irate husband appeared on the scene and suddenly I had an inkling of how callow I was, that some people were playing for higher stakes, that their whole world was in the balance, whereas I was just looking for illicit kicks, a kind of hit-and-run fix. And it could be good, that fix, it could be *very* good: purging, cathartic. Afterwards you felt a lightness of being, like all your blood had been run through a white-hot crystal and cleansed of its dross. Sometimes at the point of orgasm I thought the rush would consume me forever.

By then I was in my mid-twenties and already beginning to feel a slight decline in my physical powers. One evening, while drinking with an old schoolfriend, I was induced to take up jogging, persuaded that it could give me an endorphin high. In fact, after only a few weeks it gave me a sprained ankle, but the pack I jogged with had a drink once a week in a karaoke bar, and at one of these sessions I encountered Jo Chalmers.

The thing that first attracted me to Jo was her voice: warm, and spliced with a wry humour. She was the only person I had seen who could sing karaoke and look natural, neither vain nor awkward. She was there with a group from work, and after she sang I went over, three parts shot, and asked her out. 'Call me in the morning when you're sober,' she said. And I did.

We lived together for four years, and although we never married I still think of her as my first wife. The commitment is the same, whatever they tell you, and the break just as hard. To be fair to Jo, for much of the time I was with her I was distracted; spent long hours at work and assumed she would understand. Her own work was demanding too, and there were weeks when we talked for longer on the phone than we did in our small apartment. And maybe it was her voice I fell in love with: just listening to her sing in the shower could lift my spirits. But best of all I liked to hear her sing in the car when we went on long trips together, often to Canberra to visit her parents. And together up and down the Hume Highway we would work our way through hits from the sixties and seventies to which Jo always knew the words, crazy songs like 'Li'l Red Riding Hood', and then we would howl all along the freeway, and laugh until we were light-headed and veering into the white line.

When other people clowned they were embarrassing; when Jo was silly she enlarged, she broke open the frame. At her best she had a gift for joyful trivia that could short-circuit my analytical logic, my restless discontent. But when she was angry her anger seethed like volcanic lava trapped beneath tectonic plates, and then she would withdraw from me, and I from her, and we would play games with one another, serious war-like manoeuvres carried out on a plane of mute hostility until we both were locked into a silence that neither could find a way out of. As time went on, our life together evolved into painful periods of unspoken resentment, punctuated by increasingly lukewarm periods of truce.

And all through this time I continued to feel that strange blend of passion and detachment, of yearning and apathy, which made nonsense of the world beyond the strict, organising logic of my work. There were days when I felt an electrifying spark propel me through the day, but then there were days when everything seemed hollow, a cheerless merry-go-round, and it was an immense effort to get out of bed. Though many people thought of me as a workaholic, as obsessive, it was as if the system had crashed and I would have to lie prone on my back and run the instructions through my head: 'Now get up, then have a shower, then have some breakfast. Don't skip it, you'll regret it later. Then walk to the train, take your time if you have to, if you're late it won't matter, just get there, one step at a time . . .' After half an hour of lying there, rehearsing the moves in my head, talking myself into it, finally I would throw back the covers. Sometimes, just occasionally, I would sink back and plead a virus, but mostly I would get up and work my way through the program. And by mid-morning it would be okay, which is not to say that by the next morning the malaise wouldn't have re-settled over me, like fog descending in the night, and I would have to arc up the program again. And this could go on for days or, in a bad period, weeks. And no-one knew. Jo would just remark on me being 'moody' or 'sluggish' and make some crack about getting more exercise.

I could only have explained it then by saying that I in which the battery had gone flat. And it was true that simple things could recharge it for a while: a book; a walk in the bush; a swim. But there were whole weeks when I felt oppressed by the sheer ordinariness of life, its mindless repetition. Birth, death, decay, birth, death . . .

This was the pattern of my being. I had always oscillated between feelings of grandiosity (I deserved better) and phases of dejection (I deserved nothing) but now, in my late twenties, the periods of brooding grew longer. In combative moods I told myself that it was life that was inadequate, not me. It was life that was never quite good enough.

And then one day I had a seminal experience.

The company I worked for was one of the earliest to pick up on the faddish new corporate training methods, a whole lot of slick guff about team-building. Suddenly there was money for the new psychology and everybody was out to gain an edge.

It was nine-thirty on a wet Wednesday morning. Outside, the late summer rain was being blown onto the smoky glass windows of our company conference room, while inside, the members of my section were being solemnly addressed by a smooth young motivation counsellor called Drake.

Drake was not much older than me but full of a kind of bland certainty, worn like a sheer outer skin. He was so neat, so finely pressed, that it was hard to take him seriously; he looked like one of those square-jawed men in a David Jones catalogue, whose affectedly casual demeanour only makes them look studied and unnatural. And while he talked constantly of dynamism, everything about him suggested a stiff calculation, not least his repetition of the phrase 'in my humble opinion'. There were the usual accoutrements of the lecture: a whiteboard, a thick purple marker, a litany of trite phrases intoned as if they were the Book of Revelation revised.

In the *global* era, Drake announced, the old hierarchies would no longer apply. Management styles must change, but first there must be openness and trust. In order to develop openness and trust, team members must find a way to bond. In order to bond, they needed to put their lives in each other's hands. They needed to put sinew and bone and muscle *on the line*.

On the line? On what line? Well, on a line of thin nylon cord, as it turned out. At the end of the morning session Drake announced that phase two of the program was a day-long jag of abseiling.

Strictly voluntary, of course.

~

It was just after four on a Sunday afternoon in late March when the minibus delivered us to the door of our hotel in the Blue Mountains, a rambling colonial summer home with long enclosed verandahs that suggested secretiveness and a lazy, rich seclusion. In the evening, before dinner, we gathered in the bar, a narrow room lined with red velvet, and there, cossetted by the warmth of an open fire, we drank and joked about sudden death.

'It's the one thing that even serious rock-climbers fear,' said Greg, an earnest member of my own project team, 'because you are totally dependent on the rope. When death occurs on a climb, it's almost always in the abseiling phase.'

'Yeah, but abseiling conditions on a rock climb are totally different from what we're going to do,' said Karen. 'Greg is just trying to scare the shit out of us.'

One of the group, Phil, had done it before.

'What's it like?' Melanie asked him. Melanie was one of the company's auditors. She had been reluctant to come in the first place but had allowed herself to be teased into it by her supervisor.

'The further down you go,' Phil remarked, taciturnly, 'the thinner the rope looks.'

After the meal, half-tanked and heavy-lidded, we were ushered into a small seminar room. Here we were addressed by a guy called Dave, abseiling expert and leader of the team of handlers who were to take us over the drop the next day. Dave and his crew were all hardened climbers, a kind of outdoor priesthood for whom this kind of corporate play was their bread and butter. They might not believe in it for a minute but it paid them enough to spend half their year on the slopes of the Himalayas, or scaling some forbidden mountain in the Javanese archipelago. And I wondered why they were drawn to extreme risk. Were they nerveless optimists who knew no fear, or was it fear itself that drove them on in meaningless conquest?

Dave was in his mid-thirties, raw-boned with a shaved head and an earring. He had that taut, wiry look that outdoor types seemed to develop, but he was an appealing character, quiet and low-key.

Unlike Drake, he had a way of talking that was surprisingly poetic; even now I can recall some of Dave's talk. 'You have to remember that the body doesn't expect to be standing on the edge of a deep ravine looking down into space,' he said. 'The body expects to feel solid earth under its feet, because that's what Nature intended. The body has its comfort zone and it doesn't always like to have it tested.'

And we all sat there, like novice altar boys, and soaked it up.

The following morning was warm and the late autumn sun shone through the windows of the dining room. At least, we told ourselves, we would not have to deal with discouraging weather. At breakfast there were some who tried to keep up the sardonic banter of the evening before but by the time we boarded the minibus and were halfway to our destination the tension had begun to have a dull, flattening effect.

The bus delivered us to the foot of a cliff, where one of the trainers, Julian, was waiting to escort us up a rocky track. It was a long and tiring walk, and it gave us even more time to contemplate what we were about to do.

'Why do we have to walk up first?' asked Angus, overweight and puffing. 'Why couldn't we just drive to the top?'

'So they can scare the living daylights out of us,' said Ivo, another member of my project team. 'They have to get some fun out of this too.'

By the time we arrived at the cliff-top, Dave and another of the handlers, Ingrid, were waiting for us on a narrow ledge of rock that jutted out over the canyon below. I remember the brightness of the light, so bright the scene looked almost two-dimensional, as if painted on canvas, and I recall even now how the rock ledge was bare, save for a stunted, wind-blasted banksia, a kind of bush bonsai, its foliage bent permanently to one side.

Ingrid and Julian stood about in artificially languid poses while Dave explained the drill. It soon became clear that the only on-site preparation we were to get was a five-minute talk by Dave in which he explained the harness, how the ropes were secured and the essentials of the technique that would, if followed correctly, get us to the bottom without turning upside down, or have us spinning hopelessly in midair, not to mention swinging face-first into a wall of yellow rock.

Phil was the first to go down, because he'd done it before, and his descent went without mishap. Then Melanie stepped forward nervously and I observed the subtle change in Dave's demeanour, the way in which, while adjusting Melanie's harness and explaining how the rope worked, he stood directly between her and the edge so that she was unable to look down over the drop. But at the point where he eased her backwards and positioned her so that her heels hung over the ledge, Melanie threw an untimely glance over her left shoulder at the yawning chasm now only inches from her expensive new walking boots, and her body froze. Suddenly she was hyperventilating, and – jerking forward – she bolted like an agitated puppet towards the scrub, the rope trailing behind her in an abject tail until she reached the first line of heath. There she stopped, chest heaving, and vomited into a bush.

Dave moved across to comfort her, indicating with a nod of the head that Julian should take over at the edge.

Julian set about the work of rigging up a second harness. 'Who's next?' he asked, and I stepped forward.

The preliminaries were methodical, almost monosyllabic, and as I went about the business of fastening my helmet and adjusting a harness which dug uncomfortably into my crotch, I felt surprisingly calm. At what point, I wondered, would the adrenaline kick in? There was no time to offer a word or even a grimace of commiseration to Melanie as I stood taking in Julian's instructions, nodding and repeating the key phrases of Julian's drill, especially the bit about keeping your legs straight as you made your descent, otherwise you would fly-face first into the rock wall of the cliff.

Finally, I was set, heels hanging over the edge.

'Are you right?' asked Julian.

I nodded.

'Are you okay now? Are you ready?'

I nodded again.

'Go.'

The descent might almost have been routine, had it not been for my epiphany. Not that it was a true epiphany, more like the photographic negative of one, and it was this. Halfway down, hanging from a fine nylon cable, I realised that I was bored. This was such a surprising thought that I froze, legs braced against the ochre rock.

After some time – it couldn't have been long – Julian leaned over the edge, his hands cupped over his mouth, and shouted, 'Are you okay?'

Yes, I was okay, whatever that meant (but then again, maybe I wasn't, though not for any reason Julian might imagine). How tedious all this was. Yes, I was *okay*, I knew I was not making a fool of myself, but so what? That was the question: *so what*? Here I was, swinging over one of the great escarpments of one of the great mountain ranges in the southern hemisphere, and realising, with the acid clarity that only crystalline sunlight and a perfect blue sky could induce, that I was, at that moment, *bored*.

How could this possibly be? I could hear someone shouting at me from above, a column of words cascading down into the canyon, but I was too distracted to take it in, too absorbed in the revelation of the moment. There was something wrong here. Clearly I should be having one of two reactions. Either I should be consumed by excitement, the sheer thrill of it, or I should be terrified, all sweaty palms and a desperate anxiety to feel my feet on solid earth. Either way, I should be pumping adrenaline at a million miles a minute. But no, here I was, a young man, reasonably fit, with a mild hangover and a shocking indifference.

And then I saw myself, as if from a great height, legs braced against the cliff-face, and the thought came to me: I am a pendulum, a stuck pendulum. And with that, I pushed off again from the rock.

On the ride back to the lodge I sat next to Melanie, by now calm but morose about her failure to make the descent. Making as light of it as I could, I attempted to console her. It was all a silly game and meant nothing. She was one of the best people I had worked with in an office: constructive, diplomatic, quietly efficient and an A-grade team worker (all of which was true). Being able to abseil meant you had a head for heights, that's all, and the rest was mumbo-jumbo. These consultants were making a small fortune coming up with new gimmicks that were just glorified kids' games.

'You're so calm, Rick,' she kept saying, 'you're so good under pressure.'

No, I'm not, I thought. There's something wrong with me. It's just that I know how to hide it.

Back at the lodge we trooped upstairs to shower and change for dinner. In my room I went robotically through the motions and stood for a long time under the shower, resting my forehead against its opaque Perspex enclosure. Spacey. Light-headed. I knew the others would begin to assemble soon in the bar downstairs, and right now I couldn't face it, all that alcoholic banter, the way everything had to be made into a joke.

It was just after six when I emerged into the front garden with the intention of going for a walk. Beside the hotel was a narrow bush track that, according to the signpost, led to a lookout over the Jamison Valley. It was only a short distance through a thicket of banksias and within minutes I was on a precipitous rock platform, leaning against a steel fence at waist height and looking out over the great purple maze of ridges and canyons. At dusk the grandeur of it was somehow soothing, the way it fell down into infinity below. All around me the yellow line of sandstone cliffs caught the fire of the setting sun so that they shone with a soft orange gold, and for a few minutes I stood, breathing deeply, inhaling the smell of eucalypts and the spicy scent of the bush. The shadows were deepening and the air had the first hint of chill. I thought of how easy it would be to jump. If you were going to kill yourself, this was the place to come; you would fall through the muted glow of sunset, your body absorbed secretively into the dense rainforest below. It would be a more poetic death than most, and to those left behind, morally inconclusive, since they could never be sure that you hadn't blacked out or, in a moment of absentmindedness, slipped into the drop.

For a long time I stood there, gazing down into the blurred blue haze of eucalypt and mountain ash, and then I heard a dry, *quarking* sound above my head. *Quark, quark, quark*, it went, sly and insistent. I looked up, expecting to see crows, but there over the darkening escarpment were two cockatoos, soaring high above the canyon, their wings fully extended, two fluid white forms outlined against the charcoal sky.

And then suddenly it was dark, and I turned back.

In the dining room the others were in the early stages of an elaborate banquet. All through dinner they traded rowdy stories of their bravado, and teased Melanie, who by now was sheepish but cheerful. Some went to bed early, exhausted. The stayers returned to the red-velvet womb of the bar and drank themselves into a stupor.

~

When I tried to explain to Jo how I had felt, braced against the cliff-face, she laughed at me. It was the evening I arrived home and she was sitting in front of the mirror, brushing her hair.

'You're always hard to please,' she said, tartly. And then, seeing how troubled I was, she earnestly attempted to psychologise my ennui into something else. 'You were just scared out of your brain, Rick, but your pride wouldn't allow you to admit it. So you closed down and pretended to yourself that you were bored.'

Good try, I thought, but the fact was I had felt no fear. I knew what fear was and had no problem admitting to it – not to her, anyway. But it simply hadn't been there. But nor had I felt exhilaration. *And why not?* Nothing in the logic of my personal universe could account for it. I had hung over one of the most beautiful valleys in the world and felt indifferent. Here it was again, that question: what was my *lack*?

This fugue, this inverse epiphany on the cliff-face, was something that wouldn't go away. For days I brooded on it, until Jo became exasperated.

'Come on, Rick,' she said, 'of all the things in your life, this is a minor thing.'

What could I say? Objectively assessed, in the wider scale of things, it might be a minor thing. But for me, looking out from the knot of complication that represented my thinking self, for some inexplicable reason it was *the* thing. At night just before sleep, the image of my body as a stuck pendulum kept coming back to haunt me.

~

When finally Jo and I agreed to separate, the feeling of loss was greater than I could have imagined. It ambushed me almost immediately. I expected relief, a surcease of pain, as the poets had it, and instead felt instantly bereft, full of a hazy, unfocused sense of failure. When I came home to my apartment at night the feeling of emptiness, of energy withdrawn, was unnerving. I would sit out on the small balcony and brood on her good points: her loyalty, her honesty, her energy . . . but most of all her voice. At odd moments I would hear snatches of her singing around the house . . . in the shower, in the kitchen, in the car. It was uncanny. Once I had liked to read and resented her chattering, her interruptions; now I couldn't bear to open a book. It reminded me that I was alone. And yet I had sought this, had fantasised this . . . this freedom.

My first impulse was to go on a scarifyingly self-centred binge. If sex couldn't save me, it could certainly console me: the closeness of another body, the annihilation of taboo. One was a positive force, the other negative, but I needed both, the light and the dark, so that some dark matter could be burned off in the body's fires. The danger was that if you burned too intensely and for too long, you burned out. I knew this but thought I could finesse the odds. I had it under control. I told myself that I wasn't by nature obsessive. Or was I?

One night a friend came around to announce that he had split with his wife. We sat hunched over the low coffee table, drinking our way through a bottle of Bundy until he began to cry. As I watched his body crumple, shoulders heaving into a boneless, watery hump, I struggled with a rush of contradictory feelings: on the one hand, disgust, and on the other, awe. I couldn't bear to see any man in that state; it made my skin go cold. And yet when he had gone, I found myself reflecting on this scene with a kind of furtive envy. Yes, *envy*. I couldn't remember the last time I had cried. I was incapable of it.

All through my relationship with Jo I had asked myself if I loved her, deciding in the end that I didn't know what love was. There was a comfort zone, sexual and social, and there was pride, not least in possession. And then there was that deep yearning to lose yourself in someone, or *something*, that had called to me for years. But what Jo and I had between us, was that love? My intuition told me it was not. Why, then, was I hit so hard by separation? Where would I find union? Was it possible? I was haunted by the idea that I would never find a soulmate; that no-one would ever truly understand me. I heard myself bleating: my wife doesn't understand me. And then I wondered why I could never have a thought, or experience an emotion, without some little voice in my head commenting on it at the same time. Who or what was this other self that stood back and mocked what 'I' was feeling? Was it like this for other people? Never mind; in the end it was all words, words, words, and I was a dangling abseiler stuck halfway down a cliff-face, hanging from a thin cable like a human pendulum and waiting for a shove.

One afternoon, as I gazed out my office window at the sun glinting off the trees, my project boss, Leigh, called me over. 'I'm going down the shaft for a gasper.' he said. 'Fancy some fresh air?'

This, I knew, was not a casual invitation. We rode down in the lift together, all twenty-eight floors to street level and the charmless grey concrete plaza where office workers hung out for a smoke.

It was here that Leigh told me about a position with a hot new IT firm in the UK.

'It's a great opening,' he said. 'I'd go myself but the wife won't come at it. Too much upheaval for the kids.'

I could see that he wanted to go, could see it in the fraught, frowning way he dragged on his cigarette. He was only in his late thirties but already his life was fixed.

I must have looked stunned, for Leigh patted me on the shoulder. 'Don't worry,' he grinned. He dropped the butt of his cigarette to the asphalt and ground it underfoot. 'I've already filled them in on your background. They want a phone interview,' he added. 'How are you placed tonight around eleven?'

Within a month I was on a flight to London.

the villa

The essential thing was this: in the old world, Europe, there was enough novelty to drive his brooding self underground. He stopped asking questions; he stopped asking why, and what is the meaning of all this. He was too distracted to think about whether or not he was happy. He wasn't bored, because everything had the electric charge of the new. He could see why people travelled; it refreshed the senses, it broke the cycle of repetition.

His new employer, Panoptica, was just two years old. It was owned by an American, Jim Hagen, an ex-hippie and Stanford dropout with a gift for developing software that enabled ever more dazzling special effects in movies. 'We are masters of the reality effect,' Jim had boasted to Rick somewhere in the middle of his late-night London–Sydney telephone interview, which went on for almost four hours, a free-association rave that made him wonder if Jim was on something.

But once he arrived he found that Jim was okay. He met Rick at the airport, where he danced around him like some manic sprite, all arms and quick, jerky gestures and a staccato patter that Rick couldn't absorb because he was bleary-eyed from jet lag. Jim packed him into an open-top silver Porsche and dropped him at a hotel in Chelsea, where he lay awake all night. In the morning, Jim rang around six to say he would be collecting Rick at seven and to be outside on the sidewalk. When Jim pulled in to the kerb in the Porsche, Rick could only stare at him in a daze; strung out from lack of sleep, he felt light-headed, with a curious sensation of having been relieved of a burden. Before long he was being guided through a glassed-in atrium down by the docks, where Jim had his offices. They walked onto a wide sunlit floor, where Jim shouted, 'Hey, listen up, everyone. Here's our new man. This is Rick. Rick from Australia.'

He suspected that Jim might be some kind of genius. Aged in his early fifties, he had a long, narrow face, a beaky nose and pale eyes behind rimless spectacles. His sandy hair was thinning and he chewed his nails to the quick, yet he was shrewd and sharp-eyed, with the air of a predatory child. He treated his programmers not as employees but as junior siblings and confided in them about his hectic past, and how he had moved to London to get away from a cocaine-fuelled work culture that had destroyed his second marriage. Jim was an unreconstructed baby boomer and had never given up on the idea of utopia. He even had a utopian view of the workplace. With a detestation of what he called 'corporates', he had installed his company in a spectacularly renovated warehouse on the Thames. It was less like a suite of offices than a home away from home – if you could call a brick cavern with a soaring glass roofline a home.

'As close to heaven as heaven can be,' Jim would say, which made no sense at all.

One of the Canadian programmers, Carl, told Rick that he had once corrected Jim on this. 'You mean "earth"?' he had said. 'As close to heaven as earth can be?'

'No,' Jim replied, 'earth doesn't come into it.'

So this saying of Jim's, which had become a catchphrase, was a kind of enigmatic nonsense, but to the degree that it was both lyrical and generous it seemed somehow in the spirit of his vision, and they were all happy to bask in the luxury of Jim's dream space. There was ergonomic furniture designed in Milan. There was a coffee machine in the middle of the first floor with a full-time barista, a young cockney with a line of patter that could prove distracting. At one end of the second floor there was a performance space, where a stark glass wall overlooked the docks. There, every Friday afternoon, Jim arranged for some musicians who played at his favourite pub in Deptford to perform for the staff.

'Treats,' he would smile, in his high, boyish, transatlantic accent, 'treats are the key to happy, happy workers.'

The net result of Jim's civilised work site was that for most of the gang the office was a more inviting space than home. They would get to work by seven, take their meals in the coffee lounge and leave around eight at night.

And the work was absorbing; they were the artists of their profession and thought of themselves not as programmers but as virtual sculptors. The sculptures existed in the mind's eye of the analyst and were traced into virtual reality via the pathways of Booleian logic. These pathways enabled the materialisation of the endpoint, the image on the screen, but this was just a thin layer that sat on top of the core. They, the analyst programmers, constructed the core. Jim, with his manic elan, would frequently refer to them as the Lords of Creation.

With work like that, who needed a private life? They were mostly young single men and they banded together like a pack of work-crazed siblings. You were in the zone, and it was hard to share anything with those who were outside it. Time and the conventional routines of a working day were disassembled, not so much rearranged as dissolved. The normal boundaries became fluid; you could eat and drink, work and nap whenever you pleased. Some days it felt as though you were suspended in a space station, living in permanent daylight.

It was not long before Rick was invited to the Hagen mansion in Notting Hill. Jim was perched on a corner of his desk where he had been spouting forth plans for a new project. 'Come to dinner,' he said, suddenly.

'When?'

'Tonight. Come tonight. Meet Leni.'

Everything with Jim was about now. He had an idea, he acted on it. So it was that just after eight Rick climbed out of Jim's car, double-parked in a leafy street of grand Victorian façades.

That night he met Leni, Jim's third wife, a former art curator from Boston whom Jim gave every appearance of worshipping. Leni was a small, elegant woman with an angular jaw and sleek blonde hair cut in a bob. She was whippet-thin but strong-boned, and her shoulders had an almost military set beneath her elegantly tailored silk shirt. Her fine tortoiseshell-rimmed spectacles suggested precision, and there was a quality of refined androgyny about her.

Rick could not help but be impressed by her poise, which was such a contrast to Jim's jerky animation and the way he seemed at times to dance around her. And yet, despite their differences, or perhaps even because of them, they appeared to have realised a kind of affectionate symbiosis; there was something about the way their bodies related to one another that was beyond even the sexual: they were like two limbs of the one animal. They existed in their own private aura.

The dining room was an internal room painted a deep terracotta red, with elaborately wrought fruit and vines moulded in plaster and so realistically tinted they appeared to be growing out of the walls. At one end of the room hung two spotlit portraits of Leni's children, an angelic-looking boy and a slightly younger girl with dark eyes. It was a warm night and one half of the huge dining table was laden with food, though there was only one other guest: the Hagens' architect, Marc Peltier, a Belgian. It was Marc who had renovated the warehouse for Jim. A year later, in the gloom of a London winter, Jim had presented Leni with the keys to a villa in Tuscany and Marc had been commissioned to restore it.

Leni sat at the head of the table like a presiding magistrate. She had a quality of stillness, of willed composure, the very opposite of Jim, who sat on his hands with shoulders hunched, rocking back and forth with a kind of nervy glee. Though the food that night was delicious, it seemed somehow secondary, a mere courtesy extended to the guests. Neither Leni nor Jim ate anything, not so much as an olive or a crouton, and Rick began to understand why they were both so thin. Marc the architect ate heartily, as did Rick.

Leni got out a photograph of the villa to show Rick so that he could follow the discussion of Marc's plans. It was assumed that he would find them absorbing. The villa was not what he expected; there were no arches or verandahs, only a compact cube, faced with white stucco, sharply geometrical in form with no windowframes or mouldings. Leni explained to him that the villa had no gardens; that it had for a long time 'stood aloof' from nature. But she and Jim had plans to put in a formal Renaissance garden, perhaps with a wild area to one side – a *barco* or hunting park.

'Could feel like living in a corset,' said Jim, on the subject of formal gardens, 'but I do like the idea of some kind of maze.'

'Why a maze?' Rick asked.

'So Leni can't find me,' he said, slyly.

'This will be my home,' said Leni, gazing at the plans, and Rick saw how her finely chiselled cheekbones caught the light with an almost luminous sheen.

But the villa didn't look like a home to him, more like a museum: stonily elegant, monumentally impersonal.

'I grew up in the ugliest steel town in Pennsylvania,' she said, turning to him with a quiet aristocratic candour that was disarming, and as if this statement explained everything. 'One knows that one's real home is out there somewhere. I guess you just have to live long enough to find it.' She had a breathy, almost swooning drawl, at odds with her sharp features. 'I hope you'll come and visit us, perhaps in the spring.'

And so it went on, an evening of the most urbane pastoral talk. The focus of their discussion was an extension that needed to be added at the back of the villa, a modern kitchen and a spa bathing area as well as an office, something that would not mar the lines of the façade. There was much talk of purity, of simplicity and of austerity, and how they could build a rustic-looking barn-shaped shelter for Jim's collection of old Porsches, any one of which, with his love of puzzles, he could take apart and put together again himself.

'It's the only time you'll ever see him relax,' said Leni.

'Does he actually drive them?' Rick asked.

'Oh, he goes for a spin, now and then, but that's not really the point, if you know what I mean.'

He didn't, but he had heard Jim boasting of his Porsches more than once, though Jim's boasting was as engaging as the rest of him, and amusing even, in light of his buffoonishly inept driving.

'I do hope you'll come and visit us,' she said again. 'You know, Jim has been toying with the idea of setting up a work space at the rear of the villa where the staff can fly over for weeks at a time. Kind of a working retreat.'

'I try and talk him out of this,' said Marc. 'You should never mix work with holiday.'

'Why not?' Jim exclaimed. 'Work should be play, and play should be productive.' He locked his long, bony fingers together into a knot. 'The whole person, eh, Rick?'

Rick smiled. It was all part of Jim's utopian dream, that there were places and things that could be perfected and where everything would come together and all would be well.

Leni was gazing at the drawings, her elbows leaning on the table. 'This will be my home,' she said again, as if she could will it into being.

Jim gave his wide, glinting grin. 'As close to heaven as heaven can be.'

In the summer of that year, Rick began a relationship with one of the Canadian programmers, Mira Gospadarcyzk. Mira had what he thought of as a Polish look, the blonde hair, the creamy skin, and she was plump, something he liked in women. He liked that feeling of solidity between the sheets. She also had a sharp wit, and she was lazy, another quality he found attractive. He was drawn to her insouciance, her way of lounging at full stretch on one of the orange sofas in the coffee bar like a big, blonde cat. She was a gifted mimic in a way that Jim too found amusing: he would quite often get the giggles in her presence. Rick wondered if it were this, or the fact that Mira was clever, that induced such tolerance in a man who was a workaholic. There was also something in the teasing banter between them, the way it struck the odd note of cruelty, that made him suspect they might once have been lovers. Who had rejected whom? Mira perhaps. She used her wit to keep her emotional distance, and that was fine with Rick. After the recent disaster of his love life, all he wanted was a companionable relationship plus sex. It seemed to suit them both.

In late summer, he and Mira rented a van and took a five-week break in Europe. When Rick told Jim he was taking a holiday Jim slapped him on the back and said, 'Great! That's great! You know, come May, Leni and I will be at the villa. Why don't you drop by, stay a while?' Mira, on learning of this offer, rolled her eyes. But all through the drive across Belgium, France, Germany, the Czech Republic and Austria Rick found he was looking forward to a few days in the Tuscan hills; it would be the apotheosis of what he had begun to think of, wryly, as his European experience.

~

They arrived at the villa at dusk. The house stood in shadow, a mysterious cube. It was a palace, but it was also austere. In the distance the hills were soft in a fading light, but the grounds around the villa were bare and unkempt.

Leni and Jim were not at home. A taciturn housekeeper greeted Rick and Mira at the grand entrance and then showed them to a bedroom on the third floor. It was a large, impersonal room, like a gallery; long and narrow with a high ceiling and walls of flaking pink limewash. An imposing bed of dark wood stood against one wall and there was little else in the room apart from a cupboard of massive dimensions, elaborately carved. It had a wad of cloth under one end to prevent it tilting forward on the uneven floor.

Mira opened the cupboard; inside was a row of old garments. 'Look!' she exclaimed, her head disappearing into folds of satin and velvet, but the smell from the cupboard was musty and when she drew out a green beaded dress and held it up to the light, the silk was moth-eaten.

Already he felt claustrophobic. He needed to go for a walk but by now it was dark. 'Let's see if we can find something to eat,' he said.

They stepped out into the corridor but took what proved to be a wrong turn, and after making their way down three levels of a narrow stone staircase found themselves in a stone-walled ante-chamber with a faded *trompe l'oeil* of a vineyard at one end and no apparent doorway. It seemed they had come to a dead end. Why, they asked one another, would anyone build a staircase that led nowhere? There must have been a doorway once that was now bricked up.

Just as they were beginning to feel disoriented, they heard a car roar into the driveway and could tell from the sound of the engine that Jim was at the wheel.

That night over dinner Leni and Jim took up the conversation from the evening at Notting Hill as if they had never left off. They had no interest in where Mira and Rick had been. All they talked about was the villa.

'Those two are nuts,' said Mira as they walked up the main staircase to their room. Rick was silent. The villa had begun to exert a spell over him; it was both strange and familiar. 'I feel I've been here before,' he said.

Mira gave him a look of affectionate contempt. 'Yeah, as a servant,' she said.

When they entered their room she went straight to the massive cupboard and flung open its doors. Now it was her turn to be seduced. Like a woman in a trance she began to browse through the crush of hanging garments, fingering the embroidered silks and velvets, exclaiming, with a kind of reverent awe, over this or that detail.

'Do you think anyone would notice if I took some of this stuff?' she said.

'Are you kidding? I'll bet Leni has an inventory of everything in the place.'

Mira began to sneeze from the mould but it did not deter her. After a while he left her and went out into the long corridor, which led to a gloomy bathroom at the far end with an ancient lavatory, a cistern high on the wall with a rusted chain. When he returned she was lounging on the bed in a voluminous ball gown of silver-grey velvet embroidered with intricate loops of black beads that flickered in the light.

It had the desired effect.

The next morning, under the shower, the skin on his chest stung from the soap. He looked closely and could see a fine network of pink abrasions, left there by the beads.

At breakfast on the terrace, Leni appeared with a folder that she presented to him over coffee. He glanced at its contents and saw that she had prepared a detailed itinerary for him and Mira, which mostly consisted of visits to art treasures in the surrounding towns. He began to formulate a polite way of saying that he didn't like churches and would prefer to go on some walks, but at that moment a chauffeur-driven car pulled into the driveway and Marc the architect got out. Bounding up onto the terrace with all the eagerness of a large, friendly dog, he took his place at the table and began immediately to consume a pastry. 'Where is Jim?' he asked.

'In the war room,' said Leni, referring to Jim's office off the rear courtyard. 'I'll send Nina to fetch him.'

Mira yawned and got to her feet. 'I need a hike,' she said.

'Lunch is at two,' said Leni, stirring her coffee. She didn't look up.

As they set out on their walk he told Mira about Leni's itinerary and she pulled a face. 'She's a control freak. All she cares about is her precious limewashes and her fat architect.' Then she gave that alluringly acerbic laugh that never failed to arouse him.

For a lazy hour they strolled in silence around the grounds of the villa. He liked the fact that Mira never felt the need to talk. He found it drew him to her, the quiet between them, and when they came upon a derelict farmhouse he tore the splintery shutters from an unglazed window and they climbed across the stone sill and made love on the dusty floor. Every room smelled of sage and cat's piss but behind the house were the remains of a garden, and there they lay on the warm earth, and dozed for a while beneath the uneven shade of a deformed apricot tree. It was as if here, at least, they were beyond the gaze of the villa.

When they returned to what Mira now referred to as HQ, Nina ushered them to the rear terrace, which was lined with lemon trees in terracotta urns and shaded by a canopy of mauve and white wisteria. Leni and Marc were already seated for lunch and Jim was approaching from his office, dressed in white drawstring pants and a white singlet, an outfit that might have made him look positively ethereal were it not for a ridiculous straw sombrero perched above his rimless spectacles.

After an indolent lunch, Leni called for Nina to clear the table. Marc had been gone all morning to investigate some local stonework and it was time now to discuss the maze.

Jim had more or less settled on a high hedge design in a blend of laurel and holm oak, but he could not decide on a 'goal'. Every maze had to have a goal but he and Leni couldn't agree. Leni liked the idea of some Etruscan antiquity, still and contemplative: a terracotta canopic urn or the head of a maenad set on a marble plinth, or maybe a tomb fresco set in the ground, a stone slab with winged lions and sphinxes in relief. But Jim wanted something more 'interactive'. He loved the maze at the Villa Garzoni, where, in the grotto at the centre, there was a tap that activated water jets set along the paths so that the first person to arrive at the centre had the fun of turning them on and drenching anyone who had the misfortune still to be lost in the maze.

'What if you wanted to go into the maze alone?' Marc asked. 'There would be no-one to sprinkle.' But this, as Leni said, only showed how little he knew Jim. Jim would never go into the maze without company. What would be the point of that?

'Why do you need a goal?' Mira asked. 'The objective, Jim, is to find your way to the middle of the maze and then to find your way out again. To not get lost. Isn't that enough?'

'Oh, that? That's boring,' said Jim with his high, abrasive whinny. 'And what a letdown. You spend all this time figuring out the right path and when you get there, zilch!'

'It would betray a lack of imagination not to have something in the centre,' Leni said, coolly. 'Like you couldn't think of anything' – she gave one of her elegant shrugs – 'or you didn't care.' She gave the impression that carelessness was the quality she most abhorred.

It was clear that Leni didn't care for Mira. As was becoming her habit, she turned to Rick. 'What do you think?'

'Put something you love at the centre,' he said, 'otherwise what incentive will you have to find your way there? After a few times the novelty will wear off, you'll get sick of it and you'll just be paying someone to trim the hedges.'

'Exactly,' said Leni, softly.

'The problem is,' said Mira, 'that Jim's in love with a sprinkler.'

Leni ignored her. She was gazing at Rick now with a certain look. As though she thought him *simpatico*, a kindred spirit. He saw then that her identification with the villa was complete; Leni was the villa and the villa was Leni. When she conducted them on a tour and smiled with satisfaction at the restoration of the *trompe l'oeil* she might have been gazing at a flattering portrait of her own face. The stone staircases were the pathways of her body, the lime-washed stucco her own skin. He knew nothing then about how some women, and men, became the houses they live in, how the house is a substitute or ideal self. The self is not perfectible but the house is. Leni was trying to create a paradise on earth, a perfection that would forever elude her, and it was not inherently to do with wealth, although money was one of its pathways. Jim, on the other hand, was more interested in the game, the puzzle.

That night Mira came down with a fever. Already he had learned that, when sick, she wanted to be left alone. He tried to be solicitous but his hovering seemed only to annoy her. Apart from bringing her water and helping her into the antique bathroom, he was at a loose end, and so, after a day of just hanging around, he succumbed to Leni's itinerary. For the next two afternoons he allowed her to drive him around the neighbouring towns.

Unlike Jim, Leni was an expert driver and he enjoyed the authoritative verve with which she negotiated the steep bends. And after the first hour he felt oddly comfortable with her, even though, as he had suspected, she was bent on guiding him through a series of churches.

A few looked like medieval fortresses, blunt with a primitive beauty. Inside they had been remodelled and Leni instructed him on the finer points of their Byzantine geometry or, if from a later era, their baroque parabolas. Some of these churches, she told him, had been built over the original Etruscan temples of the pagan era, constructed on the ruins. One or two had even incorporated elements of the original: a stone wall here, a few temple pillars there. That would be right, he thought: the world reinventing itself, over and over. But he ventured few observations, for he was intimidated by her learning. Instead he was alert to her body language, to the merest hint of flirtation. He thought about how he might handle it if she made it clear she wanted him. He waited for the first subtle sign. But there was none: she was bent only on his instruction.

Meanwhile, he was struck by the contrast between the madonnas of the frescoes and Leni, who revered them; the madonnas so passive, so ample, so voluminous in their flesh and the folds of their skirts; Leni so willed, so streamlined and thin. At one still point in the afternoon they sat on a stone bench at the rear of the nave of a small chapel and Leni slipped off a sandal and rubbed her foot. For the first time he noticed her feet. They were peasant feet, short and broad, yet she had a way of wearing a plain leather sandal that was aristocratic, like everything else about her: the cuff of her shirt; the single strand of pearls around her neck; her antique gold earrings; her calculated perfection, which was both artifice and yet of her essence. It was difficult to imagine her looking ruffled.

How startling, then, that night when he got up for a leak and surprised her in the dilapidated, high-ceilinged bathroom on the first floor. She was vomiting into a white sink surrounded by green tiles, and perhaps it was the colour of the tiles but her skin had a sickly greenish hue. It was a shock, for she seemed so touchingly vulnerable, despite the high-handed manner in which she waved him away. He can still recall that wave, the elegant white hand fluttering against the green tiles.

On the fifth day Mira revived and they packed their things into the van without regret. He had decided he did not like the villa. The spell was broken. In every room the air was redolent of lost promise, of unfulfilled dreams, and he doubted that Leni could restore that promise. Despite all the plans and extensions, all the attention to detail, somehow the villa seemed to remain uninhabited. It was as if Jim and Leni were children playing in an abandoned house, or travellers passing through.

The day before he and Mira departed, he sat on the sunny terrace and watched as two men laid out a pattern for the maze with radiating lines of string. He thought of something he had read in one of Leni's coffee-table books, about how the formal gardens of the villa were meant to be complemented by a hunting park, a wild area 'where the irrationality of nature could be accepted', but it struck him that even this was contrived. Everywhere in Europe, Nature seemed fully under human control; framed and mounted and polished and trimmed; fenced and cultivated, with every square inch of the land owned. It was so unlike the wild, formless bush of his childhood, its surreal monotony, its white light, the infinite gape of its horizon.

Even Jim's Porsches had failed to interest him as much as he thought they might. The garage had been completed and the inert machines stood there in a row like stuffed panthers in a museum. Their lines were beautiful but they seemed excessive, overwrought. A frozen potential. Everything that in Jim and Leni's telling, and in his own imaginings, had had immense charm now impressed him as lacking a vital force, some inner spark. It was all so . . . so calculated. Leni, for example, had a whole wall covered with samples of limewashes, and her precise, softly spoken monologues over lunch, mostly on the look of things, made him irritable and restless. By the fourth day of his stay Jim and Leni had seemed to him to be like sleepwalkers in a waking dream; a lavish and sometimes engaging dream, but a dream, nevertheless. The obsessiveness, the fussiness of both was somehow beside the point.

But what was the point? It was some years since he had asked himself this question, and this Arcadia here in the Tuscan hills was the last place he might have expected his sensual parachute to be deflated by metaphysics. For the first time since leaving Sydney he had been ambushed by his old ennui.

~

In London they resumed their lives as before. But then, in the last week of November, everything changed. Jim and Leni were driving home from the Midlands, where they had been visiting Leni's children in boarding school. Their car skidded into the path of a bus on the M1 and Leni was flung out onto the road, dying within minutes.

There was not, as Jim was to say over and over in the early weeks of his grief, a mark on her. It seemed characteristic of Leni that she should die with her beauty intact.

Jim's way of grieving was to work day and night, sleeping on a couch in the coffee bar and buttonholing anyone who was passing for a three-hour rave. It was exhausting. Furtively they began to tiptoe around him. Because they wouldn't, or couldn't, console him, Jim began to resent them, became sullen and withdrawn. For weeks he didn't come into the office at all, and then one Friday afternoon he appeared with a sharply dressed guy in his late thirties – *in a suit* – and announced that he was taking indefinite leave of the company and installing McCarthy as his CEO.

They were stunned.

McCarthy was a Harvard MBA and the bottom line kicked in fast. No frills, no concerts, no coffee lounge.

The place lost its heart.

Mira took up an offer from a firm in Montreal and suggested, in her flip way, that Rick come with her. This surprised him. Maybe she cared more for him than she had revealed. Was he so insensitive that he didn't know, couldn't tell, when he was loved? Or could it be that she was apprehensive about going alone? Wanted him as a crutch? Although he was not in love with her, he was aware of how she might be a catalyst for him to lead some other kind of life; it was a time when scenarios began to scroll through his head like endless trailers from forthcoming movies, and it seemed, for a while, that he might go anywhere and be anyone he chose.

One bitterly cold morning he drove Mira to Heathrow, enclosed her in a bear hug and said he might come and visit her at Christmas. 'Sure you will,' she said. Then he went up to the viewers' deck and waved her off until the plane was out of sight. It was a sentimental gesture, and it was unlike him.

Now, for the first time since arriving in London, he felt dislocated. On the day after Mira left, it entered his head that he might return to Sydney. For a day or two he thought about it, but idly, not with any real intent. The shameful fact was that he hadn't once felt homesick. But then, as if something dormant had been activated in his brain, as if someone somewhere had flicked a switch, one Sunday afternoon asleep on the couch he had a dream. He was standing by a fence in a suburban backyard, and beside the fence a cluster of Cootamundra wattles floated in a haze of blue foliage, the grey-green, smoky blue of his childhood, a blue he had never seen in Europe . . . Beyond the fence he could see a beach, wide open and deserted, with steep white sand dunes that fell away to the edge of a sunstruck sea, and in a sudden rush he ran towards the water with an overwhelming desire to dive in, to break its glittering surface and be enveloped in its surf . . . He woke, flooded with nostalgia, and sat up abruptly, feeling dizzy, almost sick with a spasm of yearning.

The next day, he got a call from his sister. Gareth had collapsed from a brain tumour and was on life support.

'You must come, Rick,' Jane said. 'You must come.'

He booked a flight for the evening of the following day.

At Melbourne airport he stumbled out of the plane like a zombie. Jane was there to meet him, and before long he was in his brother's house in Ivanhoe, which overlooked a leafy park. The living room was a cruel tableau: on the couch his mother sat, ashen, holding the hand of his sister-in-law, Allie. Through the glass doors he could see his father alone on the sundeck, smoking.

Jane knocked on the glass and Ned turned, saw Rick was there and walked in through the open door. They shook hands, and when Rick looked into Ned's eyes he knew then that his brother was going to die.

For the first time in his life he wanted to embrace his father but instead they stood, face to face, two stone pillars, until Ned turned and said, 'You'd better get yourself a drink.'

That night he drove with Jane to the hospital. In silence they took the lift to the third floor, and when they entered through the grey doors of the ICU he felt an odd sensation of déjà vu. The ICU was a square room with six separate cubicles radiating off like the spokes of a wheel, and in the middle of this space was an elevated platform of waist-high benches inlaid with central monitoring computers, a corona of screens reflecting obscure patterns and emitting low-level beeps. The whole place looked like a circular flight deck. Beyond the platform, each body in its cubicle was wired up to the central consoles; it was like an assemblage of futuristic pods.

Silently he followed Jane to the bedside of their brother. And there was Gareth, looking really quite well, as if he had just that moment fallen asleep. *Not a mark on him*, Rick thought. It was three years since he had seen Gareth, at a family wedding, and he saw that his hair was much greyer, and that it suited him; it was as if he had only now, on the point of death, come into his looks.

Jane sat in the chair by the bed and held Gareth's hand. On the drive over she had explained that Allie spent most of the day beside him, squeezing his hand in the hope that somehow this might prevent him from slipping away; might keep him anchored to his life, to the earth, to her. But now she was exhausted, so they had set up a roster and Jane would be taking over for tonight. Ned would come in at midnight and Rick could come in when he had recovered from his jet lag.

Over the next four days he spent the mornings with Gareth. He suggested to Ned that, as a younger man, he should take the midnight shift, but Ned wanted to be there through the night; Rick suspected that this was when Ned feared Gareth would die, and that he wanted to be with him when he did. So Rick would get up at six, shower, eat a large breakfast (for some reason he was extremely hungry) and buy all the papers in the hospital kiosk downstairs. Then he would take the lift to the third floor and sit by Gareth's bed and read aloud to his brother, *sotto voce*, omitting any violent or depressing news but dwelling in detail on the financial and sports pages. Gareth had been an enthusiastic small investor, and it seemed logical that if anything could reach his brain, could bring him back from whatever blind or chaotic landscape he inhabited in his coma, it would be the rise and fall of his money.

It was a ritual, and like any ritual it had the power to console. There were whole hours when Rick felt absurdly cheerful until, without warning, the newspaper would turn to ashes in his hands. Then he would sit and brood on the nature of the body, its hidden malignancy, its death wish. He had taken his older brother's life for granted, even more than he took his own. Gareth was always the cheerful one, gregarious and with lots of friends. In his youth Gareth had played First Grade cricket, and later he had become a scratch golfer. But here was his body, that magnificent machine, hooked up helplessly to other machines.

When Allie relieved him, Rick would walk to the coffee shops down the road and eat out on the pavement in the sun. One cafe opened out onto a pleasant terrace, and it was as good a place as any to just sit. One morning, after he had collected his coffee from the counter, he becalmed himself in a corner of the terrace and gazed out at the trees in the park opposite.

Something odd had happened to him that morning. He had awoken from a dream in a state of inexpressible homesickness, a kind of sweet sadness that flooded his body like an ache. And, of all things, he had dreamed that he was back in Leni's villa, wandering its corridors for what seemed a very long time, until, at last, he passed through a narrow door behind a *trompe l'oeil* hunting scene and found himself in the Intensive Care Unit. At first he thought there was no-one there – the beds were all empty – but when he looked again he saw Leni lying unconscious in her pristine cubicle, and in the cubicle beside her was Gareth. Gazing ahead at the planes and angles of the ICU, he saw also the planes and angles of the villa, and how the one led into the other, and with this thought came an unexpected pang of consolation, as if there were some fearful symmetry at work here that might one day endow all their lives with meaning.

At two-thirty on a grey afternoon they assembled at St Stephen's. The church was modern and built in red brick and glass, with pale blue panels at either side of the main door. It was one of those dull, humid days when it seemed as if the flinty Melbourne sky was suspended only an arm's reach above the red suburban rooflines.

His brother had been an active man and the church was crowded. In the eulogy, Gareth's friend Neil referred to the optimism of their generation, how they had grown up with the feeling that they could do anything. The priest was a young man with a barrel chest who said and did surprisingly little. The hymns were a series of dirges so solemn and dreary that they mounted no challenge to the heart. It was not until the very end, when they switched on a tape of Van Morrison, croaking out the true anthems of Gareth's generation, that sobs became audible in the church. A shiver went through the mourners, the first shiver of collective grief, as if they were mourning for themselves, the outrageousness of one of their own dying young. The words, Rick reflected, made no sense at all, but the voice was full of a sweet if rueful surrender.

Around the grave, the mourners stood patiently and waited for the signal to cast their clods of sticky earth into the hole. At that moment it came to him, as if it were some sudden unexpected piece of news, that he would never see his brother again. He felt his knees give, and in a dizzy funk he stumbled, then righted himself, awkwardly, with a feeling of shame.

As he walked back to the car park, across the manicured lawns of the cemetery which were such an unnatural shade of green, he observed his father put his arm around his mother. Both were crying. He began to think of how he had never cared for Van Morrison, of how Gareth's taste in music had always been a bit retro. There was no way that he could respond to the vague, pseudo-mysticism that infected every phrase, that rumbling, hazy lyricism of dope-smokers. Although, come to think of it, there was that one song, 'Moondance', that Jo and he had liked to dance to . . . The image of Jo dancing with abandon brought him up with a jolt. He was only metres away from his brother's grave, and for several minutes he had been thinking about why he didn't like Van Morrison.

The next day, at Gareth's house, he saw that Ned looked much older than he had a week ago. He saw through the window his brother's children, playing on the lawn with their fat old beagle as if nothing had happened. Out on the deck, the deck that Gareth built, they sat down to a solemn lunch. They were remnants of something that once had been larger, a broken family gathered together under an indifferent sun. Someone handed him a beer but he let it sit while he looked out across the backyard and began an inventory of his brother's garden. What trace of him remained?

In the eastern corner a tyre hung from the sturdy branch of a big red-gum; along the back fence a line of Cootamundra wattles merged into a grey-green blur; beside the deck a firewheel banksia sprouted candle-shaped orange cobs, a study of upright stillness, while beneath it a trio of starlings pecked at the lawn. Starlings, such dull birds, nesting and shitting beneath the eaves.

the raft

I did not return to London. If asked then why I had stayed, I could have – would have – given several clear reasons that, looking back, I recognise as mere rationalisations, transient structures of thought that cleared a space for some deeper instinct or intuition to do its work. I didn't go back because it felt right not to; because some inchoate resistance, some feeling that didn't need a name and would never acquire one, welled up in my chest and said *stay*.

Sometimes you just did things. You surprised even yourself.

Within weeks of returning to Australia I was working for a corporation with headquarters in North Sydney. Just a few kilometres away in Kirribilli, walking distance from the office, I rented a shoebox apartment overlooking a small park and began to settle in to my new life. Compared to what I had been doing with Panoptica, the work was dull – devising programs for the setting up of new accounting systems – but I intended within the year to break out into my own consultancy. When I had settled in. When I had found my line and length.

At night I thought of Gareth and for the first time in my life I began to suffer from insomnia. Almost every night I would wake around three in the morning. Sometimes, if I couldn't get back to sleep, I would turn on my clock radio and listen to the BBC World

Service. News from remote borders, of warring factions of the Mujahideen, rendered in civilised English tones, seemed calibrated to run exactly the right kind of interference on my zealous mind: sometimes I would be dozing within minutes. But other data was less reliable. The English football results made me think of pleasurable hours on the West Ham terraces.

Then I would wonder what Mira was up to. Had I allowed a good thing to slip through my fingers? Perhaps I should call her. What time was it in Montreal?

Time passed. Occasionally I would have a drink with a friend. Th ere were company social nights when I would turn up and play my role (and these were not unpleasant), and there was a regular game of squash with three old schoolfriends. They invited me to dinners and barbecues, but these were the lowest level of distraction and, if I were not in the mood, would only aggravate my condition of restless grief.

One night he ambushed me. Gareth. Came to me in a bittersweet dream. He was standing below my window and calling to me to come out into the street. Though he was four years older, he had often given in to my pestering and agreed to batting practice in the lane beside our house after school. The lane was steep and he would order me to the bottom end so that I had to do all the running to retrieve a missed ball, and I would enter the house for dinner in a state of sweaty exhaustion. It was a dream that could not have been more potent: the smell of scuffed leather and damp grass, the sound of car horns honking, the melodic whistle of a neighbour as he walked home from the station, the way the cool evening gloom began to close in around us until we could barely see the ball.

The next morning I found it hard to get out of bed. Once again the program had failed and I had to lie prone, inert, and run the instructions through my head. 'Now get up, have a shower, have some breakfast . . . just take it one step at a time . . .' I hadn't been in this kind of funk for years. After an hour of lying there, rehearsing the moves in my head, finally I threw off the covers and sat up, only to sink back into bed. And this went on for a week.

One humid Sunday afternoon, lounging on the balcony of my small apartment and basking in the last of the autumn sun, I read my way absentmindedly through a feature article in the Saturday paper entitled 'The Emotional Male'. It was a shallow article of the kind that pretended to a seriousness it was too lazy to pursue, but in it I came across this sentence: 'A feeling of being jaded is often a mask for depression.' I looked up and out over the rail of the deck to a flock of currawongs on the wire.

Boredom is often a mask for depression? Were they talking about me?

Depression. I had heard of it, had read about it. I knew that everyone, at some time or another, felt depressed; knew that as an occasional affliction it was common, one of the prices you paid for being alive. But beyond this was a biochemical condition, some taint of being that never went away, that rose and fell like the tides but was always there. Perhaps, all along, this had been my problem, some chemical imbalance.

The obvious thing was to consult a doctor. I knew a GP, the father of a friend. I had met him at a wedding and liked him, so I booked myself in. And as I sat there in Des's surgery early one Thursday morning, I didn't beat around the bush. I said I thought I might be suffering from depression. It was an embarrassing

admission, difficult to put into words – but after all, it was an ill-
ness, wasn't it? Still, how should I have framed it? 'I've been feeling
a bit down, lately?' In my case, the 'lately' part wasn't true. Obviously the death of my brother hadn't helped things, but the
problem of my discontent had been with me for most of my life.

For much of the night before I had lain awake, rehearsing the
ways in which I might get this confession out so that it sounded
manly and credible, not whining and self-indulgent. I thought too
of the shape I would give my account of why I thought I had this –
my 'depression' – and what in my life might have contributed to it.
After what seemed a long time of lying in the dark, I had glanced
at the luminous clock dial: it was just after four in the morning,
and I was still rambling through the fractured narrative of my life
like some insomniac Sherlock Holmes of the psyche, looking for
what vital clues might be there in key incidents: recent events that
had caused me pain (Gareth), recent events that ought to have
caused me pain and hadn't (Mira) and the more general problem of
why it was that I was always the first to spot the worm in the apple.
Was I more perceptive than other people? Was the worm even
there?

To my surprise, Des didn't want to hear any of this. 'Not unusual,' he said briskly. 'Especially at your age.'

Age? What did age have to do with it?

'Yours can be a difficult age,' Des was saying. 'You're in the run-
up to forty. It's all been a bit like playschool up until now.'

But I was still, I protested inwardly, a young man. Hardly a
midlife crisis.

'Don't underestimate the role of hormones,' Des continued.
'Your testosterone levels are starting to drop sharply around now,

and medical science is only just beginning to look at the effect this has on the brain. We know a lot about women's hormones but a lot less about the male of the species. Your hormones start leaking in when you're around seven or so, not just in your teenage years but earlier than you think, and then at around thirty the levels start to wane . . .'

I didn't quite hear the rest, distracted by the thought that, come to think of it, it had been around the age of seven that I had first apprehended that the universe might be a magnificent but meaningless spiral of matter, behind which lay a terrifying void, and beside which any small human gesture was ultimately pointless . . . but it was also the time when I began to experience that feeling of homesickness, of primeval exile and loss, like a prisoner yearning for freedom. It was as if I had brought this yearning into the world with me, that it was latent in every cell of my being and it had nothing to do with grief. But what was I yearning *for*?

When I looked up, Des was writing out a prescription for antidepressants. 'You just need something to tide you over a bad patch,' he said.

This was not what I had expected. Not that I had anything against antidepressants, but these, surely, were for the suicidal, or for the non-functioning: people who couldn't get up out of their bed, or chair. I was neither. Okay, I had a few days when I had trouble getting out of bed, but I had no desire to end my life. I went to work every day and did more or less the right things. I had expected to be referred on to a psychiatrist. In those days psychotherapy was not the commonplace it would soon become, but I knew enough to know that you didn't have to be mad to qualify. And there was a sense in which I was almost looking forward to the on-the-couch experience as an intellectual puzzle: a match of wits, an elaborate and redemptive game.

But no, here I was standing outside a pharmacy in the Chatswood mall with a handful of pills in silver foil. 'Take one tablet twice a day and come back in four weeks.' What could I do? I drove to my office, downed the first lot with some lukewarm coffee, took another one at lunchtime just before a meeting and on the way home dropped the rest into a litter bin at the station. Then I had second thoughts, went back and retrieved them. Luckily, they were sitting just on top of a folded newspaper and I didn't have to rummage like a vagrant, though the thought crossed my mind that I *was* a kind of vagrant. *Here I am, rummaging in the bin of my psyche, hoping to pull something out of the lucky dip, some better than average prize.*

For the next two days I took the antidepressants as prescribed and then I threw them away again, this time for good. Yes, I was a moody bastard, but I had always been like this, and I just had to learn how to handle the bad days, days when I felt myself teetering on the edge of becoming bored even by my own ambition. And that scared me, because without ambition I was robbed of the future. Ambition was the cool wind that kept me airborne; it had carried me through my twenties; it was the one thing I confidently expected would never fail me.

The following Monday I couldn't get out of bed. I stayed there for the rest of the week, feigning flu. I would sleep until noon, lurch into the shower and spend the afternoons watching snatches of talk shows or the mindless perambulations of golf. Or raid my bookshelves for something that wasn't stale or trivial and absurd. It occurred to me that I did nothing but work; that I had stopped buying books and that maybe I should start again; that my mental focus had narrowed in the way that an artery becomes thickened and clogged by plaque. It even occurred to me that I might be suffering from sensory deprivation; I rarely listened to music anymore; I never went for a walk in the bush; I couldn't remember the last time I'd had a swim. I've got to do something, I thought. I have to act. I have to deal with this thing. I can will myself out of this.

Meanwhile, I had stopped wearing my watch. It felt like a diver's weight.

~

In late April, out of the blue, I got a call from my cousin Julie. She and her husband, Kieran, had just been transferred back to Sydney from Auckland, where they had spent the past five years. She had got my number from Jane. Would I like to come over for dinner?

Driving across to their house in Tamarama, I thought of the last time I had seen Julie, not long before I left for London. But my most vivid memory of her was from a holiday when our two families spent Christmas together at Terrigal. I remembered her then as a tomboy: a short, muscular girl with sun-streaked hair and a deep tan, a powerful swimmer who moved in the water with the slow, lazy focus of a fish.

That first night she came out to meet me in the driveway and I was relieved to see that she had scarcely changed, apart from a slight thickening around the middle. The house was a nondescript brick bungalow, and she led me through a cool hallway and out onto a concrete terrace that looked out to the water. The ocean was calm and shimmered in the hazy evening light. In one corner of the terrace a thickset man with a beard was wiping down the metal plate of a primitive wood-fired barbecue. Below him, on the grass, two small boys in wet bathers chased a featureless brown mutt around the yard.

Julie introduced me to Kieran as 'my clever cousin', and I thought this was not perhaps the best start. Kieran shook my hand a touch too firmly and went on with preparations for the barbecue, while Julie and I looked out over the rooftops and spoke the lingua franca of Sydney life: real estate. All the while I was alert to Kieran, his intense preoccupation with the barbecue, the way he sighed as he adjusted the firewood and poked at loose woodchips, and I wondered if he was not so much gruff as tired. He moved with the stolid weariness of a man who had worked all day in the sun.

'Kieran's been working on his boat all day,' Julie said, as if reading my thoughts. 'He bought this old whaling dinghy off a friend and now he's restoring it.'

Kieran looked up through a waft of smoke. 'Huon pine, beautiful timber.'

'Why don't you show Rick the boat?'

Kieran poked at the fire again. 'Like to have a look?' he asked, and his asking was a courtesy, as if to say: I don't want to bore you with this.

'Sure.'

The boat, covered by a tarpaulin, sat in the side lane. Kieran became more animated as he removed the tarpaulin and ran his palm along the polished surface of the wood. Now he was at ease and happy to deliver a laconic discourse on glues and varnishes. Every now and then he would pat the side of the boat, as if it were an old friend, and nod his head in confirmation of its worth, while I did my best to ask the right questions. I thought the shape of the boat ugly, too wide in relation to its length, which gave it a squat appearance, but the wood was ravishing, a golden honey hue with the softness of a subtle grain. I saw that you could have a relationship with this wood and was about to ask where it came from when Julie leaned over the terrace and said, 'Let's eat. The kids are getting ratty.'

'Such beautiful wood,' I said, looking up.

'Well, enjoy it,' she said tartly, 'because by the time they finish logging old-growth forests there'll be none of it left. They'll have to put boats like that in a museum.'

'Now then, Jules, you're winding up into a rant,' said Kieran, quietly, looking ahead. His eyes were hooded and his weathered lips set firmly against causes.

With this, I felt a prick of annoyance; I did not like to hear my cousin rebuked. But Julie seemed oblivious. She had moved away to the other side of the terrace, where she was calling to the boys. Her husband had thrown out the net of his words but she was not caught.

Up on the terrace, bread and salads were laid out. Kieran set about the serious business of searing the meat while the boys, Ryan and Matthew, whooped around the garden. Conversation over dinner was broken but accommodating. The boys, though shyly deferential to the visitor, were ragged with fatigue from a blustery afternoon on the beach with their mother. After they had tired of tormenting the dog, they whined and fought over who would ride the bike around the lawn and show off for the visitor. At last, Julie rose with deliberate calm and bundled them into a bath.

Despite the way they had interrupted my every sentence, I was sorry to see them go. Watching them reminded me of the hours I had spent with Gareth, in that same enchanted hour of dusk, our subliminal sense of the light of the day falling away behind us, our innocent faith in its renewal.

With the boys in bed, we settled into recliners on the deck and sniffed at the smell of meat and barbecue smoke, still wafting tantalisingly in the air. Kieran wasn't much of a talker and the wine soon sent him into a soporific slump. The small talk trailed off into a companionable silence, and for a while we just sat and gazed out at the horizon. After a while I turned to Julie and said, 'Do you get much swimming in these days?'

'Not much. If it's hot, I go for a swim at night, when the kids are in bed, and if Kieran's home. That's the best time. The wind's dropped, there's no-one on the beach.'

Swimming in the dark? This struck me as foolhardy. 'Can you see what you're doing?'

When she looked at me there was a gleam of the old mischief in her dark brown eyes. 'No,' she murmured. 'That's the point.'

I remembered how she used to wade into the surf at Terrigal, swimming beyond the breakers like a sleek porpoise, so evenly, so smoothly, as if she were in her element, as if she might never come back. It seemed to me then that there was a mystery in her, something unfathomable.

A warm breeze wafted up from the water and the sky glowed pink at the edge of the roofline. I saw that at night a trance came over these beach suburbs, a subtropical stupor in which all fear, all resistance was dissolved in the warm penumbra of dusk. Nature giveth, and Nature taketh away.

Beside us, Kieran snored gently on his recliner.

I drove home around nine, the last glow of daylight rimming the horizon. I wondered if I, too, could live like this, in the suburbs, a father of small children with a sundeck and a barbecue, a double garage and a frangipani tree. These were the surfaces, and then there was the reality. Reality was the man polishing his boat on land and the woman swimming in the dark, but they were a riddle, one that I was not yet ready to unravel. Supposing I were to enter into this riddle? What would it make of me? Who would I be?

My mind drifted again to surfaces, the form of the thing. I saw my weary commute home in the evening, backyard cricket with the kids at twilight, supper on the beach on hot summer nights, an enigmatic wife who would form the impenetrable substratum of my dreams. This was the core of it. Everything depended on this last figure in the landscape: the woman on the beach. Without her I was just a cog in the machine. And with her? With her, we were mysterious creatures at the edge of the tide: liminal, amphibious, entwined.

I drove on, into the dark, and felt that I was some great, displaced sea creature, splayed on a vinyl seat behind the wheel of a car; a beached merman waiting dumbly for the next enveloping wave.

~

For the next nine months I lived like a monk. I did nothing but work, and for all of that time I was celibate, the longest period in my life since I was seventeen.

I began to frequent a Korean bathhouse near Taylor Square in a run-down building that looked out onto the grimy columns of the Supreme Court. That bathhouse became my refuge. You went up a seedy narrow staircase and into a foyer hung with paper scrolls; you rang a small brass bell and a chunky Korean who spoke no English appeared, nodded and indicated the change room. Once undressed, you entered naked into the bathing area. This was a dimly lit room with two circular pools in the centre, raised above a surrounding deck of white tiles. The smaller of these pools was a warm spa bath filled with an infusion of ginseng, its leaves floating on the surface, and as you stepped out and down onto the tiles some of the leaves clung to your skin, creating the brief illusion that you had just stepped out of a brackish lake.

After this you slipped into the larger pool, which was cooler, and bathed until you were ready for the steam room at the far end. At any given time there might be seven or eight men in the pools, some in the water, others sitting at the edge, dangling their feet and waiting to be rubbed down on one of the futons spread along the deck. Once you were prostrate on a futon, another of the masseurs would come and kneel, and begin to scrub your body with a loofah, scouring the skin hard, almost to the threshold of pain, stopping every few minutes to sluice you down with warm water out of a long-handled bucket that attendants constantly refilled.

This was the best moment of all, the sluice of clean water across your shoulders, your lower back, thighs and feet. The warm, willing cascade of it; the luxurious blur of expectation just before the next deluge; the grateful exhalation of relief as you lay there like a slippery fish foetus in the womb of the pool room, with its dim, steamy air and its becalmed bodies.

And I would walk out of there, loose and light, and drive home, and often eat nothing that evening because I felt clean. Purified.

One night after a session at the bathhouse, I had a dream. I was in the big circular pool, or a space that resembled the pool, only it was not. And there was no-one there but me, floating outstretched and naked on a raft at the centre of the water. And I dreamed that the raft was also my bed, so that it was not as if I were somewhere else; rather, it was a sense of being on my bed in a state that was half-awake, and the surface of the bed was the surface of the raft. And all the while the raft was bobbing idly on the surface of the pool . . . And every now and then I would wake . . .

It was such a long, drifting dream, but even in the waking state a mirage of water persisted in my brain, like an hallucination, so that when I looked up in the dark I could see the water eddying across the ceiling, around the fan in a soundless swirl, rippling on and on across the blackness. And after a while it came to me. *I can't get off the raft.* Any moment now I will fall and sink to the bottom of the pool, and there's no-one here and they'll never find me, and my body will be flushed away through one of the corner drains.

That's when I saw the woman. Standing at the end of the pool was a woman in a white dress, and in her arms she was holding a baby, an amorphous white bundle wrapped in swaddling clothes, wrapped so tight that all I could see was its eyes. And the woman? She was familiar to me; I had seen her before. But where? And as I stared at them, thinking – who are they? and what are they doing here? – slowly, the baby began to glow. At first it shone faintly but then it began to glow brighter, the white shimmer of the image growing more and more intense until at last it flared into a blinding cone of light. At that moment I felt a tight, nostalgic sweetness in my chest, a terrifying vertigo of joy, and I knew then that the light was coming to annihilate me . . .

And I woke with a gasp. And lay in the dark, open-mouthed, holding my breath. That feeling . . . that feeling was indescribable. For a moment I had felt as if I were falling . . . falling into bliss.

And the feeling stayed with me for the whole of the day, until late afternoon, when it began to fade. As it receded, I tried to hold on to it, to wilfully recapture glimpses of the dream – the tilt of the raft, the hem of the woman's dress, the glow from the baby – but inevitably it grew more and more faint, like a silk fabric dissolving in the mind's eye. It could not be hung on to, and by late evening I had ceased even to try. The yearning around my heart had evaporated, the painful joy in my chest was gone.

~

I began to look forward to my visits to Tamarama. I grew fond of the boys, remembering on each occasion to bring them some small treat.

One night, when Kieran was away on business, Julie packed some cooked sausages in buttered rolls smeared with tomato sauce and we walked to the beach. After a no-frills picnic on the sand the four of us played beach cricket until it began to grow dark. At one point Matt lobbed a ball into the water.

'I'll go,' I said.

'No, I'll go.' And in one supple movement Julie had slipped out of her shorts and waded into the surf.

Later, when the boys were in bed and we were sitting out on the deck, she asked me about Gareth. Oddly, we had never dis-cussed it. I wondered if she had raised the subject before then and I had brushed it aside, or lapsed into mute resistance. But that night a rush of pain ambushed me behind the eyes, like the prickly, needling onset of a migraine. I faltered mid-sentence and it was clear to her that I had tripped an internal landmine.

Julie was unfazed. She turned her gaze away from the sea and stared at me. 'You should talk about it, Rick,' she said. 'And have a good cry. Just cry your eyes out for as long as it takes.'

'I can't.'

'Can't what?'

'Can't cry. I've never been able to cry.'

'You must have cried as a child!' She was looking at me in astonishment.

'Not that I recall.'

'You know, Rick, you should talk to someone.'

'I'm talking to you.'

'I mean a professional.'

'Like who?'

'A friend of mine has been going to a therapist, a woman. Sue thinks she's really good. Do you want me to ring her and get the number?'

I shrugged.

I thought Julie must have misinterpreted the shrug, because she made no effort to move, but a week later a business card arrived in the post with a note on the back in her handwriting. 'Thought you might want to hang on to this for future reference.'

I read the card.

SARAH MASSON

psychotherapist

It gave an address near the Manly Corso.

The next day I rang and made an appointment.

~

The house was set well back from the road behind a high, cream brick wall. There was a Norfolk pine in the front garden, like the ones on the Corso but with more life in it, more density and spring. For a moment I was distracted by that tree; I was willing to be distracted by almost anything, since I had misgivings about being there.

It was the realisation that I was becoming almost catatonically unable to speak to anyone much about anything that had finally driven me to this door.

Julie had said: 'You just need to talk to someone about the way you feel.'

That sounded reasonable. Unthreatening. Or so I thought when I rang and made an appointment. But at the moment when I stood there, staring up into the radiating fronds of the Norfolk pine, it felt confronting.

But I knew why I had come. I wanted to cry, and I couldn't. Perhaps this Sarah Masson would teach me.

I was a week off my thirty-fourth birthday.

I stepped onto the verandah. Next to the stained-glass door was a brass plate inscribed 'Holistic Therapy Centre'. Suddenly I felt nervous, like a child about to sit some kind of unorthodox examination. And I didn't like that word 'holistic'. It had a phoney ring to it. What'll I say? I thought. I'll just say that I have depression, that in the past year it's gotten worse. I'll just set out the facts, flatly.

Describe the situation. Tell her about Gareth, and before that, Jo. And maybe about the dream, the one about the woman and the baby. Yes, definitely the dream. What could be difficult about that?

I pressed the brass button.

A short, muscular woman of around forty with prematurely white hair opened the door.

'Rick,' she said, as if she knew me. I looked at her, sizing her up sexually, as I did with any woman I'd just set eyes on. It was a reflex, even in that state: one I imagined would never leave me. To my relief there was nothing there for me; it would make the encounter easier. Sarah wore loose-fitting white pants, an orange top and leather sandals. I noted she had good skin, a good healthy tan and deep green eyes. She put out her hand and I shook it. As I stepped into the hallway she indicated a room to her left. It was light and cool and carpeted, with a sofa and two nondescript armchairs. She gestured at one and waited for me to sit down. We sat, facing one another, a metre apart.

When I was settled, she looked at me and said, 'What is it that you want from this, Rick?'

I leaned over and put my head in my hands, my elbows resting on my knees. For a few moments the room blurred around me until I became aware of the silence. I couldn't speak. Something lurched and began to rise in my chest, and I thought, then, with a pinprick of amazement, I might be about to cry. Could it be this easy? But no, my eyes were dry.

Finally I managed to open my mouth. 'I'm sorry,' I said. 'I'm tired. I've been working long hours. I'm not usually like this . . .' The truth was that I was increasingly like this: unwilling, or unable, to communicate.

'Everyone who comes here apologises for something.' She smiled. 'They always say they're tired and they're not usually like this.'

I stared at the floor. I heard myself sigh, and that sigh seemed to come from a point just beyond my hands, which, unaccountably, were still pressed up against my forehead, as if glued.

'What is it that you want, Rick?'

'I want to lose my fear.' I heard myself say this with surprising matter-of-factness. Out it came. Clear, sharp.

'What are you afraid of?'

'Everything.' I heard myself sigh again.

This wasn't true. I hadn't been afraid of abseiling. I hadn't been intimidated by Leni when the rest of Jim's staff were in awe of her. Nor was I afraid of many other things. *What was I talking about? Where did these words come from?* In my chest the black wind-bellows were squeezed hard up against my ribcage.

'What does this fear feel like?'

At last I lifted my head. 'How do you mean?'

'What's your body telling you? Where can you feel this fear?'

'In my head, I suppose.' I paused. 'All over.' Silence. 'Nowhere in particular.' It was excruciating; my lips were made of sticky latex and I had to force the words out.

Sarah looked at me. 'Alright. Let's get down on the floor.' She stood, and slipped out of her sandals.

I continued to sit, woodenly.

'You okay with that?'

At last I got my mouth open. 'Should I take my shoes off?'

'Whatever you're comfortable with.'

I left my shoes on.

Sarah pushed her chair back against the wall and walked over to a wooden box by the door. It looked like a child's toy chest. She lifted the lid and took out a roll of pale blue foam. Glancing into the open cavity, I could see a basketball there, and other things I couldn't identify before she closed the lid.

'My box of tricks,' she said, smiling, and unrolled the foam onto the floor. 'Just lie on your back, and get comfortable.'

I followed her instructions.

She knelt beside me. 'Alright, now, take a deep breath.'

Breathing deeply was an effort. Plus, it had always been my experience that as soon as someone told you to breathe deeply, you couldn't. I tried to make my mind go blank, to relax my stomach muscles. Then, with effort, I inhaled deeply – but the air seemed to get stuck above my navel.

I turned my face from side to side, away from her, and began to sigh again, almost as if hyperventilating, though not quite. Then I covered my eyes with one hand.

'Why do you cover your eyes?'

'So I can't be seen, I suppose.'

'Why?'

'I thought for a minute I might cry.'

'What's wrong with that?'

'It's ugly. People look ugly when they cry. Ugly and weak.'

'Say, "I look weak when I cry."'

'I never cry.'

'Alright then. Say, "I would look weak if I cried."'

'I would look weak if I cried.'

'Who mustn't see you cry?'

'Anyone.'

'Who's anyone?'

'What do you mean, "Who's anyone?"'

'Can you be specific? Name names? Who musn't see you cry?'

'Friends . . . colleagues . . . my parents . . . teachers . . . friends . . . anyone.'

'What will happen if they see you?'

'I'll feel stupid . . . ashamed.'

'And?'

'They'll ask questions. I'll have to explain myself.'

'How does that feel?'

'How does what feel?'

'Explaining yourself.'

'I don't know. It feels tight.'

'You're holding your breath.'

'I know. I always hold my breath.'

'Holding the fort?'

Smiling, I exhaled, and the smile stayed with me. It occurred to me that I liked her. Had from the minute I set eyes on her. I started to relax. She put her hand on my stomach, a large, square, practical hand. I liked the feel of it. 'If I do, or say, anything you're not comfortable with, tell me,' she said. 'Okay?'

'Okay.'

'Okay. Now, tell me . . .'

As I talked, occasionally she removed her hand and shook it away from her, as if she were flicking off some dross or contamination, some negative charge. It was weird, but I didn't care.

By the time I walked out of there I felt lighter. I felt as if I had handed over my problems to someone else, had stored them in some kind of psychic safe.

I felt also as if someone was on my side. It didn't matter that I'd paid her to be on my side. In fact, it helped: there was a freedom in the cash nexus, in the clarity of the transaction. For one thing, if I didn't feel like it, I didn't have to pretend to be interested in her. It wasn't a date. I didn't have to worry if I was talking about myself too much, if I was boring her. I could fall into myself and wallow about in the childish pain of all my stored-up sense of grievance, all my hatreds, my buried sense of outrage and grief, not just grief for Jo and Gareth, but for every blow ever dealt to me. Though I still had the problem that I wanted to impress Sarah, wanted her to think well of me, to think that I was a decent, sensitive, mature human being, so much more appealing than all her other clients, whoever they were.

And then she spoiled it. On my fifth visit she began to talk astrology. If there was one thing I couldn't bear, it was prattle about the stars.

'You're an Aries,' she said, one hot afternoon, 'but you're holding your power in. Give yourself permission to be powerful. You're locking your energy away in your head, and this creates a sadness in the heart area, this feeling you describe as boredom. *Breathe.* Unlock the channels and the breath will flow through your body and enliven the surfaces of your skin. Enlarge your aura. If we lock our energy away, our skin is vulnerable. If we let the energy flow, our surfaces are stronger. We're stronger all over. We're not contracted inwards, we radiate outwards. Our aura is enhanced. People *feel* our energy, our strength. They think twice about attacking us – if that's what you're worried about . . .'

There I was, beginning to trust her, and she started in on that astrology shit.

'. . . it's partly about learning to trust your environment. But only up to a point. There are times when something in the environment *is* hostile, *is* threatening. What you have to learn to trust is yourself. And your ability to deal with it.'

'It?'

'Whatever it is you're afraid of.' She got up off the floor. 'Let me look up your moons.'

'My what?'

She walked over to her bookcase and took a thick hardbound book off the middle shelf, began to flick through the pages, and stopped. 'You've got a moon in Capricorn,' she smiled, 'the goat. This means you're ambitious and single-minded. Ambitious, dogged, can be overfocused . . . mmmmm, let's see . . .'

Somewhere in the vault of my chest I gave a low, silent groan of dismay, but at the same time I found I was listening intently, despite myself.

It was after this session that I experienced a sense of massive let-down. I had been a fool to succumb, to get my hopes up. None of this stuff was going to work for me; for other people, maybe, but not for *me*. I had too sceptical an intelligence to enter wholeheartedly into the game, the spirit of it. Ninety per cent of it was faith in the cure. Faith. And no-one with a first-class intellect (why be modest?) was going to come at that.

Not that I hadn't at times been open to it, in a jokey kind of way. You got through the river of your day, sometimes wading, sometimes floating; sometimes it was a slow, anguished crawl, sometimes an effortless sprint. And all the time you wondered if there was some other model that made sense of things, some other dimension that you were separated from by only a thin membrane. You felt this most when you were drunk, or stoned, like a mirage of the senses: a dreamy, floating state succeeded by a ravenous physical hunger that brought you down to earth with a pleasurable thud. The plainest food tasted sublime, like manna, and I remembered once eating a packet of ginger cookies that felt like the first meal, although the delayed effect, the wash-up, was more like the Last Supper and the taste of ashes. But that's all it was, a perpetual question mark in the mind, a disinclination to be a dogmatic nay-sayer rather than a yearning to be a true believer. *As if* the configuration of the planets meant something; *as if* there were a benign destiny moving through the heavens . . . Maybe all these counsellors were secret fruit loops. Behind those smooth, caring façades they were a bunch of cultists, waving incense and burning cow dung at midnight.

The next week I cancelled my appointment. And then, when that felt hollow, I rang to make another one. That night I dreamed about the baby again, almost the same dream in all its surreal detail . . . the floating on the water, the woman in white, the swaddled infant that began to glow. And then, tormentingly, the sweet, sharp pain behind the breastbone, so that I woke this time and sat bolt upright in bed with my chest heaving, my hand pressed hard against my heart. Was I having a heart attack? Was there some blockage or genetic weakness there that I didn't know about? But beyond that, I felt I had just had the most profound dream of my life. *Again*. I was unnerved and I was exhilarated. And I had no-one to tell.

No-one except Sarah.

I went back because I liked Sarah, and because I couldn't think of anything else to do. Her house, that room, was soothing.

One evening when I knocked on her door I could hear the light soprano of a woman singing in German, and it was her. She was still humming and trilling the odd musical phrase as she unlocked the iron grille.

'Very nice,' I said.

'German *lieder*.' She grinned. 'It's an acquired taste.'

At the weekend I went into a shop in Oxford Street and bought a CD of *lieder*, only to find that while they had a certain charm, and the singer was no doubt more technically proficient than Sarah (I didn't have a musical ear and wouldn't know), they were not what I had heard from *her* lips. They were too studied; they lacked the same . . . the same *blitheness*. Did this mean I was becoming attached? I didn't think so, not really. While I might think of her between appointments in an 'I must raise this with Sarah' way, there was no more to it than that.

But there were layers to her that I had not guessed at, and this compelled my respect. I discovered she had once been an industrial chemist and worked for the Bayer firm in Frankfurt, and that she spoke fluent German. In many ways she was salty and down-to-earth, and after my initial surprise I realised this wasn't so out of character; there was that hard-headedness about her that I'd sensed in the first session, and that had made me trust her, something about that basketball in her box of tricks – and then she'd come up with that astrology drivel, though only the one time, as if she sensed I didn't like it. She never mentioned it again.

But she did eventually get the basketball out of the box, and with me stretched out on the futon we began what Sarah called 'bodywork'. Lots of deep breathing, some massage, some acute pain in surprising places. I never knew what to expect, or where it was supposed to go. Sometimes I thought it wouldn't have mattered much what she did; it was her weekly dose of dispassionate warmth that kept me going, like taking the car to a garage to get the battery recharged.

To begin with I saw Sarah once a week, every Monday evening after work, and then once a fortnight, and then more irregularly. And it seemed to help. Not in any dramatic way but with each visit some kind of minor catharsis took place, some discharge of toxic energy or emotions. I joked with her that she was a sixteenth-century physician of the psyche, that she bled me with invisible leeches, that she saw to it that I was opened up just enough to leak out enough of my angst, my black blood, to keep the circulation moving, to stop all the circuits congealing up with the thick bile of despair, the grey clag of sadness. It was, I imagined, a bit like being on a kidney machine, like having your psychic blood rinsed.

One evening I found myself rambling on about Leni and the villa. For a long time Sarah listened, and then: 'Were you attracted to Leni?'

'Not sexually. She wasn't my type. Too skinny. And obsessive.'

'But she made an impression on you, obviously.'

'She sought perfection. In everything. I'd never met anyone before who was so uncompromising about it. And thought it possible to achieve.'

'You admired her?'

'Yes and no. I felt a kind of weird kinship with her, but I felt she was barking up the wrong tree.'

'And what would be the right tree?'

This was one of those times when I was lying on the mat, staring up at the ceiling. I turned towards Sarah, who was kneeling above me, sitting back on her haunches like a relaxed muse. 'If I knew that,' I said, 'I wouldn't be here.'

'From what you say, it sounds like Leni was simply trying to create beauty, and unlike most of us she had the means to do it.'

I knew that. I wasn't a clod. I had no objection to beauty; it was a worthwhile project. I had no objection to comfort either, as in Jim's London office, the converted warehouse. I had loved working there. Every morning that I walked into the atrium of that building I felt my spirit quicken. There was a lot to be said for a personal barista.

But talking about Leni was a dead end. I wanted to ask Sarah about my recurring dream, about the woman and the baby. 'Why the baby?'

'I don't know,' she said. 'In some schools of thought the baby is said to represent the self.'

'So the baby is me?'

She smiled, mischievously. 'Maybe. Some dream therapists believe that everyone in the dream is you: the baby, the woman, even the water. You can see the logic of this. If it's coming out of *your* brain, *your* mind, it must be you, all of it. *You* create the dream.'

'What do you think?'

'I think it's possible to pay too much attention to dreams. If you wake up and the meaning is clear, then listen to it. If not, forget about it.'

In later years I would come to think of Sarah as a kind of transient angel in my life, someone I had the luck to find when I needed her. In some way I have never quite comprehended, she kept me from drifting heedlessly over the edge. She didn't 'cure' me but she stopped me from becoming more careless and self-destructive. It was a conservation phase, a shoring-up of the best of what was already there.

Of course we had dealt with 'issues': my emotionally remote father, for one. Didn't everyone have one of these? I had asked.

'I'm not treating everyone,' she had said, 'I'm treating you.'

Whenever I attempted to generalise she would always pull me up and bring me back to myself; what *I* experienced, what *I* felt. I could see the logic of it.

But what I was to recall later, in the light of subsequent events, was the time I told her about my inability to cry. She had looked at me in amazement. 'You can't recall a time when you cried as a small boy?'

'No.'

'Never?'

'Not that I remember.' What I remembered was being caned at school and standing alongside other boys, and how they had cried and I hadn't, and how elated I had been at the hardness of my heart. Whatever else they did to me, they could not reach me there.

Sarah shook her head.

'I've wanted to cry, many times. But I just can't do it. I remember once, when I was nineteen, this girl dumped me. I felt I was on the edge of tears, and when they wouldn't come I put my fist through a wall.'

'A *wall*?'

'It was plasterboard.'

Sarah was silent for a while. Then she tapped me lightly on the arm. 'Don't worry,' she said, 'Tears will come in their own good time.'

ground zero

He met her at The Basement late one Friday night when he was having a drink there with a friend. Then, exactly a week, later he bumped into her at a jazz festival at The Wharf.

'I know you,' he said.

'Zoe,' she replied. 'Zoe Mazengarb.'

She was small and dark and earthy, and he was transfixed. Although a little heavy in the hips, she had an exquisite waist and within minutes of their meeting she had made him laugh. Later, over a drink, he learned that she was a social worker at the Royal Prince Alfred Hospital but more on the managerial side, and he sensed that she was grounded, a woman who might be able to shake him out of his periodic torpor. There was something about her demeanour that suggested reserve, propriety, but in fact they made love on the night of the first date and the sex was good from the start.

It wasn't a grand passion; in truth he had never known one, and for all that he had had his share of infatuations, they tended to dissolve with intimacy. But Zoe and he were a fit. Whenever he saw her he felt a sense of relief, as if, at last, he was where he should be: in the right place. And there was trust. Zoe was straightforward, honest in all her responses, unlike Jo, who had been avid one minute, cool the next, always nurturing some unspoken resentment. The fact that Zoe seemed uncomplicated was a large part of her appeal. After all, wasn't he complicated enough for both of them? Jo had been soulful and highly strung, and what at first had seemed fascinating and romantic had become, in the routine of day-to-day living, both enervating and unsettling. The ground was always sliding out from under him in tiresome and hysterical ways. Zoe was more fixed. She was practical, well organised and athletic. She would be loyal and dependable, and in the protective aura of her common sense he would be relieved of his angst.

Summer came early and they began to spend their weekends at the beach. He found himself basking in the mindlessness of it: this was how life should be. In the past he had wanted too much, made things too complicated.

And there was something else. Zoe had a warm family who welcomed him into their comfortable home, and he was especially drawn to her father, Joe Mazengarb. Rick had never met an older man who was so engaging and demonstrative, or such a vibrant and energetic talker. Joe was also a great and cynical reader, a kind of wily *littérateur* who liked to quote from the classics.

The two men began to play squash together every week in an edgily competitive way. Joe was small and lean and fit, with cropped hair and a black, close-trimmed beard with so little grey in it that Rick wondered if he dyed it out of vanity. For Joe was vain, meticulously tailored and, unlike many men, not afraid of colour, being especially fond of a bright red cardigan that Zoe had given him.

In some ways Joe was the kind of man Rick had once aspired to be: prosperous, successful, comfortable in his cynicism. His worldliness was seductive. Joe had a way of taking liberties with any room he happened to be in. If he dropped in on Rick at his office (they worked within a block of one another), he would stub the butt of his cigar out in the paperclip tray on the desk. At home it would be the tea tray, sometimes even the soil of his wife's bonsai maple that sat in the middle of their coffee table. If they met in a restaurant, Joe treated it as his private club. He had a kind of man-of-the-world ease and assumption of privilege that Rick envied, and he wanted to fathom it. No-one, he felt, could be that sure of himself. Beneath that suave surface there must be some self-doubt.

The rapport between the two men had been instant. Each recognised in the other a common apprehension that life was absurd, only in Joe's perception it was comically absurd, in Rick's more gloomily so. Joe was particularly fond of telling stories of idealists who had got it all wrong, utopian dreamers who had made a mess of things. In this way he liked to demonstrate his superiority as a hard-nosed thinker and rationalist. As a litigation solicitor, he was full of stories so preposterous they could only be true, but these amused him less than the follies of those he thought of, and tended to disparage, as 'dreamers'. When Zoe and Rick came over for dinner on a Sunday evening Joe would wait until Zoe and her mother, Sally, were exchanging confidences in the kitchen, and then he would get out the whisky and draw Rick into some long and rambling narrative that only ever had the one moral point: to illustrate the comic pathos of that absurd animal, Man.

On one of these occasions, Joe was keen to discuss a book he had just read, a biography of Byron. He relished the story of Byron's efforts to bury the body of his friend Shelley on a beach in

Italy, for it had proved to be exactly the kind of absurd theatre of delusion that excited him. Shelley had drowned at sea when his yacht was caught in a storm, and, soon after, his body was buried unceremoniously on the beach where it had washed up. But his friends, Byron among them, wanted to stage a burial befitting a poet. In imitation of the ancient Greeks, Joe explained, they had a pyre made by a blacksmith in a nearby village. They carted it to the beach, where they erected it on the sand and stacked it with wood. Next they dug Shelley's corpse up out of its sandy grave, and it was a gruesome sight, for the face had turned dark blue from the effect of the lime. They laid the body on the pyre, poured oil and wine over it, and lit the flames. Then they stood and watched as it burned, and Joe was graphic in his description of how the skull had cracked open and the brains had boiled as if in a cauldron. (Byron proved to have a weak stomach and rushed into the sea to throw up.)

Finally, when the body had been reduced to grey ash, the onlookers found to their great surprise that the heart had refused to burn. Reaching into the fire, one of them snatched it from the coals and put it in his pocket to preserve for posterity. This, said Joe, gave rise to a romantic legend that the poet's heart was indestructible, but the joke was on the onlookers. It couldn't have been the heart that wouldn't burn – it would have been the liver, gorged with stale and useless blood and too liquid to ignite.

'All that palaver about the liver,' Joe exclaimed with satisfaction. 'How romantic is that! These men of letters, they weren't anatomists, they got things wrong.' And he banged the coffee table, lightly, with an open palm, so that the bonsai trembled. 'It's a category mistake made by all romantics. I call it the liver syndrome.'

This story gave rise to one of Joe's scornful epithets. Anything deluded he would dismiss by saying, 'We're dealing with liver syndrome here,' or, 'Sounds a bit liverish to me.' Rick was not entirely in sympathy with this line of thought, but on the other hand, he asked himself, how many fathers-in-law read biographies of Byron? At least Joe didn't talk about his investments or his golf handicap.

~

As Zoe and Rick spent more time together, he resolved to tell her about his black moods. It would be a test of their relationship because in essence he would be owning up to who he really was, and this was tantamount to issuing a warning: if she decided to love him, all was not going to be sweetness and light.

Her reaction pleased him. She told him how as a girl of fifteen she had been troubled for a whole year that her life would never make sense. But in time she had found her role as a manager. She could create order, it was her gift, and if nothing else, she could make her part of the world function from one day to the next. It was as if something clicked into place. She had no trouble giving orders and exercising authority; it came to her naturally, and others accepted what she said. Rather than her father's flamboyant and somewhat theatrical displays of conviction, she had her mother's steady self-possession, a quiet authority. And she'd learned that the thing to do was not to ask the big questions – what is the significance of this in the evolution of the universe? – but to concentrate on the small. How can I fix this problem in front of me now? And more often than not, she *could* fix the problem, or fix it enough for things to work, or go on working until, as she put it, someone came up with a better idea. She was, in short, free of the taint of perfectionism.

He decided she was the sanest person he had met.

~

A year later, they were married in Joe and Sally's garden. The ceremony was simple and there was an unlikely last-minute guest at the wedding – Jim Hagen. Jim had emailed to say he was flying in for a lightning tour of the outback – 'keen to see your big red rock' – and maybe they could meet up.

Rick was pleased to hear from Jim, and curious. He wondered how Jim would look: would he still bear the marks of grief? But no, there he was, his old self, lean and manic and accompanied by his fourth wife, Birgit, who was Danish. Did he still have the villa? Rick asked. No, said Jim, he had sold it after Leni's death. The villa was for Leni. But he knew how much Rick had 'loved the place' (where did he get that idea?) and as a wedding gift had brought him a valuable eighteenth-century engraving of the villa, which Leni had acquired. 'You always took an interest,' he said. And Rick was touched; until the day he died, Jim would be a surprising man.

Later, as Zoe examined the lithograph, she turned it over and found there was some writing on the back: 'As close to heaven as heaven can be.' Rick recognised the handwriting; it was Jim's.

'What does he mean by that?' Zoe asked.

'We never figured that out,' he said. But the engraving of the villa spooked him, and he wrapped it in an old yellow blanket and propped it against the back wall of the garage.

~

In the early years of marriage to Zoe he felt normal. Often the words would come to him: this is how life should be. At first the fires of the body burned bright, until in time the sex became more or less routine, as it always did, the flames reduced to gently glowing coals. But that was okay; he was older now, he had a more mature perspective on things, and he knew better than to think an endless pursuit of the flame, the hot flaring moment, was going to lead him anywhere new. And he loved his wife, and trusted her in a way he had not been able to trust any other woman. She had grown to know of his black moods, of the brooding and withdrawn silences that cast a grey blanket over the house, but she was an active woman and at these times, instead of badgering him, she simply got on with her life and left him to it.

And then something else came into the equation. His son was born, stirring in him an attachment he had not been able to imagine. For years he had resisted this yoke, but when it came his surrender was sudden and complete. He knew the moment he set eyes on that bloodied little body that he would never leave Luke, and that some new configuration of odds had come into his life. Clearly not all men felt this way or they wouldn't abandon their children, but something else must be going on there, some other kind of pain or blight on the soul that he had escaped. There had been moments before Luke was born when he had asked himself: how do people bear their lives? Not only their own misery, but also the misery of the world they looked out on? Then he became a father and the answer was given.

Not that he had wanted to have children: on the contrary. He knew that once he had a child, things would never be the same; it (the child) would become painfully wedged in his psyche like a troublesome diamond, a golden thorn in the heart. But he had been able only to imagine the drawbacks: the responsibility, the relentless presence, the constraints, the anxiety, the potential for loss. What he couldn't imagine was the sheer animal pleasure of cradling that little body, the smell of him, the early perfection of the bud – and he *was* perfection, he was unmarred, which was just as well, because Rick knew he didn't have the generosity of spirit to love anything less.

Perhaps because his son was the only person he loved more than himself, some of Rick's melancholy and boredom fell away. Luke became a lens, a refracting prism through which things he had once scorned, or been oblivious to, acquired meaning. His son gave him pleasure in the ordinary. Not that this was a cure for his restlessness; from the time of Luke's birth his discontent was always there, like rising damp, but never with the same degree of hollowness. With a child, you always had a reason to get out of bed in the morning. There was something more to your life than the seductive phantoms, the metallic aftertaste of your own ego. And a child had a way of making the mundane seem enchanted. Take those wintry Saturday mornings on the soccer field: the glittering white crust of frost on the grass, small boys and girls breathing gusts of steamy vapour into the air, a line of bare sycamores along a creek, the list to one side of a Japanese maple behind the goal, its perfect tilt of asymmetry. And the magic circle around the playing field, parents and grandparents stamping their feet behind the white chalk markings to relieve their chilled toes, clapping their gloved hands together, shouting at their children, earnest prodigies in floppy shorts. The skinny, awkward bow-legged kid who seemed hardly able to walk without tripping over his feet but could run with jagged speed and who scored every week, sometimes twice. The stocky boy who tried hard but miskicked so often he would beat his head with his fist, over and over, until his mother sang out, 'It's okay, Stuart, it's okay!' (Someone needed to explain to her that having your mother sing out from the sidelines was no consolation. Where, Rick wondered, was his father?) At the end of the game the two coaches would shepherd their charges into the centre of the ground, and there, massed in a weary huddle, the kids would stand awkwardly to give the opposing team three cheers. No matter how half-heartedly they were offered, those cheers could move him.

Yes, in the years following his marriage it seemed as if he were on a roll, as if he had crossed a frontier. He was head-hunted to set up the project team for innovation in a prestigious software firm, while Zoe and he eased into an affectionate groove of mutual understanding. He felt at last that he was maturing, settling equably into early middle age and that the brooding demon of his youth had migrated to another planet. At odd times he would find himself thinking of Sarah Masson, and talking to her in his head. It had been years since he last saw her, although for a while after meeting Zoe he had continued to visit intermittently in a natural diminuendo of contact, until one evening he wrote out his last cheque.

It was May 17 (he remembered the date because it was the day before Zoe's birthday) and he had brought with him a bunch of flowers and a bottle of champagne. Sarah had smiled enigmatically and said, 'Any time you feel the need for a booster, I'm here.' And he had thanked her again and kissed her on the cheek and said, yes, he knew, and he really appreciated all that she had done for him. But in his heart, he knew, he just knew, that he'd never be back again.

He had fallen into something called normality.

He had grown up.

~

Then came the drop, like a trapdoor had opened beneath his feet. Everything at work began to jar, to shudder and crack under the pressure of the recession. He had to shrivel his team from eleven into five, an impossible number, and the hours they worked were insane.

He knew that his protégé, Jason, had a coke habit but was shocked to discover he had moved on to heroin. Someone left an anonymous note on Rick's desk, someone perhaps who wanted Jason's job, or envied his preferment. What could he do about it? He was struggling to manage his own stress, in the office all day Saturday and sometimes Sunday morning. And drinking more at night. Sometimes, at work, it was as if pieces of him and everyone else were strewn around the floor, and they scarcely had enough energy to pick themselves up, like broken tin men, and put themselves back together for the evening drive home.

Anger began to fester, slow and insidious. In his sleep he ground his teeth from the strain of it and woke in the mornings with his jaw clamped and aching; that is, if he slept at all, for he was working long hours and was over-tired, and even when he did sleep it was as if he were cursed by an underlying alertness for which there was no off button. He was a machine in sleep mode, in a state of low-power readiness, a body apparently at rest but really only in a condition of diminished operation.

On the drive home, stuck in traffic, he would bang with a loose fist on the steering wheel of the car, robotically, over and over. Often now he was late, and Zoe and Luke would eat without him. Sometimes Zoe waited but he was too exhausted to talk much and wanted only to slump with a glass of red in front of the idiot box. And this was all for what? In his twenties he had thrown himself into his work in a gung-ho way and it had been not been difficult to cover his tracks during the black periods. But now the future was no longer an ocean of possibility, more like a river where the waterline was slowly receding in the face of recurrent drought.

He was forty-two and he was stalled. Too often, mostly around three o'clock in the afternoon, he felt as if time was standing still. And he wondered: was this a mid-life crisis? There were days when his mortgage felt like a leaky barge, on others a concrete bunker. There were mornings when he was fuggy, late afternoons when he was brittle.

And then it happened, the thing he feared most: his work began to bore him. He saw that there was just work and more work, the next project and the next, and the one after that. They were all just marking time until they died, pretending that the game was important, that the game could not do without them.

His old ennui returned, only now the torment was worse. There was no longer the future to look forward to; he was in it. The back end of the future had arrived and it was no different, no more satisfying than the rest of his life. As for the front end, he could read the projections. He hadn't even got there yet and already it was failing him.

He began to have night rages and would wake in the dark with fists clenched, or an aching jaw from grinding his teeth. He became increasingly sensitive to noise, and the least thing would set him off into a hair-trigger tantrum.

One night he was disturbed around 3 am by a shouting match below the bedroom window. He thumped downstairs, threw open the front door and shouted at two men and a woman who were arguing drunkenly by the fence. One of them moved threateningly to open the gate, and that gesture of transgression sent him over the edge. Instinctively he moved towards the stranger, ready for whatever might be coming, and gashed his toe on the edge of the brass sweeper, which had begun to come away from the front door. He could feel the blood trickling over his toenail as he kept his eyes on the stranger, who at that moment was backing off, retreating in an aria of screamed obscenities.

He closed the door and turned back for the bedroom, only to find Zoe at the bottom of the stairs, furious.

'You idiot!' she seethed. 'They could have worked you over well and truly! You don't know what they're on or what they're carrying. Or if they'll come back!'

He said nothing. Bandaged his toe. Poured himself a whisky and went and sat in the darkness of the living room. The toe throbbed all night.

Each day his anger bit into him more corrosively, like an acid train, stopping all stations: lungs, heart, liver, spleen, kidneys and the whole messy labyrinth of his guts. And then the chest pains began. This is it, he thought. I'm going to be one of those men who drop dead in their forties.

Zoe booked him in to their GP, David Wang.

'It could just be stress, Rick,' David said. 'I'm seeing a lot of people lately who are affected by the recession.' He paused. 'Although you do have a bit of a heart murmur. Did you know that?'

No, he didn't.

'It could be nothing to worry about, but then again, you do have chest pain.'

That night in bed, he thought: *I'm not ready to die.*

But what would 'ready' mean?

On any day death was a possibility. He might need to have a bypass, or a valve replaced. He had heard that repairs to the heart could be more complicated than a transplant. Surely that couldn't be true? For one thing, the after-effects would be fewer. And what did the murmur sound like? A whisper? A slight rumble in the rhythm? A click? A trill? Was it some kind of electrical fault?

That night he lay in the dark and mentally rewrote his will. He began by working through a series of bequests, revising them in his head from hour to hour. He allocated mementos to friends, drafted farewell notes (including a long letter to Luke) and gave instructions for his funeral: the venue, for a start (not in a church); who he would want, and not want, to be present; the music he would like played; where his ashes should be scattered – the last gasp of the control freak.

At first his mind raced, covering the bases on an imaginary spreadsheet, so that he multi-tasked, issuing instructions on several points at the one time, flicking from one provision to the next. After a while this contemplation of his demise had a curious effect: it was unexpectedly soothing. His mind began to slow, his concentration to falter, and with this his breathing deepened and he became aware of the rise and fall of his chest. Having planned his death in great detail, he was at last able to fall into a deep and untroubled sleep.

The following Saturday he walked with Luke to the university's medical library to do some research. But once through the door of the Bosch building, he was overcome by his old library claustrophobia with its memories of enforced tedium, of the brain in an institutional harness. He had always felt a resistance to books en masse; stolid, musty little rectangles of the arcane. Still, he was there now, so he might as well get on with it.

Using the keyword 'murmur' on the medical library database, he scrolled through a bewildering array of titles: *Clinical Disorders of the Heartbeat*, *The Disorders of Cardiac Rhythm Vols I and II*, *Interpretation of Complex Arrthymias*, *Electrasystoles and Allied Arrhythmias*, *Intraventricular Conduction Disturbances*, *Frontiers of Cardiac Electrophysiology* and *Ventricular Tachycardia*. Proceeding on the intuitive principle that the right book would jump out at him from the shelves, he strolled through the aisles of cardiac books while Luke rode his bike up and down the concrete terrace outside.

The books were more dryly technical than he had anticipated, and there seemed to be two hundred varieties of heartbeat, each characteristic of a different syndrome and carrying a different name, not one of which spelled out Software Analyst Programmers in Mid-life Panic. After only a few frustrated and increasingly desultory minutes, his eye was caught by the title of a slim black volume, *Sudden Death in Athletes*, written by a man with the improbable name of Jokl. Taking it from the shelf, he slumped into a reading chair and read a lurid chapter on 'Collapse Syndromes': hypothermia, effort migraine, mountain sickness and cataplectic loss of muscle tone (athletes collapsing of shock when informed of their win), the Mexico Olympics in '68 proving to be of special interest.

This was absurd. He stood up, walked outside and whistled for Luke, who was careening down a long path into the trees.

A week later he presented himself for an echocardiogram. It was somewhere around six o'clock on a rainy Thursday evening, and there he was, sitting in the antiseptic waiting room of one of those private pathology centres that smell of money and death.

He was the only one there. Waiting his time. Within an hour everything in his life could change.

It was a heavy old house, a Victorian mansion converted into medical suites with cheap chipboard partitions subdividing what were once grand and gloomy salons. Eventually a woman appeared and beckoned him over.

'Richard?'

'Rick, it's Rick.'

'Hi, Rick. I'm Helga.'

Helga was a large, Nordic-looking woman in her fifties, solidly built with cropped blonde hair streaked with grey. 'Ever had an echocardiogram before, Rick?'

'Never.'

She pointed to a cubicle. 'Strip from the waist up.'

'Shoes?'

'No, you can leave your shoes on.'

This summoned up the notion, both comic and macabre, of dying with his boots on. Draped in a clinical wrap made of pale green paper, he opened a padded door and entered a room where the ultrasound machine was waiting for him, a block of gun-grey metal, six feet at its highest point, with two video screens at the top. Helga, he realised, was its technician, its high priestess.

Lying on the surgical bed, his head resting on a pillow, he felt as if he had been taken up into a spaceship. There was a certain warm gravitas about Helga, even in grey track pants and ugg boots which on anyone else would look shapeless and woolly. On her, they looked stylish and high-tech, like she was an astronaut in a lab. Helga had a comfortingly androgynous quality, a cross between high-tech angel and Nordic *Hausfrau*, and it was clear she could read the heart like an old invoice, like the back of a cereal packet. There were no mysteries there for Helga, but nor was she jaded, for she had a quality of intense concentration, of low-key command: rapid, efficient, absorbed. She worked the machine the way that competent women cook, with the familiarity and ease of having done it all before, but also the relaxed alertness of one who knows that at any minute it could all go wrong: something malignant or fatal could appear up there, some squiggle or smudge on the screen could signify a death sentence for the hapless figure on the surgical bed. A flaw might manifest, some warp or hole, some blockage or malformation; some enlargement or tissue damage, or clot or calcification; a startling arrhythmia, like a code that's been scrambled; an electrical fault running malign interference.

Ah, but here was another alien. A man in his sixties came in and introduced himself as Dr Cullen. He was thin, grey and dry-looking, and Helga called him 'doc'.

So here he was, Richard Kline, lying in his green paper gown on a white surgical bed, reclining on his left arm like a model posing for a life class.

On the wall opposite was a print in the abstract style, a large red funnel with smaller funnels at one end. In this room everything was circuits, even the token artwork. Helga rubbed a warm gel on the end of a tube, like one half of a stethoscope.

'What's that?' he asked.

'That's the traducer,' she said, and he smiled.

The name itself conjured up trespass and violation, and Helga was placing the instrument, this traducer, firmly against his chest, just under the left nipple, pressing hard against his ribcage, so that it hurt. Without fanfare, his heart appeared on the right-hand screen.

Just like that.

He was gobsmacked. There it was, in black and white, a slightly blurred image of heaving muscle, working away with such ferocious energy that he was in awe. Even more awed than he had been when he first saw his son's foetal form on the ultrasound screen. In awe of himself? Well, that made a change. Nothing, he thought, prepares you for the experience of seeing your own heart, and he continued to gaze at it in frank arousal, almost expecting a round of applause.

Helga, of course, was disinterested. Sitting on her high stool, leaning in towards the machine, she began matter-of-factly to scan the image from different angles and cross-sections, adjusting the dials to give close-ups of certain features, like the valves, reading numbers to Cullen, who sat behind her on a low chair and repeated her observations, muttering comments in corroboration or dissent.

Helga was reeling off the numbers. '27, 28, 47 . . . good functioning of the left ventricle . . . 28, 40, 8 . . . 7, 21 . . . A good set of numbers there, doc,' she said, and winked at Rick, letting him know she was mocking the economic pundits.

Cullen looked up from his notes and peered at Rick over the top of his half-moon glasses. 'It's all numbers these days, isn't it?' he said dryly.

Rick smiled politely, thinking: it's like watching the Keno machine on TV. This was his life's lottery, his flesh-and-blood poker machine.

Suddenly there was a noise, and with a start he realised that Helga was adjusting the sound dials on the machine, and this, now, was the sound of his heart . . . whoosh-whoosh! it went, whoosh-whoosh! Like a loud, emphatic washing machine. Look at that pump, that manic, heaving pump – rhythmic, implacable – could that really be him? All those times in his life when he had suffered from lassitude, from negativity, from doubt and despair, all that time this heart had been oblivious . . . whoosh-whoosh! . . . Here it is, he thought, the prosaic soundtrack of my self. Indifferent to the dreary thoughts of my brain, it pumps on regardless. And he was moved. Yes, he had been told about it, had seen other people's hearts in TV documentaries, but let me tell you, he thought, it's different when that heart is yours.

Helga and the doc were still muttering to one another, swift matter-of-fact statistics and appraisals. By now all fear had left him. He wanted to ask a dozen questions but he didn't want to disturb their concentration in case they overlooked some small but fatal flaw. So he gazed at the wall opposite his feet until he heard Helga say, '17, 21, 28 . . . a murmur there . . .'

A murmur! He jerked his head up. This was it. This was the death sentence.

'. . . but I'd say that was trivial, doc. I wouldn't say that consti-tuted a prolapse.'

Cullen was gazing up at the screen, his glasses having slid down to the end of his beaky nose. There was a horrible pause, and then he said, 'No, not a prolapse.'

'What does that mean?' Rick asked.

'Nothing to worry about,' replied Helga, still staring at the screen. 'I'll explain in a minute.'

Then Cullen left the room, unceremoniously, with only a dry nod at Rick, who was no longer of concern, who had failed to pro-duce an interesting set of numbers. Helga switched off the machine.

Just like that.

No more heart. Heart put away, back in its ribcage, back in its box.

Helga leaned forward on her stool and adjusted her glasses. 'There *is* a murmur,' she said, 'which is what your GP heard, but it's an innocent murmur.' She said this quickly, so as not to alarm him. She called it 'trivial'.

'What does that mean?'

She brought her two index fingers together. 'This is the normal valve,' she said. Then she moved one finger up an almost imper-ceptible fraction over the other, 'and this is yours. There's just a very slight misfit, if you like, an infinitesimal gap or cusp. A slip-page. If bacteria get in through this, into the bloodstream, they like to congregate there and breed.'

He had heard of this condition. He had heard (but didn't like to say) that the bacteria eat away the valve and then you're in big trouble. Yes, he would say it.

'They can damage the valve?'

'It's rare. Very rare.'

'That's it?'

'That's it.'

The verdict: innocent. But still he couldn't quite accept it, still was holding his breath.

'I just don't understand,' he said, 'how any murmur, any deviation from the norm, can not mean *something*.' How could a murmur be innocent?

At which point Helga put her large reassuring hands on his shoulders. 'There is absolutely nothing,' she said, 'wrong with your heart.'

Back in the cubicle, he put on his clothes. He felt he would like to shake Helga's hand, or kiss her on the cheek, but that would be inappropriate. It was all routine to Helga. Helga saw eight hearts a day.

Outside. He was outside and walking down the winter dark of Macquarie Street, past the Catholic bookstore with its sombre crucifixes, its painted statues of the Virgin, its gilt candles. He paused for a moment by the window and looked for a statue of the Sacred Heart. There wasn't one. Perhaps it was out of fashion, that lurid icon of blood and fire. There had been no blood and fire on the machine, just the blurred black and white smudges, the rhythmic pulsing, the whoosh-whoosh. And Helga, the high priestess.

It was four blocks to the underground car park and he walked them in a kind of alert trance, breathing in the cool, damp smell of rain, taking in the world around him; the all-but-deserted city, the shiny wet road, the traffic lights, the grey drizzle – and all the time in his mind's eye that surging, inexorable mass of muscle and blood, *his* heart.

'So long as the heart is doing its work it may be pardoned for its innocence.' He had read that in a book in the Bosch library; a thing may not always be perfect but that doesn't mean it can't do its job. And it was nothing personal, not something he could take credit for: if they took it out of him and put it in someone else, it would go on in exactly the same way, like the rhythm of the universe, like the movement of the tides. And he felt humbled: his heart did all this work for him, without pause or rest, twenty-four hours a day for forty-two years. Such a long time for a muscle to pump without missing a beat.

Suddenly it seemed almost beyond credible. No wonder they called it the miraculous pump. The cyclonic funnels, surging and throbbing like storm channels. Relentless, that was the word he was searching for, the quality he was awed by: the sheer *relentlessness* of it. He knew his other organs were working hard but not so dramatically, so noisily, not with the same unabated, day into night, night into day rhythm. And what he felt was gratitude. He was grateful and he must show his gratitude. He must not take this heart for granted. He must find a way to exercise more. And to relax. He had his heart, and his heart was good to him, so why wasn't he good to his heart?

~

For some time after the echocardiogram he existed in a state of simple-minded gratitude. He felt good, almost invincible. Small pleasures ambushed him. Spring arrived and he began to feel that the worst of his anger had passed.

It was a Wednesday morning. He was feeling off-colour, and he rang the office to say he had the flu that was on the rampage that spring and he would not be coming into work. Zoe was late and frazzled and sharp-tongued with Luke. He hated it when she spoke to the boy like that, even though, increasingly, this was the way that he, Rick, spoke to her. It was one of those hateful mornings of family dissonance, although he couldn't for a minute blame her for what was to come.

'I'll drive him to school,' he said. 'I'll drop you off at the station first and you'll save twenty minutes.'

She shot him a glance almost of truce. 'Thanks.'

By this time he had lost the knack of patient endurance in peak hour, if ever he'd had it. Cars were banked up along the high street like a line of tin beetles, while the humidity, already rank, seeped into the car like a noxious gas and he felt he was bumper-to-bumper in thick cotton wool.

A block before Luke's school he pulled into the kerb by a small park opposite a frantic intersection. Cautioning Luke to be careful, he watched as the boy glanced from side to side, waited for the lights to change and then ambled across the zebra crossing with his distinctive bobbing walk, his backpack dangling awkwardly from one shoulder, his right arm raised in a laid-back wave.

He waited until Luke had disappeared through the school gates and then he turned the key in the ignition. And turned it off again. There was a convenience store on the corner and he would get the paper and some milk; they were out of milk and he was looking forward to coffee. He walked to the edge of the corner and stepped off from the kerb, and at that moment a flash of white metal swerved with a screech of tyres and almost ran over his foot.

The car, a dilapidated Datsun with a dent in the driver's side and a smashed headlight, stalled on the turn into the main road, and suddenly he was standing there looking down through the driver's window – it was rolled down as far as it would go – and into the glinting brown eyes of the driver, and he leaned in and with his open hand slapped him across the face – registering in a split-second that the face he was striking was black. He was a young Islander, twenty-two, twenty-five, maybe, who stared back at him with eyes of molten rage. And next to him, another face, his friend, whose mouth was open in hostile shock, though only for a second, before it widened into a spray of growling obscenities.

Not that he heard them. Or, rather, he heard but didn't register them, because his attention was focused on the driver, who had flung open the door and was lunging at him.

For a moment he considered turning and running, but his pride would not allow this. The first blow he felt against his upper right temple. The second caught him on the shoulder. Positioning his feet instinctively to maximise his balance, he ducked from side to side as the blows came, one after another. At some point he heard himself utter a sharp laugh of derision; he was laughing at the failure of his assailant to land his punches. At the same time a part of his brain looked on in horror. Who was this self-destructive fool laughing at his tormentor?

Not for a second did he consider fighting back. For one thing, he was in the wrong, and his heart was a black hole of stupefying foolishness, a sunken galleon in his chest, and for another, if he managed to respond with even one halfway decent punch then he'd really be done for: there was no way he could beat the two of them, and probably not even this one, who was younger and fitter and heavily built. The blows came at him in a flurry, and any one of them might have smashed his jaw or broken his nose if he hadn't been ducking and weaving so that they glanced off him in jolting grazes and he scarcely felt the lacerations of his skin, the bloody contusions on his scalp. But with the fifth blow he felt the hard bone of knuckle against his skull and he fell to the grass, almost in slow motion, for a moment on his knees and then keeling over onto his side, so he felt that the green blades of grass were in his eyes, the dank earth in his nostrils.

He lay there in a daze, thinking: *Here it comes, the boot in the head.*

But it didn't.

When eventually he sat up, shaking his head slowly from side to side, he looked around him. The Datsun was gone. A woman and her two small daughters were staring at him as if he might bite.

'Are you alright?' the woman asked, nervously. 'Do you want me to call the police?'

'No, it's okay,' he gasped, and his voice came out of empty bellows. He was winded. His mouth tasted of acid bile, his body felt like putty. His heart lurched rancorously into his guts, and with a rising groan he vomited into the grass.

Somehow he drove home. When he got there he made himself a cup of scalding hot tea and put four heaped spoons of sugar in it. Sugar for shock, he remembered. Then he rang David Wang, who said to come over straight away.

David pronounced him mildly concussed and wrote out an authorisation for a head X-ray at the public hospital along the road. Rick thanked him and said he would go there straight away. But he didn't. He was beginning to feel better; physically, anyway.

David had been outraged on his behalf, had urged him to report the incident to the police. But Rick knew better. It was his own fault, he had brought this madness on himself, not that he could explain this to David, who prided himself on his counselling skills. David would warn his patient about the classic syndrome of the victim blaming himself, feeling that he had somehow invited attack, that some inadequacy or quintessential unworthiness had marked him out. Everyone knew this sort of spiel by now; it was even in the lifestyle section of the papers. But Rick knew that for one thing he had struck the first blow. And there was something else, and it was this: he had looked into the younger man's eyes and seen his own madness, his own ugliness, his own rage and humiliation reflected back at him.

That night he waited until Luke was in bed. Then he told Zoe what had happened. 'I got beaten up today,' he said baldly.

What had he expected? Sympathy? Fear? Cool disdain?

She screamed at him. 'You what! You hit a black man in the middle of the city . . .' Her first shriek trailed off in disbelief. *'Are you out of your fucking mind?'*

And before he could respond, could say anything more, like 'It wasn't in the middle of the city', she screamed at him again.

'How could you? *How could you?* There were children there! Young children. And what if Luke had witnessed it, his father being beaten up in broad daylight! As it is, he'll probably hear about it!'

Her face was a grimace of pain. Tears leaked from her eyes. At that moment, he could see, she despised him. 'And what about us? Did you think of us? You could have been seriously hurt, you could have had your face smashed in, you could have had your ribs broken. You . . .' her voice cracked and faltered, 'you could have been killed!'

But I wasn't, he thought. I wasn't. I was agile, and I did okay. But those vain thoughts were just a last gasp of self-defence against a

great grey tide of self-pity that was about to engulf him at any minute. He couldn't bear the despair between them for another second
and he got up from his chair and walked through the open door of
the kitchen and out onto the back lawn. There he sat under the platform of Luke's tree house with the base of his spine against the
rough bark of the tree trunk, and when he put his head on his knees
he could feel the synapses in his brain firing and misfiring over and
over and over and over until he thought his head might explode.

After a while, he looked up. It was a clear night. The stars
blinked down at him.

When he went inside she was sitting at the kitchen table, waiting for him. She had been crying. 'Sit down,' she said. 'I have
something to say to you.'

Here it comes, he thought. Divorce. He could see Luke asleep
in his single bed and he knew he would do anything not to give
him up.

Her voice was low, quavering and grim. 'I can't go on living with
your anger,' she said. 'In the last year you've been unbearable.' She
spoke hurriedly, as if she could not afford to pause. 'Either you go
and see a counsellor and get some sort of therapy, or I'm leaving.'

Therapy, he thought, what was the point of that? He had tried
it once in the past, and while it had helped, it had not been enough.
The vessel was still half-empty. He wanted something more,
something more than – what? Something more than comfort.
But what else was there? What else could any of us offer one
another?

For most of the next day he slept.

In the evening Zoe brought home takeaway for dinner and they
barely spoke. He jabbed at his food listlessly until the silence got

to him and he stood up. 'I'm going to sit outside for a while,' he said.

Out in the shadowy courtyard he felt spacey, disoriented. There was an obscure humming in his head. He sat down, carefully, on the edge of an old deckchair, and, closing his eyes, he began, involuntarily, to relive the events of the previous day. A garish reel of film ran in his head, sometimes speeded up, sometimes in slow motion, until he could bear it no longer and blocked it out in a black dissolve . . .

When he opened his eyes everything in the garden seemed exaggeratedly *there*, larger than life but alien. His senses were acute. A mosquito buzzed his ear and he looked up. It was a warm, scented night and the brightness of the moon ought to have calmed him but his pulse was slippery, his breathing taut and irregular, and his heel drummed against the concrete slab. A slow, disengaging cog began to shift and grind in his chest . . . he looked down, looked up again, blinked . . . the back of the house was receding from him, the kitchen window panes framing little squares of golden light that seemed to grow smaller and smaller and smaller. He stood up with a start and shook his head. Any minute now he would lose his grip on reality, would tear and splinter into gaping viscera and jagged bone.

In the kitchen Zoe was sitting at the table, reading the paper. He stood in the open doorway. 'I'm going for a walk,' he said. This is it, he thought. I will start to walk, and then I will just keep on walking until I drop.

She nodded curtly. Then she looked up at him, and her eyes were full of a sadness he hadn't seen there before. 'I'll come with you,' she said, and rose purposefully.

And walk they did, he unthinkingly beside his sad, angry wife; aloof, holding his breath, oblivious to the blur of shrimp bushes in the gardens beside him, the overhanging hibiscus and the fraying palms. They walked and walked, looping around the hill and taking the long way back, and somehow the walking began to exert its spell, the simple rhythm of striding in step, feet on the ground, arms swinging, the black fog in his heart seeping down into the soles of his shoes, to be left, like an invisible film, on the grey asphalt.

~

In the weeks that followed he felt as if he were waiting.

Waiting for what?

And Zoe, too, was waiting.

And then one of his software engineers, a man named Carl Kremmer, hanged himself in the basement of their Chatswood office. The cleaners came in on a Monday morning and found him hanging from an air-conditioning pipe. The irony of this was not lost on Rick. A man had contrived to cut off the flow of air through his body by tying himself with nylon cord to a valve that was there to enable him to breathe more wholesomely, more comfortably, without the extremes of heat or cold, without noise or smog or wind or dust, without frost or mist or airborne pollen.

By the end of the month, the human resources people had circulated a memo offering free programs in stress management; a reward, as Zoe remarked tartly, for working late into the night and falling asleep at your workstation. One of these programs was a short course in meditation. The memo came accompanied by a glossy brochure extolling 'an age-old technology of the self' and promising a technique that would 'eliminate stress' and enable you to 'maximise your potential'.

Why not? he thought. He had tried everything else, and this at least would placate Zoe, would look as if he were making some kind of effort.

When the forms went back, only two from his team had elected to go. The other was Mark Paradisis. Mark was a young systems analyst, twenty-eight years old and cocksure. His reddish-brown hair was shaved with a number-one blade and he favoured a series of stylish, oversized jackets, collarless shirts, and occasional waist-coats that complemented his dark looks. Bumptious and clever in the narrow-banded way of tech-heads everywhere, he treated Rick with a respect that was part mocking, part real; he would circle around him like a teasing child, absurdly deferential one minute, taking stinging liberties the next.

One afternoon he informed Rick that currently he was 'between cars', and since they would be going straight from work to medita-tion classes – 'Oops, sorry, stress management' (winking at him) – he thought perhaps Rick could give him a lift, at least to the introductory lecture on the Monday. Beyond that, he couldn't guarantee that he'd front. 'They might be a bunch of crazies, K.' (Rick's project team all called him 'K'.) 'Know what I mean? Hip-pies, cult-struck mind-benders. Whatever.'

But when the time came Rick was glad of a younger man's com-pany. As part of a twosome he felt less self-conscious. It seemed like more of a game.

The classes began at seven and they drove straight from work, across the bridge in the lea of peak-hour traffic. On the edge of

Taylor Square they made a pit stop for souvlaki, which they ate in the parked car. It was hot and dusty, and as they sat looking out the window at the squalor of the square – its rough street trade, its sinister little patch of concrete between the traffic lights, its pungent smells of burned coffee, rancid frying oil and carbon monoxide – the absurdity of their dinner setting, only minutes away from the meditation centre, made him feel perversely cheerful and he chortled out loud, almost choking on the first bite of dry pide bread.

Mark turned his head sharply. 'What?' he asked.

Rick was still struggling to swallow. 'Nothing,' he coughed, 'nothing at all.'

Mark then began, in between wolfing down mouthfuls of the kibbeh special, to launch into a riff on the mechanics of his mental well-being, and it would have been funny if it hadn't had a certain quality of robotic desperation.

It was like this, he explained: he was not moving forward, he was not making progress in his life. He'd had a few knocks in the last couple of years; been dumped by his girlfriend, got pissed a lot, lost his licence, lost the plot, you might say. Then this free offer came up, and, well, as he saw it, it was like servicing or reconditioning your car. Things wear down after a while – the engine's not ticking over, there are some clunks in performance – you go to a good mechanic and you get it seen to. So you can move forward, so you can progress. The car you've got might not be much good but it's the only one you've got. You've got to tune it up from time to time, otherwise the wheels will fall off. You won't move forward, you won't progress.

By this time they had finished their hasty supper and Rick had pulled out into Oxford Street. 'How do you know when you've progressed?' he asked, teasingly. He could see how nervy Mark was, how he couldn't sit still and jiggled one knee up and down like it was on voltage. Hot-wired.

'You look at it this way,' Mark said. 'You check for reality statements. You ask yourself: where am I now compared to where I was? You get feedback from people you work for. It's like one of those performance assessments. They'll tell you: now you score, I don't know, say, eight out of ten, whereas once it was three, four, something like that.'

Mark was talking as if he were a machine, a machine within a machine, a bright red Honda SL encased in Rick's silver Fiat. And then he said something poetic: 'Y'know, K, I'm annoyed at having my future dictated by my footprints in the sand – places I've been, what I've done in the past, all that.'

'You read that in a book somewhere?'

He shrugged, glanced away. 'Yeah, probably.'

At that moment they turned into Underwood Street. The house they were looking for was an elegant old terrace painted in lavender and white. It stood on the brow of the hill looking down to the sweep of the bay and had a big peach-coloured hibiscus bush in bloom by the front door. It was one of those stifling summer evenings, the gardens petrified in a humid stillness; Rick and Mark paused at the iron gate, struck by the shadowy beauty of the street, the exquisite tracery of the trees in outline against the darkening sky, the rich, orderly beauty of the terraces unfolding down the hill with the satisfying symmetry of a series of perfect numbers.

The door was ajar so they went in and through to the front salon, a room of stately proportions fitted out like a corporate office: pale grey carpet, eight rows of pale green chairs, and a white-board positioned in front of a marble fireplace. On the chairs were fifteen or so men and women who, like Mark, were mostly in their late twenties or early thirties, stressed-out yuppies in casual but expensive clothes. Instinctively Rick cast an appraising glance at the women in the room; he noted Mark doing the same. Primal instinct.

They sat and looked ahead without speaking, as if they had exhausted their chitchat in the car. Before long a man in his early forties and dressed in a suit entered the room from the rear and stood by the whiteboard. Smiling at them, he introduced himself as Jack.

Jack was to be their trainer, and Rick liked him on sight. In his light grey suit, pale blue shirt and yellow tie, he presented in every way as a middle-level executive. Jack's skin gave off a tanned glow, and this, combined with his balding head and round face, gave him the appearance of a corporate buddha. He had a way of talking with an almost permanent smile on his lips, as if sharing a joke, but his eyes shone with a warm, dark gloss, insinuating that, yes, the unfathomable *could* be fathomed.

He began by telling them that meditation was a simple, unde-manding process through which the mind effortlessly arrived at the source of consciousness. *The source of consciousness?* Immedi-ately Rick's fickle mind began to play with this, punning on the idea of source. He couldn't get out of his head an image of sauce on the brain, a large brain on a plate with a lurid red sauce poured over it, and then a white sauce, and next a yellow, like thick cus-tard . . . Without this sauce the brain looked remarkably naked, uninteresting even, doughy and grey, like batter left overnight in the fridge that had begun to oxidise . . . Could this be the *organe supérieur*, the *summa cum laude*, the source of all that was bright and beautiful and inspired?

Look how his mind had wandered already! He recollected himself.

Jack was talking about peak performance. 'During meditation the body enters into deep levels of relaxation and rest, a more profound rest than that experienced even in deep sleep. The body becomes attuned to the subtle vibrations of nature, which repair the body and release the creative energies of the human organism . . .'

Next to Rick, Mark had fallen asleep, which was not surprising – the words had a high degree of abstraction, an airy quality, and Mark often didn't leave his workstation until after ten at night. And Jack had a soft, soothing voice that exuded warmth. The effect was indeed soporific. Jack was, he could see, a very contained man, though with a surprising tendency to giggle. Nevertheless, there was something attractive in his persona that was hard to define, a subtle quality.

Rick looked around him. Not everyone, it was clear, had a mind as restless as his or as tired as Mark's. Everyone else appeared attentive, and serious. Most of them were younger, and as junior executives they were used to paying attention, used to listening for the 'hook', the slogan, the key phrases, the code words, the 'open sesame'. And now they were here for the mantra. As Mark would say: if it works, it's cool.

In Jack's discourse there seemed to be a lot of emphasis on the brain. But what about the heart? As if reading Rick's mind, Jack moved on to the subject of 'perfect health' – didn't these people ever use qualifiers? – and heart disease, and how medical research had shown conclusively that meditation regularised blood pressure and lowered cholesterol. In orthodox terms, this was its area of greatest success.

Beside him, Mark had begun to snore gently. Jack's soft tones were such that perhaps they didn't need to learn to meditate; perhaps all they needed was a tape of his voice, with one of those piping flutes in the background and the sound of running water. On the way over Mark had told him about the time he worked for an IT company in Palo Alto, California, where, during a particularly tense and difficult project, one of the supervisors had had a notion to play a relaxation tape in the office, until all the programmers had shrieked that it was getting on their nerves. Tonight, however, 'the voice' was working for Mark, who had dozed through almost the entire talk: eyes closed, head slumped forward on his chest.

Jack concluded by asking each of them to say why they had come. And they all said something sensible. They wanted 'better concentration'; they wanted 'to achieve more', to double their current workload. They wanted to feel less tense, less tired, less impatient, more calm. No-one said they wanted to maximise their potential. No-one admitted to being fed up and angry. And no-one talked about 'the mysterious absences at the heart of even the fullest lives', to quote from a book review Rick had idled through in the dentist's surgery some days before.

Mark woke up in time to say that he regarded his body as a prime racing machine, and just lately he had realised it needed a bit of a tune-up.

Rick said he wanted to get more done with less fatigue. What else was he going to say? That he was angry? And that as he grew older he was getting angrier? Angry at the universe for failing him? Listening attentively to the reasons the others gave for being there that night, he wondered if they too were dissembling, camouflaging some inner vision of flames – some moment of madness, some visceral ache of yearning – with the managerial workspeak of the brochure, a language they had learned to wear like a suit of armour, like battle fatigues.

The introductory talk finished early, around nine-thirty, and he hadn't far to drive his companion, who asked to be dropped off at a club in Oxford Street. Refreshed by his nap at the meditation centre, Mark was ready to party. On the way up the hill Rick teased him about falling asleep, and with the disarming ingenuousness of a child Mark asked for a 'recap' on what he had missed.

'Fill me in, K,' he said. 'What was the gist of it?'

'Some things are too subtle to be rendered into paraphrase.'

Mark threw back his head. 'Seriously?' And then, 'Yeah, yeah, I'll bet.'

God, he was a boy, a slick, smart-arsed boy. 'You'd better stay awake tomorrow night.'

'Yeah, definitely, if you say so, K,' he said, winking at Rick as he lurched out of the car at an intersection and sauntered off up the neon-lit street.

Driving home, Rick was disconcerted by the fact that, even if there had been time, he couldn't have told Mark much of what Jack had said. Was his concentration as shot as all that? Or had it all been too vague, too abstract? He would have to say the evening had been something of an anticlimax: he had hoped for revelations but none had come. Perhaps the first night was a test, and if you persevered and kept coming back, in the end you'd get a pay-off: the magic word, the open sesame.

And you did. Get the magic word, that is. On the second night Jack told them about the mantra. The mantra was a special sound. It was like a key in the lock of their inner being, and the insistent chanting of it would open them up and put them in touch with . . . with what? On this, they still weren't clear. Everything Jack said sounded reassuring at the time but evaporated from their ears within seconds.

For the next two nights the talks continued as before. And each evening Mark sat dozing in his chair beside Rick so that Rick had to 'recap' for him on the way home before dropping him off at a club: Zero in Oxford Street, Moscow in Surry Hills, Yada Yada in Leichhardt. Clubs seemed to have a life of twelve months; Rick hadn't heard of any of them. It made him feel old. 'I don't know any of these places,' he said.

Mark shook his head in mock commiseration. 'This is what happens when you get married, K.'

Rick continued to find it extraordinarily difficult to summarise what Jack said about anything. Zoe would ask him and he would hesitate and then ramble. It was as if the words were little nodules of polystyrene filler, the kind that come as packing around white-goods and spill out of the box when you attempt to extricate the appliance. You could gag on them. At other times the words felt like ball bearings rolling around in his mouth: precise, elegant and full of weighty momentum, but also cold, smooth and hard to trap.

One night, clearly bored with Rick's struggle to condense 'the message', Mark interrupted his waffling to say, 'Y'know, K, I was really surprised when I saw you'd put your name down for this course. You impress me as the strong type. You know' – his mouth curled into a mock grimace – "'Stress? What stress?'"

'I *am* the strong type,' Rick said.

He was not about to enter into emotional correspondence with a younger man. This was taboo. And anyway, it was far too difficult to explain, especially to someone like Mark, that lurking in his consciousness, like a virus in the bloodstream, was a sliver of pain he could neither disgorge nor salve. He could think of some parodic scenario that might make sense to Mark; a virus, say, infecting his program, or that movie *Fantastic Voyage*, where something was making its way through the pathways of the body, like a microchip afloat in a vast cyclotron.

Was this pain in the shadowy background of his consciousness, or at the forefront of his *un*conscious? Whatever *that* was. When he thought of it at all he tended to think of the unconscious as a playing field where small, neurotic athletes jostled for position, and learning to meditate might enable him to marshal them into a team where all the elements could combine well, could get onto cosy terms, could resolve whatever it was that was creating friction between them. The mantra would be the oil in the 'grease and oil change', to adapt Mark's metaphor, the soothing balm that would ease the disparate elements into the right formation, and he would become a cyber program without glitches. Debugged. The perfect dream of neuroscience. At last he would be rid of that unresolved yearning that had haunted him all his life, that was so unsettling, like a metaphysical pinprick in every balloon of pleasure, in every activity, actual or potential, virtual or real.

On the fourth night, they got it. The mantra. The pay-off, the magic formula.

As usual, he and Mark drove straight from the office but this time they were late. When Mark wanted to stop near Taylor Square and get a falafel, Rick said, 'We haven't time.'

'I'm starving.'

He knew that, like many of his team, Mark would have skipped lunch, or shot out for a Mars Bar from the vending machine in the corridor. The way they worked was crazy. In the glovebox, he told Mark, there was a bag of roasted almonds kept there by his very practical wife for times like this, or for when Luke was hungry. And had he, Mark, remembered to bring the ritual offering? He'd half-expected Mark to forget this – the flowers and the fruit that they were required to bring as a gesture of respect – but was touched to find that Mark hadn't forgotten, that he had some grapes in a takeaway food container that he produced from his designer backpack, along with a bunch of violets he had bought at the station on his way to work.

When they arrived there was an air of quiet expectation. Everyone was sitting on the meeting-room chairs with their small parcels of flowers and fruit on their knees. Some had bought large, expensive bunches, wrapped in sharp peaks of cellophane and tied with twirling boutique ribbon. Others appeared to have garnered random blossoms from the garden, or purchased something cheap and already wilting about the edges from a fruit stall.

Rick was the first to be initiated.

In a small room at the top of the stairs Jack was waiting, seated in a cane armchair. Against the wall and facing the door was a table that had been turned into a simple altar with a gold silk cloth and a single candle. Jack was dressed, as ever, in his corporate suit and welcomed Rick with his usual glowing smile. Awkwardly, and with both hands, Rick held out his small bouquet of Zoe's roses and an apple and banana wrapped in foil. The ritual gifts, the token of respect. But respect for whom, and for what?

Jack accepted the gifts and placed them casually on the altar. 'This is a very simple procedure,' he began, 'and it won't take long. I'm going to say a prayer in Sanskrit in praise of all gurus, or spiritual teachers, and then I will give you your mantra.'

Spiritual teachers? *What spiritual teachers?* Could Jack be classified as a spiritual teacher? Surely not? All through the course, Rick had resolutely turned his face away from the more esoteric character of Jack's discourse, something hazy that seemed to hover on the fringes of his perception. He knew meditation was an adaptation of a practice derived from eastern mysticism, with the same origins as, say, a suburban yoga class, and beyond that he did not intend to venture. It wasn't necessary, as Jack himself had intimated from the outset. But now the presence of the altar, however minimalist, made him feel uncomfortable.

It was a low-key ceremony, simple and precise. The mantra was no recognisable word, just a high-pitched sound, an exhalation of air with the tongue against the bottom teeth. Jack said it, and then he asked Rick to say it.

After he had repeated it a few times, Jack said, 'Good,' and then cautioned him not to repeat it to anyone else as this would diminish its potency.

Rick nodded, but his neck felt stiff. He hadn't expected to be inducted into anything spiritual; he thought he was getting a technique that was scientifically based.

As if reading his mind, Jack said, 'Remember, this is not a religion – you are not being asked to adopt any set of dogmas. Just meditate on your mantra each day, morning and evening, and come back in a week for a checking.'

And that was it. Something of an anticlimax, really. At the back of his mind was the thought that some people, not under corporate sponsorship, were paying hundreds of dollars for this. Could anything that expensive be this simple? Could anything worth having be this simple? Could peace of mind ever be simple?

Mark was second-last to go in. Rick waited for him on the verandah, looking out over the dusky roofline of the hill, the purple night sky over Port Jackson. Eventually Mark emerged, exhaling heavily in a bemused sigh. 'I need a ciggie,' he said. 'Do you mind waiting?'

Like furtive children, they moved into the side lane and Mark lit up. He looked around him, up and down the lane, down at his feet, and then up and down the lane again. He seemed edgy.

'So that's it, K,' he said.

'Apparently.'

'The secret word.'

'Yep.'

'Is yours one syllable or two?'

'One.'

Mark seemed reassured by this, as his was two, which meant at the very least that they were not all getting the same mantra. This would have been an affront to them both.

'Are you seriously going to do this every morning and every night?' Mark asked.

'I'm going to try. I'll give it three months.' Something told Rick that Mark wouldn't last three days. He seemed unhappy with the outcome; his cocksureness had fallen away and he was peculiarly sombre. He was as restless and as jittery as ever, but not in his teasing, good-natured way – more irritable, hostile even, curiously offhand.

'I'm starving,' Mark said, with a sharp intake of breath, and tossed his glowing butt into the bougainvillea that ran like flame along the side wall. And then, brusquely, 'Do you have to go home? Why don't we go somewhere and eat?'

'Why don't you come back to my place?' Rick had been thinking of bringing Mark home for a while. Zoe would find him amusing.

Mark hesitated, and then with a shy, haunted look he said, 'No, no, thanks anyway. I'll grab a bite on the way home.' There was something in the way he said it, something in his manner that was worrying. For Rick, the little ceremony had been of scarcely any moment – bland, even – but Mark seemed unnerved. He felt protective towards him.

'Let's go to Miro's,' he said, mentioning a bistro only a few streets from where he lived. Mark could get a taxi on from there.

At Miro's they sat on a quilted leather banquette in a dim red light and Mark downed two quick schooners of Guinness. As he drank, he became more and more morose, straying ruefully into a reverie of his childhood dreams.

'Y'now, K, all I ever wanted to do was play Rugby League,' he said, crouched over the lip of his glass. 'Not because I wanted to be rich and famous, not that . . .' His voice trailed off and he brooded for a minute. 'Even now, sometimes when I'm watching a game on TV, I get so emotional I could cry. There's something pure about it, you know what I'm saying? Honest. No bullshit. The speed, the strength, the raw courage . . . the sight of one man hurtling through the pack like –' He stopped, lips pursed together, as if stymied by the inadequacy of mere words. 'Like a human fucking projectile. All heart, nothing's going to stop him, you can see the veins bulging in his neck, you can see the look he's got in his eyes, and it's a look of . . . of . . . pure momentum – like an arrow.' He raised his right arm in a gliding motion across his face. 'Straight . . . straight . . .' He shook his head, gazing out into space, unable to finish the sentence. 'And I cry, I cry just watching it. I admit it.' Again he crouched over the lip of his glass. 'And that's all I ever wanted to do. Ever.' He repeated it, this time loudly, with drunken emphasis. '*Ever!*' And banged the parquet table, which reeked of smoke and beer.

By the end of the night they were both drunk, slouching out of the bar with all the elan of two deflated tyres. He dropped Mark at a cab rank two blocks down the road and hoped that he would make the two kilometres home without being breathalysed.

Zoe, thank God, was a heavy sleeper. Stumbling into the bathroom for a pee, his head in a purple brown fug of Guinness, not to mention the Vodka chasers, he cut his heel on a broken tile and began to bleed, a thin rivulet of red dripping onto the white tiles. He swore, fumbled in the cabinet for a bandage and sank heavily onto the lavatory seat to bind his foot. For such a small injury the pain was acute. Softly, he swore again. So much, he told himself, for meditation.

That night he dreamed that a currawong was pecking out his eyes. Strangely, there was no pain.

Around 5 am he woke in the dark with the mantra spinning in his head.

~

After the first week he asked Mark how it was going.

Mark hesitated. 'Uh . . . on and off, K, on and off.'

'More off than on?'

'Uh, not exactly. I just don't do it at the usual times. You know, morning and evening.'

Rick didn't pursue it. For one thing he was having his own difficulties. To his surprise he found he couldn't sit still for five minutes, never mind twenty.

At his workstation he could sit for hours, scarcely moving a muscle, but without his beautiful backlit colour screen and his Boolean logic, his algebraic grammar, his magical formulae of conditionality – *if this, then this* – he was at the mercy of his chaotic and untidy brain, a jerky and primitive slide-show of trivia. Football fixtures for the coming week, what to buy for Luke's birthday, reminders to get the car serviced, had he paid his insurance? All the endless minutiae of daily life zoomed across the inner screen of his brain like balls careening across a billiard table.

The minute he settled himself in the stiff-backed chair in his study, his scalp would begin to itch, his collar chafe . . . he would spin the mantra into an imaginary space before his eyes like a bowler unleashing an imaginary ball but he could never, as it were, find his length: the mantra ball would fall to the earth with a thud and lumber along the turf, or fail to land at all and sail off, disappearing into the clouds, while his thoughts, those mad computer-game figures, scuttled about the ballpark of his neural field in a noisy short-circuiting clamour, like machine-gun fire ricocheting in a stadium.

Only a few months before, he had felt himself at a point of near despair, and now here he was, like an idiot child unable to master the first letters of the alphabet. After what seemed like half an hour he would look at his watch and find that five minutes had passed, or, on a good day, ten. Where was the timelessness, the loss of self that others spoke of? How come he never made it into the zone, not even for a second?

A week later, at the first group checking on the Monday night, he listened as the others in the class reported their efforts. Mark had only managed to 'try it', he said, on 'two or three mornings', and couldn't understand why even to contemplate the doing of it seemed an enormous mental effort. It felt like homework, he said: the mere thought of it set up an internal resistance.

Rick had smiled and patted him on the shoulder, as if it were no big deal really, and all the while he was thinking: *You're not desperate enough.*

All through the first checking Mark fidgeted in his chair as they were forced to listen to the brilliant experiences of the others. One man had seen white lights, another had drifted off into an orange haze, someone else had experienced an intense sensation in the middle of her forehead, where the Third Eye lay. With each declaration Mark looked sideways at Rick and rolled his eyes, as if to say, 'What a bunch of tossers,' or, 'There's always someone, someone who's had an *experience*.' There are always the goody-goodies in the class, the point scorers who announce with transparently fake wonder and humility that they've hit the mark, can top whatever you've got to offer, are among the chosen. Always someone whose hits are bigger and better than yours.

Jack sat quietly, acknowledging each response with his customary smiling detachment. When at last it was Rick's turn to speak, it was as if Jack had been waiting for what he had to say, as if the responses of the others had been too good to be true and what Rick had to say was real. Rick gave a brief account of the banality of his efforts and Jack nodded sympathetically. 'Firstly,' he said, 'scientific tests show you are always doing better and going deeper than you think you are. Second, don't ever force it, just witness the thoughts that come up and then let them go, while gently bringing the sound of the mantra back into your head.'

But nothing Jack said served to dispel Rick's scepticism. I'll give it three months, he thought. It seemed, then, like an eternity.

A few weeks later his sister, Jane, and fifteen-year-old nephew, Justin, came to stay. Justin drifted into the study one morning as Rick was halfway through his meditation practice, sitting up straight-backed in the dining chair he had carried in for that purpose (it was important to have the spine straight in order for the breathing to be steady and even, the lungs open and expanded). He was sitting there with his eyes closed, hands on knees, assuming the posture, he sometimes thought, of one of those stone pharaohs. He heard Justin come in and said, without opening his eyes, 'I'm meditating.'

His secret was out.

Over breakfast Jane gave him a look of bemused scorn. 'You've gone New Age, brother,' she said.

'I think it's cool,' said Justin.

But, no, it wasn't cool, it wasn't at all cool. It was impossible.

At one of their Sunday lunches with Zoe's parents, his father-in-law said, 'I hear you're meditating, Rick.'

Looking up from his plate, he saw Zoe cast a warning look at her father.

'Yeah.'

'You find it relaxes you?'

'Not exactly.'

'From what Zoe said, it sounded to me a bit like playing chess. You lose yourself in the strategy and afterwards you feel surprisingly refreshed.'

Rick laughed. 'Depends on how competitively you play chess,' he said, knowing Joe was intensely competitive and hoping to change the subject. This was one of those times when Joe's propensity to talk rather than listen was a distinct plus, since Rick had no intention of discussing this with him of all people. Later, perhaps, when he knew what he was doing, but not now, when he was at sea. As a novice, he could scarcely speak with authority. And anyway, there was nothing to say. Nothing was happening. Which was kind of the point. For a while. As long as he wasn't losing his temper and slapping strangers, the rest could be counted a plus.

Day after day he maintained his regimen. He got up at six, took a shower, went into his study, shut the door, set the timer on his desk clock and sat. There was no mystique to it, no charm, no solemnity, nothing. Yes, nothing. In a curious way he felt he had entered into nothingness. And yet it was a ritual, a process, a frame; it was *something*.

And then one morning it came to him that he would do this every day, and that it would work. It would be his cure, and the essence of that cure would be silence and surrender. But the cure would be a long time coming. He must wait, and for the first time in his life he must have faith.

currawong

Over the weeks that followed I kept to my practice. And then, out of nowhere, I had what I can only describe as a visitation. The woman in white arose in my meditation.

It was almost eight by the time I got home from work. Zoe and Luke were at a school concert. The house was empty. In the wok there were the leftovers of a stir-fry, and I carried a bowl upstairs with the intention of eating out on the small cedar deck at the rear, after I had meditated. But I was hungry, and thought that for once I might cut my meditation short.

In the bedroom I paused to look for a cushion, and then unlocked the sliding glass door that opened onto the deck and the shade of an old plane tree. It was a perfect late summer evening, mellow and warm, and I settled onto the floor of the deck. By this time I had given up the straight-backed chair and taken to sitting cross-legged on the floor; I had always been flexible, and somehow in this position I felt more natural, less of a stone pharaoh. Because I was hungry I planned on fifteen minutes only but after a while my hunger faded and before long I glanced at my watch to find that forty minutes had passed and the deck was beginning to darken. Just five more minutes, I thought, and it was then that I felt a presence and opened my eyes.

The leafy clusters of the plane tree fluttered at the edge of my vision, and the lights in the houses opposite glowed in the ripening dark. I saw that a currawong was hopping across the deck, its beak glinting, its head cocked to the side, one yellow eye looking bold and quizzical. So it was only a bird. Staring back into that eye, I held its gaze for an hypnotic moment before the bird jerked its black head and flapped up onto the deck rail, where it looked back at me as if it knew me. And from nowhere a line came to me from *Siddhartha*, the book of my youth: 'and the bird in my breast has not died'.

My arms and feet were warm in the humid dusk; I could feel the heat penetrating the fabric of my shirt; the jasmine coiled around the deckrail was heady . . . And how rare it was to sit becalmed, how soothing . . . I needed only to lay my head back and I would be able to doze comfortably for a half hour or so . . .

And it was then, as I closed my eyes, that the woman in white came to me, the woman I had dreamed of in the months after my brother's death, the woman with her strange, blank-eyed baby in its white swaddling clothes. I felt rather than saw them, as if glimpsing a fold of the infant's cloth out of the corner of my mind's eye, but not in a way that evoked any feeling. There was none of the yearning or hysteria that had welled up in my dreams. I was merely an observer, aware that my heartbeat had slowed, and that the image of the woman had dissolved, leaving the baby to float across my internal eye.

And then I felt a buzzing in my temples and my mind began to brim again with random thoughts that zipped and buzzed across my screen like manic spermatozoa, while the baby, that luminous egg, wafted on the night air.

I opened my eyes, startled again by a sense of presence, of someone near me. But again it was only the currawong, perched on the rail close to my head. Brazen, fearless. What a strange creature to come so close. By now it was dark, the sudden darkening of a sub-tropical night. Possessed by a sense of some other self, I stood, and, glancing back over my shoulder at the bird, which was still there, staring at me with its yellow eye, I opened the glass door and withdrew into the house.

~

The next morning I stopped by Mark's cubicle. Mark was on the phone, which wasn't uncommon; lately he had been spending too much time on the phone, usually to some woman or other, and I stood, disapprovingly, making it clear he should hang up and give me his full attention. But Mark, insouciant as ever, continued to remonstrate in an urgent tone with whoever was on the other end of the line.

My temper rising, I made a conscious effort to distract myself (no more outbursts) and took to studying the rogue's gallery on the wall of Mark's cubicle, a space where the analysts pinned their notices, cartoons, photos of wives or girlfriends, children, wilderness scenes and whatever fantasy objects got them through their day. The centrepiece of Mark's gallery had long been a red Ferrari and it was still there, in pride of place, but pinned beneath it was a small colour photograph of a woman in early middle age. Her skin was dark and she looked to be from the subcontinent. Her black hair was pulled back tightly from her forehead, and around her shoulders was a white shawl. Her eyes blazed at me.

Mark hung up the phone with a sigh. 'Sorry, K, I've told her not to ring me at work.'

'Who's this?' I pointed to the image of the woman on his cork-board.

'A joke,' he said, unpinning the photo and tossing it onto his desk. 'Some guru that Phoebe – my girlfriend – goes to see. *She* put it' – he nodded at the photo lying on the desk – 'up there. She's into that stuff.'

Phoebe, it turned out, had been a member of our meditation class. She and Mark had run into one another in a coffee shop near the office, and Mark, with a more than respectable excuse to strike up a conversation, had made a successful move.

'So you meditate together?' I raised an ironic eyebrow.

Mark's smirk said it all. 'Not exactly, K, not exactly.'

Later that evening I told this story to Zoe, who by then had met Mark and found him an amusing if feckless study. 'So this is where you go to meet chicks,' she said, 'a stress management class. I suppose it's a step up from cruising a singles' bar. And when the relationship falls apart you can meditate to get over it.'

Zoe approved of my meditation. How could she not? In the months since 'the incident' we had behaved with a wary affection towards one another, but I could feel that in some deep part of her I was unforgiven. She was waiting. She would see.

So I was meditating, I was a good boy, but still the black shadow hovered at my shoulder. Winter came and it was cold, and harder to get up in the early mornings. There were many days when I was irascible and withdrawn. Sometimes I would sit in the dark before dawn and think: this isn't enough. I thought of that benign field I had sometimes felt part of when I was a boy. What had happened to it? When had I lost my connection? Had it been a figment of my imagination, like an imaginary friend, or a belief in Santa Claus? Was it some kind of electromagnetic field, and if so, when had the circuit broken? And then an overwhelming sadness would take possession of me and the thought would come: no, this isn't enough. I can't do this alone.

~

It was spring, and a Saturday morning. Zoe, who never got sick, was in bed with the flu. I dropped Luke off at a friend's place and continued on across the bridge to my office. I planned to catch up on some work.

Shoppers were out sipping coffee on the pavement or strolling the Chatswood mall. Unable to find a parking space near the office, I cruised for several blocks in the direction of a car park at the eastern end of the mall, and as I turned into its entrance I glanced across at the Chatswood Community Centre, a red-brick and glass complex surrounded by green lawn. A steady stream of people were making their way towards the wide front doors, and for a moment I thought – could swear – I caught a glimpse of Mark Paradisis among them, and yet this seemed unlikely, as Mark didn't surface from clubbing until mid-afternoon. Still, I was sure it had been him; I thought I recognised the white shirt and embroidered vest, the distinctively cocky set of the head, the familiar swagger.

Inside the cavernous car park I found a place high up on the fifth floor and strode to the lift. It seemed to take an age to reach me. It appeared to be stuck on Level 3 and I felt the old impatience rising, that razor-like cut of irritability, and I thought, no, cool it, it's Saturday morning. Once out in the bright sunlight I looked over to the community centre and saw a row of posters on the notice-board, and I crossed the grass verge to look, wondering if it really had been Mark that I had seen. What could he possibly be doing in such an uncool venue as a community centre at a time some hours before he would normally rise from his bed?

Up close, the posters showed the head and shoulders of a dark-skinned woman draped in a white shawl, and instantly I recognised her as the woman in the photograph on the wall of Mark's office cubicle. So it must have been Mark.

I glanced at my watch. Plenty of time to look in. Perhaps I could catch Mark in some embarrassing posture, or see a side to him that as yet I had no inkling of, and I stepped up to the main doors.

As I approached I could see that the wide concrete terrace out-side the doors was covered with shoes, left there by members of the crowd, a disorderly spread of cheap sandals and worn sneakers. Ignoring these, I pushed open the heavy glass door that led into the foyer; I had no intention of leaving an expensive pair of almost new Italian leather slip-ons in a place where they could easily be stolen. But as I attempted to enter through the inner doors, a middle-aged man with grey hair touched me on the arm and said, 'Sir, would you mind leaving your shoes at the door?'

'Why?' I asked, sounding churlish.

'Because it's the custom,' said the doorkeeper, 'and for the pur-poses of today's program the hall will in effect become a temple.'

A temple? The Chatswood Community Centre? I felt myself on the edge of rudeness, surprisingly so, since I had left home in a good mood. Still, that was the way it was then: hair-trigger. For a moment I considered leaving and then, glancing through the open door as an (unshod) woman pushed past me, I thought I caught a glimpse of Mark again. Damn it, I would go in, barefoot or not.

Frowning, I stepped back onto the top step and removed my shoes, being careful to place them in a far corner, in shadow, where they would not be obvious. I would just look in, confirm that it was indeed Mark I had seen entering, discover what cult fantasy he had got himself into, and either tease him about it if it were harmless or look out for his interests if it were not.

Inside, the hall was three-quarters full. People sat or stood around idly, with an air of low-key expectancy. In a quick scan of the room I could see no-one I recognised, yet I was *sure* it was Mark I had seen walking up the path towards the doorway. Perhaps he had looked in, thought better of it and left, in which case I would leave too, and I began to move back towards the main doors. Too late. Something was happening.

In an instant the atmosphere in the hall changed. A group of people was clustered around the entrance, and they began now to chant in a low, sing-song inflection, over and over with a kind of hypnotic rise and fall, in some foreign tongue I didn't recognise. From the excitement by the doors I deduced that the main attraction had arrived. It could only be the woman on the poster.

The chanting intensified and grew louder. A bell rang and the back rows of the crowd surged forward towards the door, people standing on their toes and craning their necks to see, and I knew that she must be standing there, in the doorway. I couldn't see but I knew that someone was there, or at least something had changed in the room, because at that moment I felt a wave of energy move towards me – or, rather, it both came towards me from some external source and at the same time it arose within me. The cavity of my chest filled with an intense pressure that shot up suddenly into my head in a column of heat. My face flushed, my vision blurred and I began to cry.

Right there, in the middle of the hall, I was weeping. *Oh, my God*: this was my first thought. *Oh, my God, how embarrassing, thank God no-one here knows me.* I turned my face away from the incoming crowd, which was streaming to fill up the chairs at the front, and I moved across to the far wall lined with wooden benches that were empty. *I'll just sit here for a bit*, I thought, *and pull myself together. I'll get over this and then I'll go.* It must have been the chanting. Sometimes music could do that, could move me for no good reason, or make the hairs on my skin prickle. So I would just sit there, and take out my handkerchief and try unobtrusively to wipe my eyes, and then I would leave.

But the curious thing was this: the tears kept coming, and for no reason. I was weeping for no reason, no reason at all, and I kept saying this to myself, over and over, as if it were a mantra for my recovery. *For no reason . . . for no reason . . .* Finally, I leaned my head back against the wall and closed my eyes.

After a few minutes I looked at my watch and saw that I had been weeping, silently, for forty minutes. Something had cracked, something had broken; I was dripping into my shirt, I was melting into the unyielding chair. *Ah, so this was it, this was the crack-up.* Here, on a Saturday morning, on my way to the office, in the most banal place imaginable. With no fanfare, no drama, not even a blaze of temper, I had finally lost it.

The dark-skinned woman – she whose entrance had provoked my unravelling – was sitting in an armchair at the end of the hall, in front of the stage. She was indeed diminutive, barely five feet, and draped in the gentle folds of a plain white cotton sari. Her black hair was pulled back in a large bun and she wore a thick strand of wooden beads around her neck. Her skin was unusually dark and tinged with blue. There was a glow about her, and her eyes were dark pools of reflected fire. She seemed to sit within a sheath of luminosity such as I had never seen around any woman, not even at my most besotted. And yet she was, to all intents and purposes, an ordinary woman. So why was I crying? What was this wave that had swept over me when she entered the room? Nothing could have been more mundane than this suburban hall with its plastic chairs, its fluorescent light fittings, its cork notice-board and its Anzac roll-of-honour. Yet here I was, in meltdown.

Around me, blurred figures came and went while I sat anchored to my bench, waiting for self-possession to reclaim me. I've been working too hard, I told myself, I've been stressed, the chanting caught me off my guard, it'll pass. I'll just sit here for a few more minutes, and in a little while I'll be okay.

But I wasn't okay. For a time I would subside into calm and the tears would dry and I would sigh with relief, and stand up in readiness to leave, to just stroll out the door . . . and then the aching pressure would return and my eyes would burn and the whole watery miasma would start up again. It was as if even by attempting to get up off my bench I had inadvertently activated some hydraulic lever, some cranial water flow, and I would be back where I was, and the bench would claim me again.

After a while I looked up at the big round clock above the door. Eleven twenty. I had been there almost two hours.

Two hours? It wasn't possible. The jolt of this brought me back into real time and I was able to collect myself enough to look around the room. I could see that the hall was divided into two sides, and down the centre people were queuing to meet her. But the queue moved slowly so that they sat on the floor cross-legged, or cupped their arms around their knees and whispered to one another. Some sat with their eyes closed, as if meditating. As each supplicant reached her seated form, he or she rose up on their knees and she pressed her forehead to theirs and held it there for several seconds, then held them back from her, gazed into their eyes and flashed them a smile of tender recognition. I saw then that her body shone with a dark-skinned radiance and her composure was unfaltering. Sometimes she would laugh, as if all this – the hall, everyone there – was a tremendous joke.

Mark. *He must be here*, I thought, and once again I looked for him, this time through inflamed and bleary eyes. But he wasn't there, although, of course, he might well have come and gone while I, hapless at the side of the hall, was trying to pull myself together. But I was okay now, I was bled out, and it was definitely time to go. In my socks I began to walk towards the main doors, and was almost there when I turned to look back at her one last time, to reassure myself that this dizzying experience was real. At that moment she looked up, looked right at me, and gave an amused shrug that said, 'What? Leaving?' And there I was, in tears again, standing stock-still and bereft at the door, all six foot one and a half inches of me, tears coursing down my already soggy cheeks. In acute shame – or was it surrender? – I wandered across to the end of the queue, dropped to my knees and sat, cross-legged, in a daze.

By the time I had moved to within a few metres of her I was calm; I had given up all resistance. I no longer cared about the indignity of it. I would go through with this strange ritual, and then it would be at an end. I would get up, walk out the door, drive home and it would be over. No-one would know it had happened.

When I was within a short radius of her I began to feel a subtle vibration in my body. I looked down at my hands and saw that I was trembling, though only slightly, perhaps not even perceptibly, and anyway I was beyond caring. Someone behind pushed me forward and she raised her hands and held my head, and her palms were cool. She drew my brow to hers, forehead to forehead, and I caught a glimpse of her small brown feet, and then I was in a white haze, fighting back the urge to break into racking sobs. When at last I stumbled to my feet I tripped and almost fell. One of her attendants handed me a clutch of tissues and I wiped my eyes.

Outside, it was hot. The light was piercing. Somehow I made my way across the grass and back to the car. It was futile even to consider working in this state and I decided to go home, but for a long time I was in a trance, driving on automatic pilot. I was halfway across the bridge before I looked down at my feet and realised that I was wearing someone else's shoes.

~

I decided to tell Zoe about my experience – I could not disguise the state I was in – but when I arrived home Zoe was asleep.

She slept for a long time. It was unlike her but I thought of it as a blessing. It gave me the hours to compose myself.

In the days immediately following, I could never find the right moment to get the words out. 'Guess what? On Saturday I had this strange experience. I saw this Indian woman and I cried like a

baby. What do you make of that?' Then I decided it was an aber-
ration, a random event of no consequence, and Zoe would only be
disturbed by my account of it, possibly even panic-stricken; better
that she didn't know.

Soon I began to think of the experience as unexceptional, and
by the end of the week a confession had become unnecessary
because I had found within myself the reason for this strange
behaviour. Stress. I was overwrought. Working too late, sleeping
too little. And the woman had been so compassionate, so beautiful
in her ways that she had moved me at my most vulnerable. And if
for the first time in my memory of myself I had wept, then no
doubt it was because I had felt safe: among strangers. It was like
the story of the two men on the train who tell each other their
most intimate secrets, safe in the knowledge they will never meet
again, will never have to endure a relationship burdened by their
defenceless intimacy.

On the Monday I was on my mettle, waiting for Mark to sidle
up and say something, but that morning he phoned in sick with
what subsequently proved to be a severe bout of hepatitis. His
convalescence was prolonged, and carried out at his parents' home
on the south coast, by which time he had been head-hunted for a
job in Hong Kong. On the day that Mark eventually came in to
farewell his colleagues I was at a conference in Melbourne. And
thus it was that I never saw Mark again. I sent him a note at his
new workplace to congratulate him and wish him well, but did
not think to ask if he had in fact been at the Chatswood Community Centre on that Saturday morning. Mark sent me a jokey
pornographic postcard from Hong Kong, and that was the last
contact we had.

And so I forgot about her. It was just one of those turns, one of those blips on the radar screen when an asteroid careers through the heavens. Until a strange thing happened: at the point at which I had almost forgotten the experience, she began to appear in my meditation.

One torpid morning, when my daily ritual seemed stale, when it seemed to be getting me nowhere, I thought for the first time that I might abandon the practice. At that moment her face floated into my inner vision. It was nothing dramatic: no flash of light, no heart-jolting frisson. Just her dark-skinned face, hovering in my mind's eye with luminous clarity. And a few days later it happened again. But I thought nothing of this. Many images came and went in the distracting mangle of thoughts that passed in my case for contemplation. Did I believe in the process? Perhaps I never had believed in it, but I clung to it like a capsized fisherman might cling to a piece of the wreckage from his drowned boat.

As time went on, that dark, luminous face began to arise in my meditation more often, sometimes as soon as I sat down and closed my eyes. Before long she was there with me almost every day, though only for a matter of seconds. And what I felt with each visitation was entirely neutral. No tears. Nothing. And who was she? I had no idea.

~

A year passed.

One morning I saw her face on a poster in the window of a New Age bookshop in the Chatswood mall. According to the poster, she was a Hindu saint from a village in Tamil Nadu. It seemed that once a year she toured the cities on the eastern seaboard, bestowing her own peculiar form of blessing on her devotees, and on any members of the public who cared to come. In two weeks she would be in Sydney again: same time, same place. And what would happen, I asked myself, if I went to see her, this time deliberately, knowing what was in store?

When I returned to my office I checked the date of her visit in my diary and saw that I was booked to run a training program in Adelaide. Good. That settled that.

As it happened, the training program was postponed. But it was, nevertheless, a full weekend: a school concert of Luke's on the Friday evening, a picnic lunch on the Saturday, a dinner in the evening at the harbourside penthouse of Zoe's boss.

On the night before the picnic I thought of *her*, of how she might already be in the city, and I recalled my meltdown of a year ago and felt strangely indifferent, as if it had happened to someone else.

Lunch on Saturday was a barbecue in Centennial Park. Zoe and Luke and I arrived in good time and lugged the picnic hamper to the designated spot by the Federation dome, chosen because the children could ride their bikes and there was space for the families to have a relaxed game of baseball.

It was an overcast day, a bank of charcoal cloud hovering low in the sky. Zoe's brother Ben came with his kids, who were on their paternal access weekend, and he and I talked listlessly about politics. Was it me, I wondered, or did all conversation suddenly seem stale? Sentences snapped off in mid-air and hung dangling. Ben seemed to be saying the same things, over and over, but he was in a better mood than usual. Everyone was in a good mood except me.

When I looked at the others it was like looking through the wrong end of a telescope, a kind of stoned feeling where the figures in the landscape retreat from you and come increasingly to seem two-dimensional. The more stoned you become, the more the life leaches out of them. Either that or you are staring through a pane of thick glass.

After lunch I volunteered to walk the children over to the kiosk for ice-creams, and on the way I gave myself a pep talk. It didn't work. All through the day I was edgy and didn't know why. I had charred the steak, knocked over a bottle of wine so that it seeped into the bread and stained Zoe's picnic cloth, and worst of all had been impatient and distracted with Luke. Sent out to mind second base, I drifted off into some white sphere of discontent that soon had me marooned in a knot of self-reproach.

It was just after three when I looked at my watch and thought: I could just make it. I walked over to where Zoe was sitting beneath the blue-gums, as happy and relaxed as I had ever seen her. I looked down at her dark glasses and her broad straw hat and it was as if I scarcely knew her.

Bending low to her ear, I said. 'The car keys are in my jacket. I have to go for a walk. Don't ask me any questions now. I'll be back in time to take Luke to Rachel's.'

Her mouth opened but nothing came out. I could almost feel her body sag as the pleasure of the day seeped out of her and she felt, yet again, abandoned by this miserable, moody bastard she had married, who could never just surrender himself to the joy of ordinary things. I knew that if I hesitated, her sadness would derail me and then I would resent and, later, torment her, so I strode off up the hill to the road and hailed a taxi.

Once in the car, it occurred to me that I had no money. I asked the driver to stop at an ATM, but as the cab slid into the kerb I realised that – of course – I had no cards on me. My wallet was back in my jacket on the grass under the blue-gums, and it was too late to go back. The cock had flown the coop and by now he was demented. 'Just drive on,' I said to the cab driver.

Halfway across the bridge the sun broke out from behind grey cloud and the glare blinded me. *What is the matter with me?* I asked myself, but whoever had asked the question had no real interest in the answer.

When we reached the place, I opened the door and said, 'I haven't any money on me. I came out in a hurry and left my wallet behind.' (How lame this sounded.) And I took off my watch and said, 'Will you take this?' The driver – Lebanese, I guessed – looked at me as if I were mad, then shrugged. Slowly he took the watch, inspecting it as if it might explode in his fingers, and then he looked at me again with a guarded expression. 'How do I know you won't say I stole it?' he asked. I shrugged, helplessly. Something in the mordant anguish of that gesture must have attested to my sincerity because he nodded. 'Okay,' he said, and slipped the watch into his pocket.

Within seconds I was bounding up the steps to the wide doors of the hall and could scarcely slip out of my shoes fast enough, leaving them carelessly angled across an outsize pair of shabby sandals. Inside, my gaze went straight to the space at the front, below the stage, and there she was, in her plain white cotton sari, as before, and seated with the same luminous composure. Nothing had changed, all was exactly as it had been a year ago, except now there were more people and the hall was full. The queue extended all the way down the middle of the floor with monitors on either side.

I must join it now, I thought, without delay. I couldn't afford to hesitate because it would be a long, slow wait to receive her blessing, and within two hours I must be home. And now I had no watch to keep time. I looked around for the wall clock I remembered from last time but it was no longer there. Damn. I would have to ask whoever was next to me, and I patted my pockets, looking for my handkerchief, only to find I had left that behind as well. Soon the tears would come, it was inevitable, and I would have to snivel into a tissue like a woman. But what did it matter? What did any of it matter? These were mere details, and I had never been more beyond mere detail in my life.

And it didn't matter, because no tears came. I realised I had been looking forward to those tears, to losing myself in a comforting wave of self-pity. Instead, as I drew closer to her in the queue, shuffling along on my rump, I felt that a knot in my chest was loosening. How long had that knot been there? Why hadn't I noticed it before? A calm sweetness begin to course in my veins, and when at last my forehead was resting against hers I felt my heart pop like a bubble, and the bliss rose up into my head in a pink haze. Then I stood, and glided to the side of the hall, and sat on one of those bare wooden benches I had wept in, for so long, exactly twelve months ago.

After a while I turned to the young woman next to me and said, 'Do you have the time?'

It was ten past six, and Zoe and I were due in Bronte at seven-thirty. I had fifteen minutes to make it back home. Impossible! Could I drive in this state? Unthinkable, and yet I would have to go. And then it occurred to me that I didn't have the car. Propelled by some clockwork mechanism, I made it to the door, where the fresh air, humid as it was, brought me into real time and I half-walked, half-ran to a taxi rank in the nearby mall.

All the way back to my house, over the bridge, up City Road, I sat gazing ahead as if in a trance. How could I describe to anyone what I had felt in the hall that afternoon? It was not that the words were not available: the words were simple, as was the feeling. For the first time in my life I felt that I had come home.

Zoe was waiting for me in the bedroom upstairs. 'I've taken Luke to Rachel's,' she said, 'and you have some explaining to do.'

Here it was; there was no way around it. I loved my wife and I did not want to deceive her. I took a deep breath. 'I've been to see a woman,' I began.

She cut me off at once. 'I thought so,' she hissed. '*I thought so*. It had to happen sooner or later, didn't it!' Her face was a mask of venom.

At that I opened my eyes wide, as if I had just been told the most amazing joke, and almost laughed out loud, because it dawned on me that she was assuming I had a mistress, that I was on the brink of confessing to an affair. Of course: the stock figure, the middle-aged man in midlife crisis who falls in love with a younger woman who understands him, who makes him feel himself again. And it was all too ludicrous, too much of a cosmic joke, and I began to chuckle and shake my head like the condescending prick I was, until she hauled off and struck me across the face.

I sank onto the edge of the bed and put my face in my hands until I could control myself, until I could control the strange mirth that threatened to convulse my body. Zoe stood above me, seething, both fists clenched and held up to her breasts. At that moment I admired her as much, if not more than, I had at any time in our marriage. Instead of dissolving into bitter tears she was ready to batter me. And all I could do was laugh! In another minute she would think me mad, would feel the ground sliding out from under her feet again, would know that here was the all but final phase of my disintegration . . .

A cool draught of self-possession finally took hold of me. I dropped my hands from my face, looked up at her and patted the edge of the bed beside me. 'Sit down,' I said.

Zoe's first reaction was guarded. Who was this woman? Where was she from? She's from India, I said. Her name is Sri Mata, a courtesy term meaning revered mother, and she's a spiritual teacher, a yogi, a celibate woman who has never married and who has disciples around the world. I took out a thin booklet I had stuck in my pocket and gave it to Zoe. 'Here, read this.'

She sat and stared for a minute at the face on the cover.

'I have to go and see her again tomorrow,' I said.

'For God's sake, Rick, we have a lunch tomorrow with the Cranes. We haven't seen them for ages and they'll be offended if you pull out. It's taken us weeks to find a clear day.'

'Tell them I'm sick. I have to go. On Monday she leaves for another year. Why don't you come with me?'

She shook her head, and, folding the booklet neatly, deliberately, she put it on her bedside table beside the clock. Then came the quiet tears. 'It's alright,' I said. 'There's an evening program. I'll go to that. I'll come to the Cranes'.'

At around six in the evening of the following day I drove back across the bridge, this time on my way to a different meeting hall in Roseville on the fringes of the northern suburbs. And all the way there I felt a calm elation, a blithe weightlessness. I had been released from the dull round, the banality of everyday life, and I was on my way.

The old scout hall at Roseville was built of wood with a tin roof, and around the entrance the grass was ragged but the interior was warm with a mellow rustic ambience. I knew from the booklet that the evening program was a special one where those who wanted it could take mantra initiation, and I had made up my mind to ask for a new mantra. The old one that Jack had given me had served its purpose: it had brought me to her.

From the opening bars of the devotional music sung by her small entourage, to the last minutes when I helped to pack up the dusty hall at around three in the morning, the entire night passed in bliss. The seven hours that I spent in her presence seemed to last for around thirty minutes. None of it was hazy; indeed, it had a clarity that I would never feel again. Every movement, every ges-ture had a lightness, a quality of dance. The light in the hall had a soft electrical charge, and it shone on the faces in the crowd so that their skin glowed with a translucent sheen. When I knelt before her and she breathed the Sanskrit syllables of the mantra into my ear, I was beyond self-consciousness and had to stifle an impulse to touch her feet. I felt that I had merged – with the crowd, with the wooden chairs in the hall, the honour boards against the wall, the flowering shrubs in pots along the stage, the musty velvet, the bright electric light inside and the warm night beyond.

At last, around two in the morning, when everyone had been up to receive their blessing, she stood, and with that graceful and play-ful matter-of-factness I found so enchanting she walked briskly to the side of the stage, where she took up a broom and set about sweeping the floor. Others rushed to assist her, and for a noisy half-hour we dragged chairs and collected shawls and sweaters and empty paper cups and all manner of lost property.

At last we were done and she walked, a small, white-clad figure, towards the main door, where one of her devotees, a man about my age, had arrived late and was waiting for her blessing. When he knelt at her feet she tousled his hair playfully and joked with him, though I was not close enough to hear what was being said. All I could do was marvel at her relaxed focus. It was as if this man were the first blessing of the night, not the last; as if she had just arrived at the hall, fresh from a bath and a long sleep, instead of having sat there for seven hours unbroken, without food or water, hemmed in by the sweaty and tearful bodies that presented themselves. And this, I apprehended, was perhaps the most miraculous thing about her: this relationship to time. No moment was the beginning or the end of anything, only itself. She was brisk yet unhurried. At the end of the night she was exactly the same as she was at the beginning.

As for me, I had never felt less tired in my life. Along with what remained of the crowd, I wandered out onto the steps of the hall. It was a balmy evening and the sky was clear and piniened with stars. Looking up at them, I could not remember a time when I had felt so at ease in the world, so loose in the living of it. And then I was distracted by a ripple of laughter from those around me, and I saw that she was moving slowly down the driveway in the back of a black sedan while a young man who had broken away from the crowd danced barefoot beside her window, throwing rose petals across the bonnet of the car.

The car stopped. She wound down the window and reached out to grasp his hand, which she kissed, smiling at him almost mischievously, as if they were sharing a private joke. Her eyes had a fire in them and her white teeth flashed in the dark. The car began its slow crawl onto the main road but still the young man followed alongside, pulling flower petals from where he had stuffed them in his pockets and tossing them high into the air, strewing petals on the bitumen and dancing along the empty highway like a madman, while we who had gathered on the steps of the hall laughed and applauded.

On the drive home I gave a lift to a young couple and went several kilometres out of my way to drop them at their door. It was, I reflected, that kind of night, and in truth I didn't want to go home. Not that I didn't love the two sleeping bodies that lay waiting for me, but I wanted to prolong the magic, my sense of being beyond, or free of, time.

When at last I cruised into the fluorescent cavern of my garage I felt in my pocket for the small photo I had carried away with me, bought from the bookstall at the side of the hall earlier in the evening. This was one of the few discordant moments of the night: the many images of her face for sale as if she were some kind of pop star. It reminded me of the dismal church iconography of my childhood, of all I had come to abhor. For a time I had gazed at the various shapes and sizes before I purchased the smallest photograph I could find, smaller than a postage stamp and clumsily encased in Perspex, handmade but tacky in the Indian way. Perhaps, I thought, I would sit it discreetly in the top drawer of my desk.

~

Now what? I asked myself. Now *what*? I had found her and she had gone and I was left behind. To do what? Go on as if none of this had happened? As if I had had no experience of some other dimension of being?

For the next six months, in my meditation, all I could do was weep. Almost every time I thought of her my eyes would feel the telltale pressure; if I were in a public place, I would quickly have to distract myself. I tried to ration my thoughts, the amount of times I could, or would, allow her image to hover in my mind's eye. Surely this . . . this *disturbance of the field* would settle down soon.

I felt myself becoming vulnerable, exposed; all my defences were being stripped away, dissolving in my tears and leaving me open to the wind; layer after layer of crustacean shell peeled back until I was just the naked self that had come into the world. I was a child again. And one day it struck me who the baby in my dreams was: it was the part of me that was connected to her. And now I was being stripped away to that essential self.

Guru. How could I bear to use that word? It smacked of the seventies, and the Beatles, and John Lennon in bed with Yoko Ono holding a press conference between the sheets of some five-star hotel and drivelling on about love. I despised this stuff, had despised it even when I was young, never mind now. Yet here I was, caught in the net. Was I now a de facto member of a cult? The very idea was ludicrous. Nevertheless, something told me I needed to be careful. I had no intention of confessing this, to anyone.

But as time went on there was a strain in remaining silent. It meant that nowhere I went could I be myself. It felt unnatural.

What of those others who had been there? There were so many people in the hall that weekend, the predictable sprinkling of ageing hippies and young ferals come down from the hills, but the majority had looked more or less like me. Perhaps they met regularly. It would be a relief to talk to someone about my experience. Not that I doubted the experience: if it had been some kind of mania, of freaking out, it wouldn't have felt so good.

'It's all in your mind,' my mind told me. 'She is an ordinary person, albeit a benign one, from another culture, and the exotic joy of it has got to you; the eastern mystique; the charm of it; the chanting, the drumming, the cymbals.' Chanting is well known for its effect on biochemistry, like any sustained and harmonious vibration.

'Leave it,' my meditation told me, 'don't worry about it. Whatever "it" is will take its own course. Forget about it for now. You must learn to trust yourself.' Yet who was this *self* I was supposed to trust?

But for a while, trust is what I did, because that was the easiest path to follow. And life was the same, exactly the same as before. No, it wasn't *exactly* the same. On the surface, yes – but in a way I couldn't define (and by now I knew better than to attempt it) some profound change had occurred, some vibration had entered my body. I had heard about other people's experiences but I didn't have 'experiences', no visions, no flashing lights; what I experienced was a subtle but ongoing change in my relationship to the world. I could say no more than that.

And then one day when I was cleaning up at home, I picked up the pamphlet I had brought home to show Zoe. On the back I noticed something. In small print was a name, Rebecca Wilson, and a local phone number. Ah, Rebecca, I remembered her. We had met at the Roseville program, and had sat together for a while.

She had invited me to join a monthly chanting group but I had made excuses. With her long, cascading tresses she looked like a hippie, and I had no desire to hang out with people who hung tattered Tibetan prayer flags across their verandah, or stuck statues of lumpen elephant gods on their mantelpiece.

But maybe it wasn't like that; maybe I was jumping to unwarranted conclusions.

The next day, at work, I rang her number.

The apartment was in Edgecliff, one of a group of eight built in the forties on the side of a steep hill and looking out over a mass of terracotta rooflines. The apartment block itself was almost completely obscured by trees and vines. A line of cypresses ran along the boundary facing the road, and a steep drive ended in a tangle of trellis vines, of jasmine and climbing rose.

Outside the door of Apartment 5 there was a cluster of shoes and I unlaced my own. The door was ajar but I knocked anyway. When no-one came I pushed it open and walked into the cedar-lined hallway. At that moment Rebecca appeared. Her long, brown hair was pulled back in a tortoiseshell clasp. She looked lovely; she was aglow.

'Rick,' I said.

'I know,' she said, with a certain gaiety. 'We're in the living room.' She indicated a doorway and waited for me to go through.

Once inside, I was dismayed. Against the far wall, set on a shelf at chest height, was a huge Indian altar, garish in the extreme. It was made out of some kind of gold-coloured tin and built like a tabernacle, with doors that opened from the centre to reveal three chambers, each with gaudy images of contorted forms painted on all sides. A man with a peacock head-dress and dark blue skin playing a flute, a woman seated on a swan and playing a stringed instrument, an elephant head on a man's body, dancing a jig. It was grotesque, and tacky beyond belief. There were candles lit all along the front, and incense sticks in brass holders. There were flowers on either side, and a large bowl of fruit sat in front of the tabernacle. And everything sat on a red and green silk cloth, intricately patterned in the Indian way. The overall effect was of gilt and tinsel, outlandish and in the worst possible taste.

I winced. Idolatry, I thought. Worse, it reminded me of my Catholic childhood. Here we were and it was just the same, worshipping idols and crude images.

Well, then, I would turn my back on it, and I did, finding a spot on the floor where I could sit at an angle such that I was looking towards the other end of the room. As I settled into position I noted that there were around thirty others present, and they looked more or less normal – not a dreadlock in sight. That, at least, was reassuring.

But what a schizophrenic room it was. Built in the art deco style it was, in effect, two rooms separated by wide double doors that had been removed to create the effect of one long salon. The first room was the very model of a European music room. It had a green velvet chaise longue pushed back against the wall and two handsome Victorian armchairs in black leather standing on a thick Persian rug. A piano stood against the end wall, flanked by bookshelves. These were stacked not only with books but with piles of sheet music and two busts – one of Beethoven and the other I didn't recognise, though I could read the inscription: *Liszt*. Some of the books had titles in a script I guessed might be Hebrew, given the presence of the menorah that stood on top of a dark wood chiffonier near the door. The whole room might have been a Viennese parlour from the 1920s. And yet, here at this end of the salon, the other half of the owner's split self stood in flamboyant and embarrassing relief.

I never did like any of that Indian iconography in the tacky bedrooms of girls I had known in my student days, and I cared even less for it now. The one thing I could relate to was a large photograph of *her*, but even that was way too big, quite unnecessarily enlarged, and so uncomfortable did I feel that I could scarcely bear to look at it. Meanwhile, the smell of incense wafted up into my nostrils and I felt a headache coming on.

By this time Rebecca had seated herself cross-legged on the floor at a small box harmonium. When she began to sing, a devotional song in Sanskrit, I felt my heart lurch in my chest with sudden elation, and for a moment, and only a moment, my eyes blurred with tears. *Where does this come from?* I asked myself. I'm not even in a good mood, I don't like the room, I'm wary of these people, and yet I crack open like a nut the minute this woman begins to sing. Rebecca's voice was remarkably affecting. It was not the voice of the church choir, sweet and plaintive. Instead, it had a hard, ecstatic edge to it, a ruthless eros that made me shiver and brought the hairs up on the back of my neck. She played the harmonium expertly, with a kind of fluid yearning, though entirely without affectation, and the songs she sang bore no resemblance to hymns.On the contrary, they had an unnerving undertow of the wild, as if at any moment they were about to break the bounds of their notation. It was a sound I might once have called primitive, though I was wary now of that word because I realised I didn't understand it.

But the true revelation of the evening was the Sanskrit. I hadn't the least idea what these words meant, so why were they familiar to me? Familiar and enlivening, as if the bellows of my lungs were powered by their distinctive sounds, as if I drew my very breath from their long vowels, like an explosive sigh. Not that I sang along or even hummed – I was too self-conscious and it felt ridiculous even to try. Perhaps it's just the music, I thought, but then when they sang in English the effect wasn't the same: still lovely, but diminished. No, it was the Sanskrit. I had heard a little of it before, at her programs, but then it had washed over me. Now, tonight, I felt at home with it, like it was *my* language, my native tongue, lying quietly in wait for me to recognise it. As if I had emigrated alone from some other country as a child, had forgotten my mother tongue and was hearing it again for the first time. This, truly, was the most bizarre and inexplicable part of the evening.

Over supper I sought out Rebecca. She was a fey woman, delicate and with a tendency to dither, in every way unlike the authoritative presence at the harmonium that had led the call-and-response chanting. She introduced me to some of the others, and their names wafted around me in the general chit-chat of the moment. It was pleasant enough, but still I could not bear the big tinsel altar, the red and gold beast that seemed to take up more than its own space so that I felt invaded by its presence. It was too strong, too alien. How could she live with it, day in, day out?

'Where did you get the altar?' I asked her.

'In Rajasthan,' she said. 'Amazing, isn't it? When I first saw it I thought it was over the top, but then it grew on me. Of course I don't leave it up all the time – there isn't room in this small apartment. I set it up before we meet.'

Thank God for that, I thought, because I liked her, and I wanted her not to be a loony. But, I resolved, I would not be coming back.

When I arrived home, Zoe was still up. An early riser, on most nights she went early to bed but I could tell that she was curious, and possibly even anxious about this outing.

'How was the prayer meeting?' she asked.

'Not my scene,' I told her. But I had struck up one conversation over supper, had met one person I could relate to. This was Stephen Chang, a pathologist with an ironic sense of humour, someone with whom I felt I could share the self-mockery I employed to keep myself at what I thought of as a safe distance – not from *her*, but from the bizarreness of the outer trappings. Stephen and I had exchanged business cards and agreed to have a drink one night after work.

'Invite him home for dinner,' Zoe said.

'Maybe.'

~

Had I come down to earth? Not in the least. In the months that followed I experienced what I can only describe as a series of epiphanies, times when I felt infused by an absurd, secret pleasure. I would be posting a letter and suddenly feel a rush, a heightened sense of awareness. The postal system was a marvel: I put something in a steel box and within hours someone would be reading my words. I would cross a road and be struck by the extraordinary fact that the traffic lights worked; all over the city red and green lights were signalling in perfect order, and this was a miracle.

In these moments I took nothing for granted, *nothing*, and was heady from an uprush of euphoria. I was a new creature and the world no longer seemed mundane; it did not have a mundane atom in it. It fizzed and sparked with the current of an unnameable essence – and that essence had always been there, it was just that I hadn't been alive to it. I had been an instrument un-tuned.

One Saturday afternoon around five, the busiest time in our seedy local bottleshop, I stood in the queue behind an old woman, shabbily dressed. When her turn came, she shuffled up to the counter and asked the young man behind it, Tony, for a single bottle of draught beer. At least, I deduced that this was what she wanted, for she had a speech defect and seemed to choke on her words. But Tony was unfazed. 'Same as usual, Barb?' he asked. She grunted, and he walked from behind the counter to the wall of refrigerated cabinets, where he extracted a single bottle from a tightly wrapped six-pack.

By the time he had returned to the counter, Barb had decided that no, she didn't want draught; she wanted premium lager. 'No worries,' said Tony. The man in the queue ahead of me sighed deeply as Tony once again stepped out from behind the counter. This time he put his arm around Barb's shoulder and proceeded to shepherd her gently towards the big fridge. 'Which lager?' he asked, and waited while she took an age to choose, as if her brain were stuck in a groove and couldn't compute. Finally she muttered something and he extracted another bottle, this time from a cardboard pack.

Then he took her arm and escorted her back to the head of the queue, all the while keeping up a flow of amiable small-talk. Had she had a bet today? Did she fancy anything in the Derby? Just when it seemed the transaction had been brought to a conclusion, Barb opened her scuffed little purse and began painstakingly to count out the price of her bottle in small change. 'Jesus,' muttered the man ahead of me.

But Tony ignored him. He leaned on the counter, in an attitude of relaxed patience as if whiling away the time with an old friend, and studied the pile of coins on the counter. 'Been raiding the money box, Barb?' he said. He could not have been more than twenty and yet he had the ease of a young prince. He treated this abject figure with such respect that instead of appearing pathetic, she began to shine in the glow of his courtesy. As I looked on at her muddle of five, ten and twenty cent coins, silently I began to count along with her – *fifteen . . . twenty . . . twenty-five* – and in that counting something happened: the spaces of the bottleshop began to shimmer in a milky white light, the coins, the beer, the fridge, the faded lino tiles, the black brand-name t-shirts hanging from cardboard display stands, the manic figures on the TV screen above the door, all were transparent in the light.

On the walk home I felt it again, that secret pleasure; felt drunk with it, an intoxicated fool. And I asked myself: is this what they meant by a state of grace? It was easy enough to have an epiphany on a mountain top, or beside a lake, but in a bottleshop? What tricks she played on me, how mischievous her humour. Was this how *she* saw the world? And had she now granted me a glimpse of it? Something that before was hypothetical, a mere concept, was now intimate, *known* to me.

For weeks after, I felt emotionally labile, was ready at any moment to melt, as if there were no boundaries and I might embrace anyone. Looking at my wife and son over the dinner table, I would feel the familiar pressure behind my eyes and have to distract myself in some way. One evening on the train, I sat next to an overweight youth in shabby jeans and a grey hoodie who was reading a book. I glanced at the running title at the top of the page: *How to Win Friends and Influence People.* Oh, no, I thought. Such pathos in this, and I wanted to put my arm around him and grasp him in a bear hug and say, 'Look, you're fine as you are, at the core of your self is a divine flame. You are the ecstatic pulse of the universe, you are without blame.' I had a mad impulse to give this kid some money, or take him for a meal and explain to him the truth of his being. Instead, I pressed my fingers against my eyes to absorb the watery film that was forming there, at which moment he shifted in his seat and in so doing bumped against my own raised elbow. 'Sorry, mate,' he said.

I couldn't speak of these epiphanies because on one level they were, if anything, too ordinary. But looked at from another angle, I knew they would sound mad, and could easily be interpreted as an uprush of mania. I had worked once with a man who suffered from fierce oscillations between mania and depression, and I knew what the symptoms were, knew they could last for weeks, even months. But I knew I was not manic: my pulse did not race; I was not impulsive; I did not go on buying sprees.

I imagined telling Zoe about this, tried to rehearse the telling in my head, but the words weren't there. I loved her, now more than ever. Why, then, was I unable to share this with my wife, to draw her into the charmed aura of my experience? But I knew that if I attempted to articulate what I felt, the very words I used would undercut me, slice right through me like a guillotine of the trite. I would sound an eager fool. And yet my old scepticism hadn't deserted me. I was, I told myself, the same empiricist I had always been. I still believed in the reality of my senses, it was just that my senses were now attuned.

Meanwhile, to Zoe's bemusement, I had placed the tiny photo of Sri Mata on the table in my study. At first I wondered if having her image in the house would affect me in odd and unpredictable ways, but it was nothing, a mere object. And in any case the plastic image was inessential since she was always with me, a constant presence, and I meditated on her form: the delicacy of her feet, the blue-black of her hair, the hem of her white sari. She would flit momentarily into my mind in meetings, on the train, while I kicked a ball in the park with Luke; I imagined I caught a glimpse of her out of the corner of my eye, and her peculiar radiance enlarged for a moment every object, every figure in my field of vision. But I knew I would continue to lead a normal life, whatever that meant. Before I met her, I had thought I knew, but now I wasn't so sure. I had given up my old mantra, a simple sound and an old friend that had tided me over a bad period, and now I meditated on the one she had given me, a mantra that was long and complex, and I could scarcely get my tongue around the cascade of Sanskrit syllables.

And then there was the vexed question of God. I had given up on God a long time ago, without a pang, and had felt not the slightest desire to reclaim him since. But now, in her short talks, always in Hindi and translated by a devotee, she spoke of the divine; taught that there was an ultimate knowledge and source, and that a part of this, its very essence, lay within my own heart. She referred to it as the Self, an all-pervading consciousness of which we were a part, a union that we were blind to, though occasionally we caught glimpses of it. It was a teaching that sat uneasily with the old version of my empiricism, yet I could not deny that since my first meeting with her I had been granted insights into another dimension of the real.

When I tried to explain it to Zoe, I compared it to the experience of becoming a parent. When you have a child it's like you have been living in a small room and all the time you thought it was the world, and then the child comes and you discover that you are in fact living in a house with many rooms. But you are still inside the house. When you meet the guru you realise that there is a world beyond the house, and you step out of the house and into the unknown.

But there was another way to try and make sense of it, and that was to read. I discovered that there was a Vedanta bookshop in Croydon, and one Saturday afternoon I relieved myself of two hundred dollars and came home with a box of books. I read the *Bhagavad Gita*, I read the lives of the sages, I discovered that many Western philosophers and poets had been strongly influenced by Vedic mysticism. I baulked at the doctrine of reincarnation, since my senses gave me no evidence of this. But I liked the way the sages of Vedanta didn't dwell on sin, on the harsh and the punitive. There was no 'don't do this, don't do that': just 'remember your goal'. You got on the path and moved forward in your own way and your own time, doing the best you could.

I learned of the tradition of the guru and the disciple; that one did not 'seek' and 'find' the guru but that the guru found you; activated a predestined connection when the disciple was 'ripe', which often meant desperate enough and unhappy enough to open to the unfamiliar and the unknown.

I learned that the connection I felt with her was of a special kind, called *bhakti*, and that I was a *bhakta*, one who may read and think and study and intellectualise as much as he likes, but the ground of his being is this loving connection he feels to the guru.

I re-read *Siddhartha*, the text of my youth, and knew for the first time the meaning of the phrase 'wounded deeply by a divine arrow that gave him pleasure'.

I couldn't wait for her to return to the city in November, to emerge once again from her seclusion. By then I would have it all down. I would progress to the next level. I was ready.

But for now I had to contend with Joe Mazengarb.

Zoe, who was one to keep things discreetly to herself, had finally confessed to her father that she feared for her husband's sanity, that he seemed to be regressing into an infantile dependence on an idealised mother figure and might well be at risk of drifting into a cult.

When, after one of our regular squash games, Joe suggested stopping off at a bar for a drink, I knew what was coming.

'What is this thing, Rick?'

'What thing?'

'This . . . this guru thing.' Joe was choking on *that* word.

'It's nothing to worry about, Joe. I haven't lost my marbles.'

'I must say, I'm concerned.'

'It's okay, I'm still the same person. I still vote the same way, still barrack for the same team.'

'Don't humour me, Rick.'

'It's impossible to talk about,' I said, staring into my glass. There were two paths I could go down here: I could attempt to explain everything to my cynical father-in-law and listen to a lecture on the liver syndrome, or I could brush the subject away. I shrugged and opted for the latter. 'It isn't necessary. Really.'

But Joe was a professional interrogator and, having brought us both to this precipice of discomfort, was not about to give up.

I don't remember the rest of that conversation, though I do recall another one, on a Sunday evening at my in-laws' house. After a relaxed dinner, Joe produced a new book he had bought, in which there was a yellow sticky note. The heading of the marked chapter read: 'Is There a God Module in the Brain?'

I knew what was coming: a treatise on the biochemistry of mysticism and the work of the Indian neuroscientist Vilayanur Ramachandran.

'You know, Rick, those guys in San Diego found evidence of neural circuits in the human brain that affect how strongly an individual responds to certain experiences. If I have more connections between the emotion centres of the brain, like the amygdala, more connections than you, say, then I'm more likely to have' – he hesitated – 'certain experiences.'

For once, Joe was tongue-tied. 'Certain experiences' was all he could manage, so distasteful, indeed embarrassing, was the subject of my delusion.

'I've read the research, Joe.'

He raised his eyebrows, then both hands, in an interrogatory shrug, as if to say, 'And?'

'As I read the work done to date' – I tried to sound considered – 'far from invalidating religious experience, it merely indicates what the underlying neural substrate might be.'

'But it does suggest that what you experience depends on your brain, not on any external reality.'

'There may be differences between individual propensities, it's true. But we have to be careful when we talk about the relationship of the brain to what we call reality. We don't understand enough about either to be able to make a whole lot of categorical assertions about their relationship.'

Joe decided on another tack. He had been reading a book on conversion experiences, he said, by a man called Shermer, 'and this guy believes that the revelations of St Paul, Augustine, Luther and Calvin were most likely the result of temporal lobe seizures'.

At that point I might have laughed out loud. I was impressed by Joe's homework, and if I had thought about it I might have felt touched by his concern. Instead, I bristled. 'I know this stuff,' I said, 'and I've never had a seizure, so I guess that rules me out of the category of the spiritually programmed animal.'

'You're fencing with me.'

'No, *you're* fencing with *me*.' I felt the anger rising, and the scorn. 'Do you know how ridiculous all that sounds, all that neural puppetry?'

'Do you know how ridiculous it is for a man like you to succumb to some hippie guru?'

I held my breath. I told myself I owed it to my father-in-law not to lose my temper. 'Look, I'm not interested in philosophy here. I'm not debating how many angels can dance on the end of a pin. This is about my experience. You can speak with authority about *your* experience, I can speak about mine. I'm the same person I always was. I don't know about this thing called God. I can't see it or hear it or feel it but I do see and feel and hear *her*. You offer me argument, logic, words; I offer you my experience. And what if all these theories you cite are true? It doesn't matter whether they're true or not. It works for me. And why should this bother you? I'm not proselytising here, I'm not trying to convert you. Only if I were would this argument be in order. This is my objection to Christianity. It argues that it, and it alone, is right and everyone else is wrong. It wants to convert the world. It wants to gainsay the deeply felt mystical experience of others.'

'Now you're preaching.'

'You started this, Joe.'

We were quarrelling like schoolboys.

That night I went home and re-read Radhakrishnan's introductory essay to the *Bhagavad Gita* and marked the following: 'The *Gita* does not give any arguments in support of its metaphysical position . . . Dialectic in itself and without reference to personal experience cannot give us conviction. Only spiritual experience can provide us with proofs of the existence of Spirit.'

Indeed.

I began to arm myself further with the word. Goaded by my father-in-law, I read Freud on infantilism in the adult and the effects of maternal deprivation. My mother and I, it is true, had had our ups and downs, and I was not her favourite. But that was beside the point. There were thousands of devotees of hundreds of gurus. Some got on with their mothers and some didn't. How to explain the difference? There was no reductionism that could explain away this phenomenon. If I had been close to my mother, they would say I was seeking to replicate the relationship, like a man who seeks a wife resembling his mother. If I hadn't got on with my mother, they would say I was looking for a compensatory maternal figure. Psychology was a maze of mirrors that reflected back the ghosts of its own assumptions. Nothing in psychology, as I understood it, explained my connection to this small, middle-aged Indian woman, this connection that had come out of the blue and, in a vital sense, reclaimed me.

~

It was in this labile and expansive mood that I decided to take Luke camping at the Bay of Fires, where I had swum as a boy.

We flew down to Melbourne and took the boat over Bass Strait so that Luke, who had never been to sea, could experience its depths for the first time. We slept in a spartan two-berth cabin, one of many that opened off a maze of narrow corridors. 'We're like bees in a hive,' I remarked as we found our way to the cabin, and Luke nodded earnestly and said, 'Except there's no queen.' Such a literal-minded boy, with a sweet intensity that I feared he would lose in adolescence. Too excited to sleep, he perched at the end of his bunk and stared out the window until the lights of Port Melbourne were no longer visible, the sky dark but with a full moon that shone its trail of light over the surging waters of the strait.

In the morning we woke to an abrasive loudspeaker. Sitting on the edge of his bunk and pulling on his socks, Luke stared at me with a solemn gaze. 'You can feel it,' he said. I thought he meant the vibration of the massive engine beneath us, which had kept me awake for much of the night. 'No,' he said, 'the ocean. You can feel it under you. It's awesome.'

At the Devonport terminal we hired a car and bundled our packs into the boot. Then we set off for the coast, heading south-east along the highway, past the Great Western Tiers and pastures white with frost. When we turned off into the Fingal Valley we met with a cold so intense that the bare limbs of the deciduous trees were still coated in ice crystals and the valley shone like a landscape in a folk tale. We drove on, through the old mining towns with their wide streets and abandoned collieries, until at last we arrived at the top of a steep mountain pass, the edge of which fell away into canyons of dry eucalypt forest. As we made our descent, down and around the many narrow bends, we began at last to catch a glimpse of the glittering sea below, the long arc of a bay that curved towards the horizon.

At the small seaside town of Scamander I pulled in at a dusty secondhand bookshop that had a food counter with scallop pies, which we ate for our breakfast. Then we set off for the fishing town of St Helens, where we bought camp food at a supermarket and hired boogie boards and wetsuits from a surf shop. By mid-afternoon we had arrived at an area known as The Gardens, and here we took the turn-off to a narrow unsealed road that led to the Bay of Fires.

Because it was winter the campsite was empty, and we parked the car in a clearing fringed by she-oaks. I was impatient to see those magical waters of the bay again and wanted Luke to get oriented before it grew dark, so we set off down a steep track to the shore, where first we had to climb up and over a rocky promontory before we could descend to the long, white sands of the bay.

The water was still at low tide, and all along the sand lay beached puffer fish with ugly bulbous heads, squashed angry-looking faces and bloated bodies covered in grey spikes. Luke was fascinated by their sinister ugliness and began to count them, until I directed his attention to Sloop Rock, a formation of rocks just off the coast, where a single steeple of rock reared up from a cluster of smooth boulders around its base, the whole appearing to float on the water.

Luke stared out to sea. 'The rocks here are different,' he said, and I knew what he meant. In the softness of their contours they had a pneumatic quality, as if inflated with air; beneath the warmth of their pink lichen they seemed to breathe.

At the far end of the bay we encountered a group of middle-aged walkers accompanied by young guides with bulging back-packs, and I guessed they were trekking towards the expensive eco-resort that lay some kilometres north. With their bodies knee-deep in grass and their heads silhouetted against the sky, they looked like pilgrims, even if it were only the local pinot and oysters that lured them on.

I showed Luke where I had camped as a boy – behind the grass-lands, near the mouth of a creek that ran out into a small lagoon – but it was too cold to camp there in winter as it lacked shelter from the wind. I told him of how, one morning, Gareth and I had woken to find a brown snake basking in a languorous coil beside our tent, and of the day a gang of bikies roared in to drink at the other end of the beach. My father had stiffened to red alert while my mother snapped at us to stay close, but Gareth had disappeared to climb a path that ran along the rear of the promon-tory. When he returned he boasted to me that the bikies had offered him a beer.

Luke was keen to help with the set-up of the campsite. We pegged the tent beside a cluster of drooping she-oaks, and I warned him that if the wind came up at night they would make an eerie sound and he was not to be spooked. After we unrolled our sleep-ing bags I unpacked the primus stove, but Luke wanted to light a fire. Then he insisted on cooking the sausages and hamburgers, which he handled with the deft practicality of his mother, squatting on thin haunches and shaking the pan with one hand, while with the other he brushed the sparks away from his eyes. We ate beside the fire and I explained how the Bay of Fires was a favourite campsite for the northeastern tribe of the Tasmanian Aborigines, how in winter they came to live off the shellfish. When the English navigator Tobias Furneaux sailed along the coast he observed their long line of campfires glowing in the dusk and gave the bay its name.

Then the darkness began to enclose us, and the cold, but we stoked the fire and warmed ourselves by its coals.

In the morning it was freezing but Luke was determined to enter the water so we put on our wetsuits and took up our boards. When Luke emerged from the surf he was trembling from the chill. After we had changed, he was still shivering, so I suggested we cheat and drive to a local restaurant for lunch where it would be warm.

At Binalong Bay we ate out on the deck under gas burners and looked down to a wedding that was being celebrated on the beach below. The members of the bridal party were in bare feet, the men in black trousers and white shirts, the bridesmaids in tight pink dresses that barely reached the top of their thighs. We watched as the elderly male celebrant took off his shoes and rolled up his trousers so that his white, bony shins looked like the legs of a rare species of seabird.

At the culmination of the ceremony the groom lifted his bride and carried her to the edge of the water, where he whirled her around and around in the shallows. Up on the deck we, the diners, clapped and cheered.

Luke seemed bemused by this. 'Why did everyone cheer?' he asked. 'We don't know them.'

'To wish them well.' It was a lame way of saying what I really meant. We cheer because we are in the presence of a great fertility rite. Uplifted by the promise that life will go on, for a moment we love one another and are irrational in our hope.

In the late afternoon we returned to the campsite to build a fire and make supper from bread and packet soup. There was no wind and no cloud, one of those night skies where you don't so much see as feel the curve of the earth fall away under you, with the stars spun out in a swathe. Luke yawned and I suggested we put out the fire and climb into our tent early.

When I was sure he was asleep I unzipped the flap of the tent and went outside. There was a boulder nearby with a smooth, rounded surface and I sat cross-legged on the sand and leaned my back into it. For a while I meditated, absorbing the muted roar of the ocean, until I became aware that my body had dissolved into the rock, and the rock into the sand. I felt the edges of whoever and whatever I was expand out into the darkness. The night sky entered into me, and when I looked down to where my body had been sitting, upright on the sand, there were no organs, no viscera, only the white stars blinking in space.

the riddle

And so he continued to meditate, in an interregnum of calm, until the inevitable happened. He began to feel smug. He had discovered the secret; he was one of the elect. He had knowledge at his fingertips. He had read the books, he had it all figured. He couldn't wait for the next time she came out of her seclusion so that he could advance to a higher level.

And then he received an email to say that, for the first time, she would be running a long weekend retreat in a small seaside hamlet an hour outside Melbourne. No talks, no teaching, only some chanting in the evenings and silent meditation throughout the day. For three days he would live the life of a monk and go deeper into the mystery.

He flew down to Melbourne late on the Friday afternoon. On the plane they offered him food but he was too nervous to eat. Instead, he stared out at a sea of grey-white cloud that floated beneath him. For a while he closed his eyes, hoping for sleep, but, unable even to doze, he opened them. When he looked out the window, he saw that a huge cloud had risen up in a curling arc, like a frozen wave about to break. In the distance the sunset was a rim of crimson fire along a black horizon; the wing of the plane looked uncannily still, as if they were not moving at all but were suspended in space. Every now and then a gap would open in the cloud and the yellow lights of houses would blink up at him from the dry, brown earth below.

At the airport he hired a car and drove to a small town on the Mornington Peninsula. All the way down he felt an intense excitement; this was going to be it, the time of revelation when he broke through into another dimension, when he ceased to be an apprentice, when finally he got 'it'.

The conference centre was three kilometres outside a well-known tourist town, but the nomenclature 'conference' turned out to be misleading. It was in fact an old air-force barracks from World War II, and a gutted and rusting small plane stood propped beside the driveway as he drove through the main gates. Somehow it seemed symbolic; he was here to take flight from his old self. But the conditions were dismayingly primitive, even for a school holiday camp.

Following the signs, he parked outside a cream-coloured demountable hut labelled 'Registration'. It was empty. Admittedly he was late, and it was dark and he could hear chanting coming from a large weatherboard building with a pitched roof that he deduced must be the main hall. A woman dressed in white jeans and a white shawl stopped and asked him if she could help. She led him into a warm room of Laminex tables and plastic chairs that turned out to be the dining room, and there she introduced him to a man who was to take care of late registrations. Within minutes he was given a plastic wristband and assigned to a dormitory.

Dormitory. That word filled him with unease, and sure enough he had been allocated to the second in a row of wooden huts at the bottom of a steep, grassy slope beside a creek. Inside, the hut had concrete floors and double bunks and not much else, apart from a concrete ablutions wing at one end. At least, he told himself, it was inside and not a tent out in the sharp unseasonal cold that was beginning to blow in from Bass Strait.

He took a leak in the ablutions wing, which had all the charm of a prison block. Then, to his dismay, he found there was only a single top bunk left, and he swung his bag up onto the bare mattress, thinking he would make up his bed later. He had brought with him a sleeping bag, as instructed, and there were pillows and a rough army blanket. By now it was almost dark, and he fumbled in his bag for the small torch he had packed.

Outside, the paths were well lit, and a clear sky of bright stars raised his spirits. He climbed the grassy slope to the main compound, and when he entered the hall *she* was already there, seated on a low stool that had been draped in white silk. The hall was full, so full there was scarcely room to breathe. By now he felt no excitement, only deep fatigue, and he looked around for a gap of floor space where he could sit until the usual queue formed. After treading on a woman's foot and bumping the head of small child, he managed to squash himself into a space behind a pillar and felt his jeans stretch uncomfortably as he adjusted his legs into a cross-legged position and loosened the back of his shirt.

Once settled, he began to relax. The interior of the hall had an unexpected charm, with a fibro ceiling that sloped on both sides and a tiny proscenium stage draped in green and gold silk. Already he felt soothed by the chanting, though before long he wished he had sat on one of the chairs at the back. His shoulders began to ache and his calf muscles were stiff and sore. When he felt the familiar tingle in his feet he knew that as soon as the singing stopped he would have to get up and move around. And of course by now he was hungry. On the plane he had been unable to eat, from a feeling of nervous anticipation, not to mention the hectic rush of getting to Mascot, and he had made a mental note to buy sandwiches at one of the airport cafés when he landed. But then, in his haste to get on the road as soon as possible, he had forgotten all about food and so had arrived with an acid pain under his ribs, only to find he was too late for dinner. But still, here he was with her, for two full days, and who knew what revelations and experiences awaited him? What was a pain in the guts?

Craning his neck at intervals to look around the wooden pillar that blocked his view, he gazed at the small, dark-skinned figure in white who was seated in front of the stage, and who had begun now to receive the children first, as was her custom, while some of the adults began to form a queue. For him there was no urgency and he made no move; he would go later. There was all the time in the world, that was the point of being here, and for now he was content simply to sit, hands clasped around his knees, and gaze at her.

Once again he was struck by how her photographs failed to capture the aura of her presence. By now he had seen dozens of these photos, and each one could have been of someone else. The ineffable sheen of her skin, the subtlety of her expression and the light in her eyes were beyond the camera's capacity to capture and store. At times it seemed as if they were barely accessible even to the human eye, as if some emanation from her hovered at the edge of the cornea and could only be glimpsed peripherally, and then for a nanosecond. When someone asked her a question, often she would laugh with childlike good humour, revealing an appealing gap in her white teeth. When she set about explaining a point in Hindi she would use her delicate, dark hands fluidly, occasionally forming a small fist and gesturing with an emphatic elegance that was neither masculine nor feminine but that embodied an authority, a knowingness, unlike any he had experienced. When people wept at her feet, as they so often did, she stroked their cheeks, brushing aside strands of their hair and giving them a look of the utmost compassion. And yet through all this, in every mood – laughing, frowning, consoling, chanting ecstatically with her eyes closed and her arms extended – she was sublimely impersonal. He had tried once to explain this to Zoe, who had responded with the obvious: 'If she's as loving as you say, how can she be impersonal?' To which he could only reply, lamely, 'You have to be there.' Why don't you come, he had asked, and see for yourself? But she'd shaken her head, and got up to brush her hair.

As the crowd murmured around him in the stuffy hall, he closed his eyes to meditate. And immediately thought of food. Damn, how careless of him not to see to his bodily needs. He was used to Zoe doing that. It was Zoe who packed sandwiches for a long trip, or kept dried fruit and nuts in the glove box of the car. Seeking distraction from his hunger pains, he opened his eyes and saw one of the marshals browsing at the bookstall at the rear of the hall. It was Rebecca. Yes, Rebecca. He got up and walked over to her side.

'Hi, Rick,' she said, with obvious pleasure at seeing him. Feeling foolish in the extreme, he asked her if she knew where he could get some food. 'No,' she said, with an expression of quaint seriousness that was rather attractive. 'Why don't you go over to the kitchen and see if they have something there?'

'The kitchen?'

'Where you registered. Behind there.'

Outside, he searched for his shoes, which had been scattered some distance from where he left them and were now squashed beneath several other pairs. How could this be, since he was one of the last to arrive? The longer he searched, the more irritable he became.

By the time he located the kitchen, a big commercial set-up of deep stainless-steel sinks, black gas burners and giant cooking pots, it was empty. Sacks of flour and lentils were stacked up against the wall and there wasn't a loaf of bread in sight. All he could find was an urn of hot water and various teabags left over from dinner, so he poured himself a mug and loaded it up with sugar. Then he drank the rest of the milk left in the only carton on the bench that wasn't empty. He had come to his first meditation retreat in the hope of deep insights and had begun the evening by prowling around with a growling stomach like a disgruntled bear.

When at last he joined the queue for her blessing, it was after eleven and the crowd was beginning to thin. The diehards would stay until the last moment, and he would be one of them. As he approached what by now he thought of as the final straight, the few metres in the queue between himself and her feet, he began to feel the subtle vibration that emanated from her and that entered him as if through the pores of his skin, no matter how great his discomfort, no matter his mood. But when she drew him to her, brow to brow, and he felt nothing. A pleasant blankness, a certain lightness of being, but nothing more.

Afterwards, on the walk back to the hut, he asked himself if his expectations had been unrealistic. And he laughed silently. The concept of 'realism', as commonly applied, in no way belonged here. And anyway, what *had* he expected? Nirvana in a decrepit air-force barracks? Still, it was only the beginning of the retreat; he was confident she had more in store for him than this, and he must wait patiently for it to come, and not think of himself as a special case to whom anything – anything at all – was due.

That night was one of the most uncomfortable of his life. The man beneath him snored loudly in fitful bursts. The door to the ablutions block at the end of the hut was weighted in such a way that whenever anyone got up in the night for a leak it banged loudly in a sudden thud that jolted him awake. As if that were not enough, around two in the morning the temperature dropped suddenly and he shivered under his single blanket. He disliked the constraint of sleeping bags and it hadn't seemed cold enough to bother unpacking his when finally he had climbed up onto his bunk.

As a consequence of all this, he slept in, only to find when he climbed down from his bunk that the hot water in the showers had run out. He set out for the dining room but a cold wind had blown in off the water, and halfway across the paddock he had to turn back for a jacket. By the time he made it to the dining room there was only cold semolina porridge sitting congealed at the bottom of a big steel pot, and insipid white sliced bread, which he lathered thickly with peanut butter – something he hadn't eaten since he was a child. Anything to fill him up.

All day he squirmed in a cocoon of hunger. He was unable to meditate, he was unable to sit still. The morning program went on forever, the queue afterwards was interminable, he delayed too long in joining it and soon it was two in the afternoon and his belly shouted at him with hunger. He knew he would again be too late, he would miss lunch, he would get to the bare, fluorescent dining room with its white plastic chairs and there would be nothing left to eat, it would all be gone. When finally he arrived at her feet, his blessing seemed perfunctory, as if she were barely interested in him, as if they were both going through the motions.

But it didn't matter because all he could think about was lunch. He couldn't get to the dining room fast enough, and to his relief saw that they were bringing out big new trays of food for a second sitting. Thank God for that! But it looked better than it tasted – a bland, overcooked vegetable burger in a mushy bun, accompanied by a few lettuce leaves, undressed. He swallowed it down awkwardly so that he almost gagged, conscious of a craving for coffee, real coffee, not the instant stuff that sat spilled in sticky granules on the benches, and not that disgusting coffee substitute made of roasted grass and God knows what other foul vegan brew. He was a long way from home, and not just in kilometres. He was out of his comfort zone.

By the time he had finished eating, it was almost three in the afternoon. The evening program began at six-thirty and he could go for a walk along the beach now, as some of the others were doing, but an icy wind was blowing in off the strait. He decided instead on a nap.

Back in the hut there were several prone bodies with the same idea but as he approached his bunk he had an idea. Reaching up to the bunk, he hoisted the mattress and bedding down over his head and carried them to a space at the end of the hut where there was a bare alcove of concrete floor. Perfect. He would sleep there. Before long he had gathered his things together and set them up alongside the mattress. It would be hard, and it would be cold, but he would not have to climb up onto that narrow bunk and he would be much further from the snorer and the thudding cubicle door.

Already he felt better.

He began to do a quick check of his things, and by this time a small boy had approached and was staring at his manoeuvres. There was something odd about the boy, a plump child with fair, curly hair and vacant green eyes.

'What are you doing?' the boy asked. 'Why is that thing there?' His speech was unclear, as if he couldn't be bothered to articulate the ends of words, and it occurred to Rick that the boy was in some way simple. Was that the correct term for it now? Or would it be more accurate to describe him as 'complex'? In either case, he wanted him to go away; he was not in the mood for children, he was tired, he wanted quiet, he wanted a nap. But the boy hovered. 'What's your name?' he asked.

'Rick.'

'My name's Oliver.'

Well, at least he wasn't called Bhodi or Moon, like some of the hippie kids around the place. 'Are you sleeping here?'

'I'm sleeping with my mum.'

So what are you doing in here, Rick thought, in the men's quarters? 'Perhaps you'd better go back to your own hut,' he said. The best he could offer Oliver was a charmless smile as he strolled off down the aisle between the bunks for a leak in the ablutions wing.

When he returned, the little brat was jumping on his bed and emitting a weird yodelling noise.

'Hey, get off there!' he snapped.

Oliver stood stock still, mouth open in idiotic astonishment. Rick leaned across the mattress and put his hand on the boy's shoulder with the intention of squiring him out the door, but the instant he touched him the boy keeled over, face forward, onto the bed, and lay there like a zombie.

This was too much. 'Get up!' he said, sharply, and then regretting his tone, 'Get up, Oliver. I'm going to have a sleep on that bed.'

Oliver rolled onto his back and looked up at him with a crazed smile. 'Going to have a sleep,' he droned, as if in a trance, 'going to have a sleep.'

'Not you, me.' And he leaned over and hoisted the boy upright, then lifted him under the armpits and set him down roughly in the corridor. Any minute one of the sleepers would wake up and see him molesting this kid. What a perfect day.

To his relief, Oliver made no resistance and began to stroll down the aisle, gazing about him as if he had just that minute wandered in and it was all new.

Rick sank onto the mattress and fell into a heavy, dragging sleep.

When he woke it was almost dark. Damn, he would miss dinner again, for the second night in a row. He threw off the blanket, reached for his jacket and strode to the door, where his boots were lined up with the rest. At the end of the line of shoes, Oliver was standing in shadow, looking intent. At first he couldn't see what the boy was up to and then he recognised the sound; Oliver was pissing over the shoes.

'Hey!' he shouted. The boy turned to him, staring blankly and waving his little white prick up and down. Then, as if stung by a slap, he ran off up the grassy bank, keening his strange yodelling wail.

Jesus, what next? To his relief Rick found that his own boots had been spared, but since he didn't know any of the others in his hut he wouldn't be able to alert them and they would just have to make the unhappy discovery when they returned. Or should he ask one of the monitors to make an announcement?

When he arrived at the dining room he realised he had misread the time on his watch and he was an hour early. Typical. He couldn't put a foot right. He walked back to where the car was parked and drove three kilometres into the tourist town nearby, where he bought a double-shot coffee, eggs and bacon and some chocolate, including a small bar that he planned to give to Oliver; his conscience continued to prick him over his waspishness with the boy. Oliver was without a doubt the most unlikeable child he'd ever encountered, with flapping arms, sickly pale skin, and a moronic expression, slack-mouthed and mocking, that he found physically repugnant. Nevertheless, he ought to have been able to feel some impulse to kindness. The child was disturbed and he, Rick, had failed a test. Why was it that ever since he arrived at this boot camp, his every word, his every gesture, seemed to strike the wrong note? He was not normally this inept, even when out of his comfort zone. Something was out of sync. And he might not even see the mad kid again – with luck, he wouldn't – though, as it happened, no sooner had he pulled into the drive of the campsite than he saw the boy walking through the door of his hut. Inside, he found him running noisily up and down the ablutions block and shouting into the echoing stalls.

'Here, Oliver,' he said, testily. 'I've brought you something,' and he almost thrust the chocolate bar into the pocket of the boy's shorts.

Suddenly he thought of how it would look if anyone came in. Here he was in a lavatory block giving a small boy a lolly. Terrific. In less than twenty-four hours he had been reduced to this.

Oliver just stared at him, that blank moronic stare. 'What?' he said, but Rick turned and walked away.

Oliver stood motionless in the aisle, his arms limp by his side. '*What?*' he shouted, and the cry echoed in the bare spaces of the bunkhouse. '*What? What? What?*'

When Rick returned to the dining room it was crowded but they had not yet begun to serve dinner. From over in one corner he saw a raised arm waving to him; it was Rebecca. She was sitting with a group of people and she beckoned him to join them. Later, he could not remember what they talked about; all he could recall was the loneliness that descended on him as they spoke, followed by a strange, numbing paranoia, like the worst kind of stoned feeling. He was miserable, utterly miserable. As the meal dragged on, he could hear his own voice, too loud and too emphatic, some awful desperate braying, and all the time the pain was getting worse. He felt that the others were laughing at him, that he was absurd, an awkward fool, a big lumbering bundle of bone and muscle, of sinew and fat. He and Oliver were somehow kin.

By the end of the meal he was scarcely able to speak.

That evening in the hall he fidgeted with a hostile restlessness that pricked at him as if he were being tormented by invisible flies. He did not get into the queue for her blessing, he left early – before ten – and he walked the track down to the beach, where he sat on the damp sand, his head hunched over his drawn-up knees, and listened to the roar of the incoming waves. There was no moon. He thought of seeking out Rebecca and putting the moves on. She had flirted with him, and it would restore his pride.

Later – how much later he couldn't say – he lay on his mattress in the hut and stared up at the blank ceiling. It was all a mistake, he shouldn't have come, the place was indescribably tacky and he had made a serious error of judgement. In the morning he would get up, pack the car and leave early. He would use his mobile to re-book his flight, and with luck he'd be home by mid-afternoon. He would lose face with Zoe but it would be a small price to pay.

He woke at eight and did not bother with breakfast. For a moment he contemplated not having a shower, so keen was he to make his escape. By the time he had dried off and dressed, the dormitory hut was empty and he was able to pack up his things without having to face any awkward questions. No-one would notice he was gone; everyone there was completely self-absorbed, absorbed in their own salvation, their own 'experience', and the other bodies around them were not much more than props or dummies, a human blur.

As he lifted his bag into the boot of the car, he stopped for the first time and thought about what he was doing. He was behaving like a child. He had forgotten about one thing: *her*. It would be churlish of him to go without making any farewell. Some instinct, a throb in his pulse, told him he would regret it. He would be leav-ing without closure. It was messy, it was adolescent and it was beneath him.

Slipping the car keys into his back pocket, he headed for the hall. Just as he rounded the corner of the dining-room block, sud-denly there she was, walking towards him with a small crowd in a procession behind her, the hem of her white sari trailing in the dust. Surely she should be in the hall by now? He must have looked puzzled because a man next to him explained that she had made an unscheduled walk to the beach, and as a result the program was running late. So he stood there, goggle-eyed, waiting for her to pass, but as she approached the wooden steps leading to the hall she stopped, looked straight at him and said one word, in English. 'Going?' But her eyes were more eloquent: *I have put you through all this*, they said, *and now you are going to run away like a scared child.*

What happened immediately afterwards was hazy; he staggered up the wooden steps of the hall in a daze, slumped into a chair against the side wall and wept.

In the long wait in the queue he was shaking, and when finally he found his way to her chair, she looked into his eyes with the most compassionate smile she had ever given him, laid her hands on his head and gave him a prolonged blessing. As if she knew. But of course she knew. On a low table beside her there was a brass bowl filled with rose petals, and, taking a handful of petals, she began to stuff them into his ears, to the delighted laughter of those looking on.

Drunk with bliss, he staggered back to his seat.

That night, when he rested his forehead against hers, he had, for the first time since he was a boy, prayed. *Take this absurd pain away from me, take it all. I don't want it. I'm laying it down here, at your feet. I'm giving it to you. Take my life's burden.*

~

He had booked himself onto the last plane out on the Monday evening, and when he arrived at the airport he was hungry. All the food stalls were closed, except one, and even there they had only a single packet of sandwiches. By now he was exhausted and he slumped into a seat in the departure lounge and unravelled the wrapping from the soggy white-bread sandwich in his lap. Inside

was a slice of plastic yellow cheese, two slices of pale, watery tomato
and a single leaf of limp lettuce. Great. It was the theme of his
benighted excursion. Still, he was empty, and he took a half-
hearted bite and began to chew. What followed was perhaps the
most remarkable part of the weekend. The sandwich was delicious;
the sandwich was the best sandwich he had ever eaten. With each
mouthful it grew more subtle and more satisfying so that he began
to chew more slowly, the better to savour it, to linger over its
sweetness. Now he was not so tired. Now, suddenly, he was very
focused, he was like a scientist in his lab, wholly absorbed in an
experiment.

When he boarded the plane and the steward brought him his
plastic tray with its two airline biscuits, brittle circles of flour dust
in cellophane packets, he couldn't wait to open one of the packets
and bite into the dun-coloured orb. Yes, *delicious*, and the other
one equally so! And he saw what she was doing, how she had played
with him all weekend, how she had taken pity on his arrogance, his
discontent, and was teaching him now to take pleasure in the simplest things. To be grateful.

It was gratitude that he lacked, that he had always lacked. Since
childhood it had been his curse to see the flaw in everything. This
he had prided himself on; this, he had told himself, was discrimi-
nation. No-one could fool him.

And with this thought a rush of tears welled behind his eyes
and he laid his head against the window to conceal his overflowing
heart.

What did he learn from this? He learned that he was not in
control, and that any expectations he had were foolish in their
naïve presumption. Sometimes they would be met, sometimes not;

sometimes they would be met but when he least expected it and not in the form he had anticipated. His imagination was a tantalising distraction; pleasurable in itself, often, but nothing ever came of it. Nothing was ever as he imagined it. To re-imagine the past or daydream the future was beside the point. Only the present mattered.

But this was not an insight that stayed with him. He was unable to hold this wisdom, this freedom in his heart, for long. For the first month after the retreat he lived and breathed and worked in a serene state, and the memory of that single word, the sound of her voice, its gentle ironic inflection of mock surprise – 'Going?' – was enough to make him smile to himself in the middle of a meeting. But it was not enough. *Nothing* would ever be enough for him. And later, when he looked back, he could see that this short-lived phase of serenity was nothing other than a return to his original smugness. Which is why it was inevitable that he should fall out of it, without warning.

~

Now began some terrible mood. A sense of futility seeped into his viscera like a thin drip of poison. So, he thought, so, it's going to wear off, just like every other infatuation. Every morning, in his meditation, he could feel a sharp instrument twisting in his bowels, some double-edged sword of disillusionment and longing. The pain was unbearable.

He began to brood on the boy, Oliver. He felt that Oliver and the baby in his dreams were one and the same, that the baby had come to him in human form, as an idiot boy, and he had failed to recognise it. He loved his son – of course he loved his son; the test of Sri Mata's influence was whether he could love others, and he had failed that test. He was *uncharitable*. For the first time it occurred to him that he was lacking in love, not in the receiving of it but in the giving.

He began to feel an underlying panic. One night he dreamed that he was riding in a crowded old bus with its windows wound down. He had two babies in his care, and as the bus jolted along the potholed road he feared that one of them might fall out of a window. It was dangerous – so dangerous he had to get off the bus in the middle of the busy city and carry the babies awkwardly along the middle of a road congested with traffic – and the infants were so heavy, and what if he dropped one? He asked a man loitering in a doorway to call him a taxi. The taxi came but the driver protested that he didn't know the way. He became angry, he swore loudly in the street. Someone will have to come and help me, he shouted, and, clutching the babies, he strode off up the road, shouting and weaving through the traffic . . .

And woke.

He began to resent her. How dare she do this to him? Lead him to bliss and then hang him out to dry? Why didn't she help him more? Why had she brought him this far and no further? What was the point of meditation and the energetic connection to her that they called grace if he still behaved badly? He was worse off now than he had ever been, because now he was disappointed in himself for failing the spiritual course. He had always been a good student, always done well in whatever course he enrolled in, whatever project he took up. Now he was a dunce.

He gave up meditating. What was the point?

Zoe was shocked, alarmed even. He could see that, perhaps even more than him, she had become attached to the idea of her husband as a master's apprentice. It didn't matter which master; all that mattered was that he was a good boy, that he acknowledged his problem and made an effort, that he was a horse in some kind of harness. Well, fuck that.

Even so, giving up made him uneasy. He told himself that his unease was mere superstition. Meditation had become his voodoo, his rabbit's foot talisman, his lucky charm, his anxious ritual, like those obsessive-compulsive types who tap three times on the front door when they leave the house.

He became clumsy. His energy was rough, more abrasive even than before. He began to bump into things, into people. He was febrile, a scattergun. It was no special mood you could name – not anger, irritation or depression – just an off-centredness, like his internal scales had been tipped out of balance. Could it be that since he began to meditate he had arrived at a subtle equilibrium he didn't realise he possessed? It didn't mean that he had no moods or never lost his temper, but that the moods and the temper passed quickly. It was as if he walked now on the balls of his feet, or on an invisible tightrope.

It was early April and he drove to the airport and took a plane to Brisbane. He had a one-day conference at Surfers Paradise but had decided to hire a car and drive there after lunch with his sister, Jane, at her house in Woolloongabba.

They sat out on the big, wide deck at the rear, built up high on stilts like the rest of the house, and it was like sitting in the middle of a jungle: banana palms, papaya trees and a flagrant pink hibiscus poked through the derelict fence of the low-rent apartment block next door. The run-down apartments had token balconies that were all but obscured by an overgrown garden, luxuriant trees with branches laced together by creeper and spiderwebs.

Moments after Jane brought out coffee, they heard shouting. A skinny, shirtless man ran out onto one of the balconies, waving his arms. His brown tufts of hair stood on end, his grey beard was matted and he was raving. 'The flies, the flies, they're everywhere, the flies . . .'

His sister pursed her lips. 'Him again,' she said. 'Last night he was hurling pot plants at the wall of the girls' bedroom.'

A police car pulled up, and then another, then a van. Suddenly there were nine uniformed police in the street. Three of them opened the iron gate to the garden and stood on the cracked concrete path, looking up at the balcony.

'No arms, no weapons! No arms, no weapons!' cried the wretched figure. He was clearly terrified and dropped to the floor of the balcony like a ragdoll. 'Look, look, I'm lying on the floor. I'm lying on the floor. No arms, no weapons.'

One of the policemen stepped back to get a better view. 'You'll have to come down, sir.'

'No, no, it's the flies, the flies, they're everywhere. You have to spray the bushes. I'm not coming down till you spray the flies.'

One of the policemen tried the door, which was unlocked, and the three entered. Before long they had picked the ragdoll up off the floor of the balcony and were frogmarching him across the road to the van.

Rick turned to his sister. 'What will they do with him?'

'What they always do with him. Take him to hospital, and after twenty-four hours they have to release him. And he comes back and he's quiet for a while, then it starts all over again.'

Yes, he thought, *it starts all over again.*

By the time he drove into Surfers it was late afternoon. He checked into his hotel, one of those white behemoths that line up behind the Esplanade, and he was too tired, too apathetic, to do anything but order room service. It was years since he had been to Surfers, and in the morning, before breakfast, he went for a walk through the seedy streets, past a whole arcade of empty shops plastered with 'To Lease' notices. On a corner, outside the brass framed doors and glossy plate glass of a Louis Vuitton shop, a drug-raddled youth, whey-faced and reed-thin, was begging for small change, his eyes glazed, the palm of his left hand extended listlessly.

He turned and headed for the Esplanade, the great white beach, ever lovely with the waves rolling in like layered motion in series of eight or nine . . . two, three, four, five . . . And as they surged to the shore they broke simultaneously as if orchestrated, rolling crests of surf that gave off a muted roar and a sea mist that wafted across the Esplanade.

Already a portion of the beach was set with red and yellow flags, so narrow a space for permitted immersion, so limited a licence to frolic. The lifeguard was tall and lean and muscular but surprisingly old, in his forties at least. Or was it just that he had weathered into premature age? He had attached a resistance band to one of the steel columns of the lifeguard tent, and as he stood there, gazing out to sea and waiting for the raised arm that signalled distress, nonchalantly he worked the extender, in–out, in–out, first with his right arm, then with his left. The day had begun quietly. No-one was drowning.

Rick had an impulse to dive in, to swim, but he had no togs.

And in any case he did not want to challenge the series of the waves, to immerse himself untidily in their rhythmic formation. The bodies in the water, between the flags, looked like flotsam. They did not belong; they trespassed and flailed. A lone surfer, outside the flags, pitched from his board, his body tossed into the air in an arc before folding neatly into the oncoming waves.

He walked on, past the Anzac memorial, a simple stone at the ocean edge of the Esplanade, its rigid, immobile form set against the relentless surge of the tide . . . five, six, seven, eight . . . He paused beside a bronze statue of a lifesaver, larger than life, a man in Speedo trunks, racing for the surf like a sprinter out of the blocks, eyes fixed ahead on the water. He read the plaque beside the bronze form. It said that this man died in his fifties. He was a world champion lifesaver, had won gold medals. But now, here he was, stalled in frozen motion. Forever on the cusp of rescue.

He looked at his watch. It was time to return. On the way back to the hotel he stopped at a shop that had opened early, and he bought a cap for Luke and a pair of crazy thongs in the shape of alligator paws.

In the hotel conference room the air was uncomfortably chill and they put on their jackets. He hated air-conditioning. Outside, the air was muggy, it clung to the skin, but in the artificial light of the conference room little draughts of icy air began to chill their shoulders, their forearms, the backs of their necks. They were at the mercy of controlled temperature.

Before dinner he went up to his room on the twenty-second floor, and sat out on its small, vertiginous balcony. Across the way a giant ferris wheel rotated slowly with a pulsating neon eye at its centre. The fairground looked fragile, as if temporary and constructed from Meccano. On the other side of the street was a new shopping plaza with a mock medieval tower and a clock that gave off soft musical chimes on the hour, like muted church bells heard from a distance. The boxy white towers of the hotels rose in stark outline against the blue mountain range in the distance. The ridges of the mountains rose in curved, flowing shapes that looked kneadable, as if made of a smoky charcoal dough.

Later, a small group of them dined at a yum cha palace on the Esplanade, desperate to escape the chill of the air con. After dinner, some went off to look for a bar, others sat on the ruffled sand, still warm, and gazed at the waves . . . five, six, seven, eight . . . He counted the series rolling in, the mesmerising order of it. Did he imagine it? Was he imposing order on chaos? The answer didn't matter, never would matter, for in his heart he knew suddenly that there was no chaos, anywhere, not in the commonplace sense of the word, and he was consoled by the knowledge of this.

In the burgeoning dark they strolled back along the sand to the street that turned off to their hotel, past the pandanus trees with their naked roots and their phallic growths hanging from the trunk, uncircumcised and pointing down to the concrete pavement.

Back in his room he watched the late news, thinking he should go outside again, should go out onto the balcony and watch the neon ferris wheel while it spun its slow compass through the warm, salty air. He opened the sliding door and settled onto a wrought-iron chair, so hard, so uncomfortable.

After a while he looked over to the wheel. It had stopped turning and its neon eye was dark. He got up, went inside, didn't bother to undress and lay on the bed, waiting for sleep. It fell on him, a depthless surge of something powerful, and he dreamed he was standing on the Esplanade, gazing at the waves, their exquisite unending series, rolling in . . .

When he woke there was an unbearable tumescence behind his eyes, and he felt grateful, not for anything in particular, just that he was alive. It was the dream; some resistance in him had dissolved. But why had that dream been so powerful? After all, it had merely repeated what he had already done that morning on his walk, when he had looked out to sea. But the dream version had been infused with a powerful presence, unsought, given to him as a gift.

Now he was awake, and the reliable Gold Coast sun was shafting through the heavy drapes, and he wrenched himself upright on the edge of the bed. He glanced at the bedside clock: it was late and he would miss his flight. He phoned down to the reception desk for a quick checkout, lurched into the shower, drowned himself in over-chlorinated water, dressed and packed his overnight bag. Then he drove out to the airport. There, brandishing a pair of alligator thongs, he joined the queue for home.

The very next morning he returned to his meditation practice, only he got up earlier, at five instead of six, and he meditated longer. He made no resolution about this, it just happened.

Now, truly, he began to feel as if nothing important was within his volition. He had had a dark night of the soul, had bumped into things, and he was meditating again. Stuff happened, and he was moved on. And where was 'on'? He hadn't a clue. He felt like a knight that was being picked up and slid about on a chessboard.

What he needed was someone to talk to. He had a secret life, and he needed to make sense of it.

Sydney Park

I rang Rebecca.

No, I didn't want to join her chant group (I said this as politely as I could, making the excuse that I often worked late and she lived on the other side of town). But could she suggest someone I might meet with on a regular basis?

Well, she said, she knew of a Vedantin monk who lived in the inner west, not far from me, a man called Martin Coleby, who taught yoga and ran classes from his home.

'I did a workshop with him once,' she said. 'He's pretty cool. Not pious, or anything like that.'

Didn't monks live in monasteries?

'Not Martin. He went to India when he was young, spent time in an ashram. Now he's a renunciate.'

A renunciate?

'Celibate, vegetarian, all that.'

'Where?'

'In St Peters. In a crummy little terrace. He doesn't have much money, only what his students can afford to pay.'

I thought about it for a while and the idea was plausible. It would be private, no-one would know. I rang this Martin Coleby.

Martin suggested I come on a Thursday evening after one of his regular yoga classes and we could take it from there. Perhaps he had something to offer me, perhaps not.

As instructed, I arrived promptly around seven, just as his students were rolling up their foam mats and saying their goodbyes at the door. I waited to one side until they were gone, all the while observing Martin, a muscular man of medium height, lean and with a kind of tensile strength, as if he might once have been an athlete. He wore loose white drawstring pants and a grey t-shirt, and had a tattoo around his right bicep, an inscription in the alphabet of some exotic language. His head was shaved and bullet-shaped, with a long, narrow face, high cheekbones and hollowed-out cheeks. His eyes were a pale icy-blue but the most striking thing about him was the ugly red welt that ran along one side of his skull, as if it had been seared with a hot poker.

I must have stared a moment too long, for Martin smiled ruefully and said, 'I had a tumour removed late last year. I think I might be onto my ninth life.'

I hesitated, wondering if I ought to ask politely after his prognosis. But I just stood there, feeling like the interloper I was, until Martin waved me across the threshold and into a dark living room, shabby and sparsely furnished. It smelled of incense.

'Some tea?'

I nodded, though I never drank the stuff. He indicated I should follow him down the narrow hallway into a big glassed-in area at the rear of the house.

At one end of this space there was a small alcove of a kitchen, where he stood by the sink and waited for the kettle to fill, waited with a quiet focus that I sensed he brought to every task, no matter how menial.

When the water had boiled he poured it into two mugs and added a fine green powder. Then he handed me a mug and said, 'Okay, Rick, tell me why you're here.'

It had been a long day at work and I hadn't yet been home; I hadn't thought of what I might say, had rehearsed no line of inquiry, had fronted up in a state bordering on irritability. But I opened my mouth and some words fell out. 'I seem to have acquired a weird attachment to a woman I hardly know.'

'Attachment?'

'Well, you could call it that. She creeps into my thoughts, all hours of the day and night. It's like . . .' I sighed, conscious of deep fatigue. 'It's like she inhabits me.' I might have been describing one of those office infatuations to which men of my age were supposedly prone.

'And who is she?'

I said her name.

'Ah.'

'You know her?'

'I know *of* her.' Martin gestured at a small fold-up table by the window and I pulled out a chair and set down my thick ceramic mug of tea. Martin sat opposite. 'Tell me what *you* know about her,' he said.

'I know some of her personal history, but not much. I know she lives just outside Chennai, and that she seems to have followers around the world, whom she visits every year. I've googled her and she doesn't have a profile. She's not a big name.'

'No, she's a bit of a recluse. She pretty much works under the radar.'

'Meaning?'

'India has many sages, but few of them travel. It's only in the last few years that she's decided to emerge from relative seclusion.'

'Yes, but who is she?'

'She's a holy woman. A saint, if you can live with that idea.'

A saint. Saints in my boyhood religion were dead. I stared down into my tea, which I still hadn't touched. It looked green and unappetising. 'I've never had any interest in this kind of thing, but now, for some reason, I'm drawn to it.'

'Then you're lucky. It's your time.'

'My time?'

'You must be ready for what she has to teach you or you wouldn't be having this experience.'

Riddles. It was all riddles. 'Yes, but what *is* this experience?'

Martin looked at me from over the rim of his mug. 'You tell me.'

So I began, more or less at the beginning, to give an account of my experiences with Sri Mata. I tried to be matter-of-fact, almost to the point of sounding offhand, but the more I talked the more I doubted the wisdom of my being there; it all sounded limp and nonsensical. Finally I lapsed into silence, and ventured a sip of the tea, which by this time was lukewarm and made me feel nauseous.

Martin had listened with eyes closed and now he opened them. 'That's it?' he said.

'That's it.'

'Okay.' He laid his palms flat on the table and looked down, like a cabinet-maker assessing the grain of a piece of wood. 'Sounds like you learned to meditate because you were desperate. And when you're desperate you become open to change, which in your case was finding a teacher.'

'I wasn't looking.'

'You don't need to. When you're ready, they find *you*. That's how it works.'

'It?'

'The practice.'

'The practice? You mean meditation?'

'That and more.'

'There is no more.'

Martin shrugged, as if to say: that's what you think. 'You can't do it all on your own. Well, some people can but it's rare. Mostly we need a teacher, a recognisable form, someone we can relate to. When you go and see a being like Sri Mata, you're viewing the ultimate truth by proxy. You see that she's different. She seems to be in possession of something you'd like to share in. You're drawn to that.'

'To what, exactly?'

'Well, to begin with, her energy. She's at peace and yet alive, magnetic even. She's realised the truth and makes it visible to you through her bodily presence.'

'What truth?' My tone was cynical, churlish.

'The unity of the field, of all things. You had a glimpse of that, your experience in the bottleshop. But that's how she sees the world all the time. And that's how the world really is, only for most of us there's a film over it.' He raised his hand and lowered it like a curtain. 'And she's like a light socket or a cable that plugs you into it, *it* being what lies beyond the appearance of material objects, a unified field of consciousness that pervades everything.'

I found I was holding my breath, perhaps because there was no logic here that I could recognise. 'If it pervades everything then I'm already a part of it, so why do I need the connection to her?'

'Because, like most of us, you're blind. You think you're a goldfish in a bowl, when really you swim in the ocean. But before you can strike out freely you need to develop your stroke, as it were. She is your life jacket.'

'I'm inflated?'

Martin smiled. 'With grace.'

'Why me?' I said, and it wasn't really a question, more that I was thinking out loud. 'I'm hardly a prime candidate for this stuff.'

'Think of it this way: why not you?'

'You said I was "ripe". How was I ripe?'

'You meditated, didn't you?'

'That was stress management.'

Martin nodded. 'For some people, yes.'

'And why not for me?'

'Well, obviously not for you. Because you're here, asking these questions. And because you left your family in the middle of a nice picnic and hitched a ride in a taxi.'

A *nice* picnic? Something about that word 'nice' made me want to laugh out loud. Who was this man? Had he ever led a normal life? 'I don't know why I left the park that day. It was out of character.'

'You felt out of control?'

'Not exactly.'

'Then maybe this "character" you were out of is worth looking at more closely. Who is this Rick Kline?'

I was weary. I had come here for answers and all I was getting were questions. But what had I expected? Some kind of comfort, maybe? Instead, I was swimming in sand. I turned to look out the window, where it was still light. In the drab concrete courtyard there were pots of herbs and a bush of bright red chillies. On both sides of the courtyard rows of tall tomato plants were tied to stakes. They grew in a narrow strip of earth between the concrete and a high paling fence, and though the fences were dilapidated the patch of garden was neat and carefully weeded. The tomato plants were laden with green fruit, glossy, abundant and looking as if they were about to burst their skins.

I turned back to Martin. 'I've never thought of myself as anyone's disciple,' I said. 'I don't have the temperament for it.'

'No, I can see that. But then, maybe you're not the person you thought you were.'

This, in truth, was a large part of what was bothering me. For years I had constructed a version of Richard Kline that now seemed beside the point. I was a snake that, instead of sloughing off an old skin, had retained it, and now I was forced to impersonate an old self while I grew a new skin underneath, and the two skins were suffocating me. I struck out on a tangent. 'I don't like the group thing. I don't like the way people behave around her, they're like children. It's cultish.'

'And yet you like to sit with her.'

'That's one way of putting it.'

'Is that devotion?'

'It doesn't feel like it.'

'Then how does it feel?'

Good question. *How does it feel?* Impossible to describe that feeling. A cluster of words and phrases swarmed in my head until, finally, one word fell out, one lame word. 'Emotional.'

Martin nodded.

'But not in the usual way,' I added, hastily.

'In an unusual way?'

'Unusual for me. I tend to choke up.'

Martin seemed to know what this meant. 'And these are sad tears?'

'No.'

'Happy tears?'

'No, not exactly.'

'Then they're guru tears.'

'Meaning?'

'Meaning tears of recognition.'

Recognition? This was a striking thought. 'Meaning I recognise her?'

'And she recognises you. It's called *darshan*, a special form of seeing. It's a two-way thing. Relational. Not a passive viewing but insight, a direct vision of the truth. And a particular kind of truth, one we always knew but had forgotten. You see the truth in her and she sees the truth in you.'

'Maybe.' I hesitated. 'I don't know.'

Ah, but I did know. Or I thought I knew, at least for a while, but then that early euphoria had left me. More than that, my old self had returned, a feral dog dumped in the bush that had somehow managed to find its way home to lie under my bed and growl through the night. Now I experienced prolonged bouts of insomnia, was consumed by a restlessness that left me enervated. The initial glow of my romance with her had passed and I felt dumped, dumped by the guru wave. Back where I started. Yes, I was meditating again, but to what end? I thought of her often but I was not, after all, a changed man. The spark of that rare love was gone, extinguished. My meditation was empty, robotic.

'It feels like I've been experiencing an infatuation, and now it might be over.'

'I doubt that, Rick. What's over is the *honeymoon*. You've been too comfortable. Doubt comes, disappointment, and with it anger. This path is not a comfortable one. It's not meant to be some kind of poultice, it's meant to be a sword that cuts through your defences. So if you are pissed off, no longer in your comfort zone, ask yourself: are you willing to take the next step?'

What next step? Hadn't the sword already sliced into me, long before I encountered *her*? Hadn't my imagination always been an open wound?

'No-one promised you it would be easy.'

'No-one promised me anything.'

'Didn't they? Think about that.'

By now it was dark outside, the last faint flush of summer daylight gone. Martin put his hand up to his mouth to suppress a yawn, and I saw that he was tired. My eye went to the ugly welt on his scalp; in fading light it looked like a black shadow.

I stood and said it was late and I had better be going.

Martin rose and walked me to the door, where he laid his hand on my shoulder. 'Just go with what you have, Rick,' he said. 'Be patient and think of the self as a laboratory. Whatever experience you are having, explore it, test it out.'

'Well, thanks for seeing me.'

We shook hands but the mood was flat.

I walked out into the dark street, a leafy avenue lined with plane trees. I was a man who had strayed into a cul-de-sac. It was unseasonably mild, a humid Sydney night when the warm stillness feels like an embrace, a random blessing.

Soon I would be home, back to base, and then what?

Slowly I walked towards the car, and when I reached it I looked back to where Martin was still standing in the open doorway, leaning against the frame, the palm of his right hand resting on the dome of his head, a buddha in the porch light.

Suddenly he straightened up and stepped out onto the footpath. He waved, and called to me across the street, and pointed in the direction of Sydney Park, just a few kilometres down the road. 'I go for a stroll every Saturday afternoon in the park, usually around four. If you feel like a walk, come by.'

~

Sydney Park. I had never liked it, never cared for its attempts at renewal, which had about them a whiff of morbidity. At that time the trees were young and immature; from a distance they looked flimsy. The remnants of the old brick factory remained, its sombre industrial chimneys, its rows of abandoned brick ovens like small prison cells, the stolid Victorian masonry of the arches where homeless men slept at night, rags and cardboard flaps left in abject piles during the day.

I met Martin outside the western entrance to the park at the bottom of King Street. It was a fine, cool afternoon with a glint in the air, and we began our walk beside a stand of eucalypts where bark and leaf debris crunched beneath our feet.

I felt a kind of sap rising in me, an expansion of energy in my chest, and thought maybe it was too long since I had gone for a walk, and should do it more often, and take Luke along with me. By then we had come on some young men who were kicking a ball. One of them held the ball in his right hand, having just retrieved it from the bottom of a low rise, and he turned and kicked it directly at Martin. I found this provocative, but when it came spinning towards us, just above head height, Martin raised his right arm and caught it effortlessly, one-handed, before dropping it onto his foot in a practised stab kick. The youth who had kicked it fumbled the ball and the others jeered.

'Not bad.' I said. 'Signs of a misspent youth.'

Martin grinned. 'I'm out of practice, but they,' indicating the boys, 'like to keep me on my toes.'

In the days leading up to this meeting I had thought a lot about Martin. Until my encounter with Sri Mata, my own life had been conventional, but where had Martin Coleby come from?

Zoe was curious. How did you get to become a middle-aged suburban monk? she asked. Disappointments in love? Trauma at an early age? Psychically poleaxed and left with no other option but to retreat from the world? Or maybe an obsessive will to self-mastery? Women always wanted to know these things, always wanted someone's history, but I was not about to ask; it felt too personal.

Instead, I asked about the guru–disciple relationship. Had Martin ever been to see Sri Mata?

'No.' He shook his head. 'I have my own teacher. I used to live in his ashram outside Chennai. For twelve years.'

He said this slowly, almost haltingly, as if it had been a long time ago.

'Why didn't you stay there?'

'He told me to leave, go home, teach others. He said I'd become too comfortable in the ashram, too pleased with myself.'

'Were you?'

'Probably. I didn't want to come back here, that's for sure. I was unhappy with the idea, very unhappy, but here I am.'

I felt an urge to ask him more about this 'unhappiness', but sensed it was off-limits. But it did embolden me to pose a question that had troubled me since Joe Mazengarb had raised it. Was the guru a substitute parent?

By then I was familiar with Freud's argument, not only from my reading but also from my irascible debates with Joe; any kind of god or guru was an idealised parent, a desire to regress to the infant state and to seek safety and psychic security in submission to the wise man (or, in my case, woman). It had been Joe's abrasive dialectics that had led me to read Freud in the first place and to discover the troubling notion of transference, that in my attachment to a guru figure I was unconsciously transferring unresolved feelings and desires from my parents to another adult. In other words, I was just a big baby and needed to get over it.

To my surprise, Martin was not dismissive of the idea.

'I think there's an element of truth in that,' he said. 'None of us has perfect parents. Some of us do need to be re-parented, for a while at least, and the teacher does that. At the same time,' he added, 'this feeling of something missing, which you experienced as a child, is not just because you've been expelled from the womb, or because your parents weren't perfect. It's hardwired into us, a divine discontent. The fact that we experience this nameless discontent is a sign that we are attuned to an unconscious knowledge of something else, something larger than ourselves. God, the Mind at Large, cosmic consciousness, call it what you like. It's a part of us and we are a part of it. In the *Bhagavad Gita* Krishna calls it the Knower of the Field. And this is what meditation leads to, getting in touch with the Knower, who, by the way, is always there within us. Has always been there, both without and within.'

This resonated for me. Hadn't I experienced moments when I intuited this? As an adolescent, I had often heard some other voice in my head, offering a dispassionate commentary on my actions. Even in the depths of my angst, that voice would arise, cool and appraising.

'I think the psychologists call that dissociation,' Martin said wryly. 'They have no model of the transcendent, or of the god within. It's too radical, too confronting an idea for the Western mind. And, it has to be said, too open to abuse if the individual is not on a disciplined path and under the guidance of a teacher. Without a teacher it can become what psychology calls inflation, an ungrounded sense that "I am God".

'The teacher begins by taking us into a protective cocoon where we can begin to feel our way. He, or in your case she, can relieve feelings of emptiness or isolation, can be a refuge that gives us relief from pain. But if we persist under her guidance we will be forced to confront our vanity and self-righteousness. What Freud didn't see was the later stages of the practice, which go beyond that infantile shelter. That's just the beginning, just as childhood is a beginning, not a phase you stay in all your life. The meditative path is one where the psychic residues of the infantile state must at various times be gratified, then confronted, and ultimately aban-doned. At first the teacher gratifies them for you, then she pushes you to confront them. That's when the going gets heavy. That's when more is asked of you. And that's when some people give up.'

'So you move from a position of early dependence to some other state?'

'That's the idea. Meditation can begin as a narcissistic exercise, a way of propping up the wounded ego. It can give rise to egotistical thoughts. "I am special, other people are ignorant." New Age self-righteousness.'

I could see that this might have been the case at first, in the early days, when I started to feel smug, and even superior, but not now. Since the temporary euphoria of my baffling initiation I had had too many experiences of my own limitations, too many of what I now thought of as my mad Oliver moments.

'And then it becomes about the exploration of that something else?'

'Uh-huh. But how do you know if you're not deceiving yourself? Are not delusional?'

'Only you can figure that out. Do you trust your experience, or don't you?'

'How do I know if I *can* trust my experience?'

'Just keep meditating, Rick. Do that and everything else will sort itself out. You don't have to believe in anything. Just do the practice.'

'To do the practice you need to believe in it.'

'No, you don't. You need faith, and that's a different thing. Belief is clinging to a set of doctrines, usually based on what someone else has said. Faith is opening the mind, without preconceptions, to whatever comes along. Faith is a plunge into the unknown. Faith is what underpins any science that's not dogmatic. Faith accepts that we cannot know everything and can control only a little. We surrender our need for certainty.'

'But *you* believe in certain things.'

'I do. Or, rather, I know them from my practice. But that doesn't mean you have to. Whatever I tell you won't stick. You have to find out for yourself.'

'Then why are we talking?'

Martin laughed. 'Who knows? You've turned up, so we've talked. Things just happen.'

~

For the next twenty-one weeks I walked with Martin almost every Saturday, and in that time he instructed me in the rudiments of Eastern mysticism. It was not my habit at the office to stop for lunch, but on the Monday after that first meeting I walked to an office supplies shop on High Street and spent a good twenty minutes looking at notebooks. I was drawn almost immediately to a medium-sized ring-bound journal with a bright red plastic cover; I liked the look and the weight and feel of it. I hadn't owned a notebook since I was a boy, and the very idea of handwriting was enough to give me a rush. I had forgotten the promise of the blank page, and I felt youthful again, ready to be initiated into an as yet unwritten scripture: not a diary, nothing so banal, but a playful scroll, a white space of possibility. I bought a dozen of the notebooks and took them home that night. When I stacked them on my desk they seemed to emit their own aura.

Every Saturday, in the evening when I arrived home, or sometimes the following morning, I would make notes of my conversations with Martin, never wholly confident of their accuracy. Whatever Martin said sounded simple and convincing but the next day I couldn't recall it precisely, or only a flattened-out version of it. In the translation into my own phrasing something always escaped, some spark of energy and conviction, some gleam of intensity that was Martin. This bothered me, but when I complained of it to Martin he was offhand. 'You don't need to remember anything,' he said.

For Martin it was all about the practice, but when I pressed him he did agree to recommend some reading, beginning with Aldous Huxley's *The Doors of Perception*. It seemed at first an odd choice but I soon discovered the logic of it. In the nineteen-fifties Huxley had taken mescalin and it changed him, induced in him something that he described as a sacramental view of reality. It was, said Martin, not unlike what I had experienced in the bottleshop, only more prolonged, more intense, more lurid in its detail.

From this, Huxley developed a model of the brain as a kind of filter, a reducing valve for a reality that is overwhelmingly complex and multilayered. When we look at a table we see a table but it's really a pattern of vibrating atoms; if we saw everything in this way all the time, saw the whole world as a cosmic dance of energy, we would not be able to function. The brain had evolved as a mechanism to filter information so that we can process it in a manageable way. What comes out the end of the valve is, in Huxley's words, a mere trickle of consciousness. But every so often we get a glimpse of the 'more', as when drugs open the cortex and we get to see what lies beyond our limited perception. We perceive the wondrousness of things, what the mystics cognise as the vibratory hum of a divine consciousness, an energetic maelstrom that Huxley calls the Mind at Large. Something that is transcendent, yet at the same time present to us as 'a felt immanence, an experienced participation'.

These last words came closest to describing my experiences with Sri Mata. Since my first meeting with her, and on my good days, I had begun to feel that I participated in the world in a new way, as if she had drawn a magnet over my field to realign my internal compass. She lived in my head now as a presiding presence, but it was as if she had always been there, as if I had known her before and it was only now that I had become able to 'see' her. And in enabling this re-cognition, she had altered the way I saw everything else, had opened the valve a little wider.

As time passed, my walks with Martin became the fulcrum of my week. I looked forward to them. I looked forward to other things as well – I was far from being a recluse – but not in the same way. *She* had given me a field of meaning and for two hours on a Saturday afternoon I was able to inhabit it fully, without distraction. And while there were hours of earnest debate with Martin, there were also times when we strolled in companionable silence. Sunlight filtered through the leaves of the feathery wattles and the boys shouted into the dusk. They seemed always to be there, lofting their ball high into the hazy air and swearing with careless vehemence if they misjudged its flight. Sometimes they would aim the ball straight at Martin and each time I would feel my temper rise. There was a needling quality to these gambits but Martin was unfazed and would enter momentarily into the game. One evening, as we left the park, we came upon the boys beside the western entrance. They were sitting on top of the old brick ovens, smoking. One of them called out. 'Hey, Martin!'

Martin waved.

'You know them?' I asked.

'In a fashion. The first time I ran into them they tried to mug ·me but we've progressed from there.'

I wondered what this 'progress' had involved. 'Perhaps you

should invite them to a yoga class,' I said.

'I've tried that. I think the idea of it scared them. I'd have more luck with martial arts.' And he told me of how a year earlier he had approached a state juvenile detention centre and offered to teach weekly classes of yoga and meditation. But the authorities had passed. Martin shrugged. 'Too soon.'

And yet, I could see, these boys wanted to get to know Martin. They prodded at him; they sensed there was something there for them, even if they didn't know what it was. Perhaps it was the tattoo on his bicep, a badge of credibility. And, had they known it, they might even have liked the translation from the Sanskrit: *Salutations to the destroyer and re-creator of worlds.*

This was the intriguing thing about Martin: he could be so ordinary, ordinary in a good way, in a way that I could never manage. When I watched him kick a ball I reflected on the fact that in no way was he exotic. *She* was not a normal human being, that much I was sure of, but Martin was not so removed that I couldn't measure myself against him. Only four years separated us in age, and before anything else we were men together, and men from a common background. What lay between us was the depth of Martin's experience. Above all, I envied his naturalness, for it seemed that if 'spiritual' progress meant anything, it meant a natural and spontaneous embrace of the moment, an embrace that was generous in its response to others, unfettered by any painful self-consciousness. Wherever he was, Martin seemed at home. One afternoon when we were discussing meditation, he stopped suddenly and said, 'Sit here and meditate with me now.'

'Here?' We were out in the open, not even under a tree. I glanced across at the boys who were nearby.

'They're alright. They're used to me. I often sit here.'

But I baulked. I would feel like a fool, and even though I knew that this was what I most desired – to be a happy fool and not to care – I was an ocean away from that particular landing.

'Well,' remarked Zoe, one Saturday evening in autumn as I lit the barbecue on the deck, 'these talks with Martin always put you in a good mood. If I were a suspicious woman I'd think maybe you had a mistress.' Indeed, my walks with Martin did enhance my mood. I felt at last that I was coming to grips with the core of the riddle; that slowly, strand by strand, I was unravelling a knot that had sat between my shoulder blades for a very long time.

One school holiday, when I mentioned that Zoe and Luke were away, Martin invited me to his house for dinner. In no time at all he prepared a simple meal of kichari – 'I lived on this at the ashram' – with a delicious side dish of coconut chutney, strong on the chilli he had grown on his balcony and dried above the sink. And he had no objection to me opening a bottle of wine, though he declined to share it.

While Martin was stirring the rice and lentil mixture, an enormous black cockroach flew at him, and he swatted it so that it dropped to the floor in a sudden dive. Then he ground it with the heel of his bare foot. You could hear the crunch.

I couldn't resist. 'And the sanctity of all life?' I asked.

'I've given this a lot of thought.'

'And?'

'And I make an exception for cockroaches.' With this he ladled the kichari into two deep bowls and set them down on the table.

That night over dinner, relaxed by the intimacy of the occasion, not to mention the wine, I asked Martin about his past. What had brought him to a fate so unlikely? Where had he grown up?

'All over the place,' he replied. His father had been a major in the army and the family had moved around from base to base. He was a normal kid, he said, only interested in girls and surfing, and he didn't get on with the Major, who ran the home like a barracks. 'He had rules about everything,' said Martin. 'He was afraid, afraid that without his rules he wouldn't know who he was.'

I nodded. I knew the type.

At the age of twenty, he continued, he dropped out of a science degree and began to drift up and down the coast with friends, doing seasonal work, living out of a van and hitting the surf as often as possible. 'I think I knew then I wasn't cut out for normal life.'

'Who is?'

'Well, some adapt better than others.'

The turning point had been an experience on acid. He was staying with his girlfriend in a caravan park in Kiama while his van was being repaired. Often he and his friends would drop a tab on the beach, lie on the sand and stare up at the clouds, comparing notes. Always for him these experiences were benign. But one evening when the weather was wet and steamy and it was just him and the girl in their cramped and gloomy caravan, they lay on the bed naked, dropped a tab of acid, and within what seemed only minutes he had plunged into a vortex of horror.

The caravan had a long wall mirror at the foot of the bed and when he looked into it he saw that he was melting, his whole body liquefying. First his head dissolved into a puddle of viscous red and yellow fluid that pooled on the sheet. Then it began, slowly, to trickle over the edge of the bed, and drip onto the floor. Next the right arm, then the left, the two legs together, until only his molten torso remained on the bed, and he could see his own heart beating on the sheet, a lump of pulsating meat. Before long, this too began to melt, and the horror of it was paralysing; he tried to shut his eyes but was unable even to blink. Any minute now there would be nothing left of him, he would be just a tiny speck in a gaping void that grew bigger and darker by the second.

Then, in the midst of his terror, a thought came to him: *who is observing this disintegration?* Something or someone remained. Some other self was present, something larger than the scared little Martin figure melting on an unmade bed. Then he knew: at his core there was a part of him that was indestructible, some other self, and here it was, quietly observing this lurid fantasy of the brain.

In the months that followed, a single question possessed him. Who was that observer? Where did he come from?

'I'd never been a reader, but after that I began to read whatever I could get my hands on, all the acid literature I could find, and then some. What was the brain chemistry on this?'

'And what is the brain chemistry?'

Ah, he said, this was a big question, and if I wanted to pursue it he would give me some books. But in the end those books had failed to satisfy him. The brain was just a transmitter, like a television set, infinitely more complex but a transmitter nonetheless. The question was: where were the programs coming from? From that moment a new restlessness took hold of him. He returned to the city, resumed his studies and worked part-time as a security guard, and occasionally as a bouncer at a club in George Street. One evening he wandered into a yoga class in Chinatown run by Tadeusz, an eccentric Pole and former martial arts instructor.

They hit it off. Within three years he had become one of Tad's assistants. At the age of twenty-seven, he set off with a backpack for India.

I couldn't imagine Martin as a bouncer and said so.

He smiled. 'The Major taught me to box,' he said. 'Insisted on it. Not that that's much help when you're wrangling a crowd of drunks. It just gives you a false sense of security.'

I was distracted, and thinking of my youth. 'I never got into drugs,' I said.

'Never?'

'Just dope in my twenties, nothing more. I was too much of a control freak. I didn't trust the suppliers.'

'Well, I suspect they were more reliable then than now.' And in any case, Martin added, the problem with drugs was that they were not practical, just a temporary holiday from normality. Once the effect wore off you were back where you started, back to your old neuroses. What you needed was a practice that could weaken old behaviour patterns and destructive ways of thinking, weaken them permanently. You needed to recondition the neocortex. 'You have to change the game, Rick, change it for good.'

'The game?'

'The Rick game, the Martin game, all that accumulated shit that builds up from childhood. The crazy wiring of the ego. The ego is a necessary organising principle that gets us through our day, but as we age we begin to tire of it, we tire of our own con-structed persona. We start to experience it as baggage. This is the paradox of human maturation. Once the ego is established, in maturity it becomes stale, a burden. It tires of the game. After a while it begins to struggle for its own extinction.'

This was one of the things, he said, that in later life made us restless, and could lead to erratic or bizarre behaviour, a desire for radical change.

Later that night, writing up my notes, I found myself lingering over a phrase, the *burden of personality*. I recalled a book I had read not long after I met Zoe, a book I had found on Joe's shelves. It was a reflection on the nature of melancholy. In it the author had described his claustrophobia, his sense of being smothered by the barnacle weight of his own personality. He had used that same word, had compared his state of mind to that of a man trapped beneath the hull of a capsized boat, unable to dive deeper and swim free. Maybe this was a male thing. Did women feel it? At a certain age you felt the encumbrance of the identity you had constructed for yourself, or had thrust upon you: all those leathery accretions of habit, those barnacles on the psyche that are both you and not you. And you felt the need to be rid of them, to have it all – this construct, 'Richard Kline' – dissolved in whatever merciful solvent you could find.

One morning, early, when it was still dark and after I had settled on the floor, cross-legged and with my back straight against the wall so that I did not sag and doze off, almost the moment I closed my eyes I felt that I was sitting beside a lake. And although the glazed surface of the lake was uncannily still, as if painted, beneath its waters lay a fathomless abyss, a ceaseless hum of meaning, a fertile chaos in which some force was endlessly giving birth.

Morning after morning this lake appeared. I didn't seek it, I made no mental effort to summon it to mind; it was simply the case that as soon as I sat on the floor and closed my eyes I was there, beside its dark water. The lake was rimmed by a forest of trees that fruited a kind of nut, like a chestnut, and all around me lay a glossy carpet of these small brown nuts so that I knew, if I grew hungry, I needed only crack open their shells. The lake was so vivid, and yet so soothing, that I was reluctant to open my eyes, to get up, leave the room and begin the rest of my day. But then one morning I was taken by the fear that I might no longer be able to go on leading the life I now led. I saw an image of my son, alone on the lake in a small canoe, and I shivered and grew cold. I opened my eyes, suddenly and with relief, and got up and left the room, and was especially attentive to Luke over breakfast.

Not yet, I thought. *Not yet.*

But when I mentioned the lake to Martin, this internal landscape that seemed to me so portentous, Martin was dismissive. 'The mind plays tricks,' he said. 'Different images will arise in the meditation of different people. It does not further your practice either to resist them or to become attached to them. Just go on repeating your mantra. Don't get distracted.'

~

After a while the deal I had struck with Martin seemed one-sided. What was I giving in return? Martin had little money but would, I knew, have refused any I offered him. You didn't bring alcohol to a monk, and he was particular about his food. Plants? I wasn't a gardener and didn't have a clue and, besides, Martin had little space and what he had was already covered in carefully tended growth. But Zoe suggested I take him out for dinner once a month.

It was a tentative suggestion, for she wondered if Martin were one of those purists for whom commercially prepared food was a pollution, but he accepted the offer cheerfully and suggested an Indian restaurant in Marrickville where they were 'easy on the salt and the sugar'. He liked the owner of this place, Rajesh, a former accountant from Cochin and one-time member of the Indian Rationalist Association.

On our first night there, Rajesh came to our table with the intent of resuming his friendly argument with Martin. 'You Western soul-seekers, you fall for all that ancient mumbo-jumbo. And why? The sun comes up in the morning and makes things grow, but tell me this, do you worship the sun?'

'I worship everything,' Martin replied, and gave his good-natured laugh. 'I bow down to you, my dear friend.'

'Yes, yes, you bow down to me, I bow down to you, we all bow down to one another. But you come from an advanced country and then you decide to go backwards. What is the point of that? All this superstition.'

'You know I have no choice, Rajesh,' said Martin, with mock dismay.

'You patronise me. You patronise me and I am not deceived. You are a clever man.' At this point Rajesh turned to me – 'He is a clever man' – and then back to Martin – 'you should know better.' In this way their banter persisted for a few minutes, with Rajesh's wife, Lila, shushing at her husband discreetly in the background until, with a display of resignation, he turned his attention to other patrons.

That night I reminded Martin of a remark he had made the previous week about divine discontent. The phrase troubled me. What was the import of this 'divine'? Discontent was an experience I knew all too well, the prickly self, the restless spin and burn of it. But I choked on the 'divine' bit, and I took up Huxley again. I could relate to Huxley's computer-like model of the brain but flinched from the idea of a Mind at Large. Was this another way of talking about God?

'The God question can't be answered,' replied Martin, cheerfully, helping himself to another portion of naan. 'Don't worry about it. It gets in the way.'

'In the way of what?'

'Your practice. You can chew on it for years and end up where you started. Without your practice the brain will play the same games over and over. You could read ten volumes of theology and be none the wiser. You could *write* ten volumes of theology and still doubt. If you must think of God, think of being itself, not *a* being. Forget the divine, if the word bothers you. However we label it, there is the ground of all being.'

'That's too vague. It's like, "God is what I say it is."'

'There is no God, not in the biblical sense. There is a cosmic consciousness, a form of intelligence that pervades everything. You can choose to tap in to it, or you can ignore it and try and go it alone. Not that you can ever truly go it alone, because you swim in the ocean of that consciousness like a fish in the sea, and the particles that make up that sea are the same as the ones that make up you. But you can swim blind or swim with your eyes open, so to speak.'

'But the fish survives, whether its eyes are open or not.'

'It's a metaphor, Rick. Think of that ocean as something dynamic, not static. Some modern theologians talk of the theology of the event. They distinguish between a *name*, such as "God", which is a static entity, *out there* –' he gestured into the distance – 'and a dynamic process, a movement of energy that is constantly evolving. The name is a convenience that we use to refer to the event but it cannot capture the event, which constantly seeks new forms and new ways to express itself. Think of it as a physics we don't yet understand, a vast, all-encompassing intelligence. We are within it and hence it's most likely beyond our understanding. But we can tune in to it. When we meditate we don't go into stillness, not in a static sense – that's a common misunderstanding – we go into a zone where we can connect directly with that current.'

'We go with the flow?' My sarcasm was intended.

'More to the point, we learn to trust the flow, we surrender to it. Surrender is the hard part. And in any case,' he added, 'consequences follow from actions without any supernatural intervention. It's about how energy works. The law of karma functions like the law of gravity. You don't need a god. If there *are* gods, then they are minor deities who look on while we sort ourselves out.'

That night I went home feeling elated. Two men in their forties sitting in a cheap restaurant over a ferocious curry and debating the form of God seemed, at that moment, to be the height of pleasure. Every part of me, every atom, had been wholly engaged. I had held nothing in reserve. The ordinariness of my surroundings meant nothing.

Just the weekend before, Zoe and I had sat through an interminable dinner party in a penthouse apartment, during which our hosts had outlined in detail their plans for the renovation of a farmhouse they had bought in the Dordogne. The prospect of this farmhouse – this elaborate pastoral fantasy with its own plumbing, rewiring, re-roofing and collection of rustic furniture – seemed to illuminate their lives with so intense a glow of possibility that I was reminded of Leni and her villa. What *was* this obsession with dwelling places? It was as if time could be defeated by creating the perfect space, by the conversion of the evanescent into the stationary. Time could be objectified into something solid and reassuring. And yet I had never much cared where I lived. I could easily imagine going on the road, as Martin had. Perhaps one day I would.

On the drive home I remarked on this to Zoe. The house in the Dordogne was escapism, I said, an avoidance of death.

'You *would* see it that way,' she said, tersely. 'Other people might see it more straightforwardly as a fairly normal pursuit of pleasure. They can afford it, so why not?'

'Pleasure? They moaned constantly about the obstacles.' But I knew the obstacles were the point. It was the quest that mattered, the need for a goal.

Zoe had stared ahead. 'You're so judgemental. And anyway, everything after a certain age is an avoidance of death.'

The unspoken lay between us: What you do, your newfound conversion, is just escapism in another more self-righteous form. At times like this I heard my mother's voice: *Why can't you just accept things as they are?*

~

For some weeks my meetings with Martin continued on as before, in what I think of now as a holding pattern. Occasionally I got a niggling sense that Martin was withholding something from me, something he judged I was not yet ready to hear. Maybe he felt that I could cope only with one big idea at a time, in this case the self as a laboratory, an experiment. It was a point he returned to over and over, his touchstone.

'You are a thinker, Rick,' he would say, 'but thinking can only take you so far. Nothing I say, nothing you read, will make much sense without your *experience*, and especially your experience of her, your teacher. She is the substratum of your knowing, and everything else is tested against that. It takes root – or not – in that experience. You can think of this as "spiritual" if you like, as metaphysics, but you are never not an empiricist in the broadest sense.'

On the last Saturday in August, he appeared to be unwell. He looked pale, and throughout our walk he coughed in intermittent spasms and spat phlegm into the bushes. It pained me to see him so distressed. Maybe I was insensitive but for the first time it occurred to me that Martin led a lonely life. If he fell ill, who would look after him?

'Are you okay?' I asked.

'Bronchitis. A weakness of mine. I tend to get it around this time of year.'

This was followed by another coughing fit that had him hunched over with an arm clutched to his chest. His body shook.

'You need to see a doctor, get some antibiotics. I can drive you there.'

'It's alright, I'm on a course already.' For a moment he was breathless. Then he straightened up, and with some deliberation turned to face me. 'I've had some news,' he said. 'I'll be going away soon.'

'Away?'

'New Zealand. My guru has a centre in Auckland and he's asked me to run it for the next six months. Maybe longer.'

'When do you leave?'

'Two weeks.'

Ah, so it had to come to an end. 'I'm sorry to hear that. I'll miss our walks.'

'So will I.'

I asked him if he needed any help. His furniture put into storage? A lift to the airport?

'No,' he said. 'No, it will all be taken care of.'

~

And now I was at a loss. With Martin I had felt more at home in my skin, had breathed more easily, walked more lightly on the ground. We had shared in a rare intimacy, rare because it cut to the core of things. In the circles I moved in there was no-one I could talk to about what mattered to me most.

I began to reflect on what had brought me to this point. I recalled certain events, and relived them, searching for clues as to what I should do next. I sat in my study and read through the notebooks I had inscribed after my meetings with Martin, read them over and over, obsessively. I would read them if I couldn't sleep at night, or first thing in the morning in the quiet minutes before I settled to meditate. I scrawled certain phrases on bits of paper and stuffed them in my pockets, or in my wallet.

After a while I decided to enter the contents of the notebooks on my laptop and created a set of files, one for each meeting with Martin. In this way I sought to construct a conversation with myself, since I could no longer speak with Martin in the flesh. But this was frustrating, and only resulted in me asking more questions that

Martin wasn't there to answer.

One night, late, when Zoe and Luke were in bed, I deleted the files from my laptop. Then I carried the notebooks downstairs and squatted beside the wood heater. I tore off their plastic covers and fed the notebooks into the flames, one at a time, and waited. They took a long time to burn. In the morning there was nothing left. The grey metal corkscrews of their ring-binding lay scattered in the ashes.

on the escarpment

In early September he got a phone call from Rebecca. Sri Mata was flying to Australia and would be staying on for six months, an unprecedented length of time. She would live on a property in Kangaroo Valley, owned by one of her devotees, but every Sunday morning she would be emerging from her seclusion to hold regular programs in the city.

He could scarcely believe it. So, he told himself, I have not been abandoned.

Though she lived within him as a daily presence, in her physical form she had been so remote for so long, so inaccessible as a phenomenon within Nature (Martin's words), that it seemed barely conceivable that she would appear on Sunday mornings in a house at Strathfield to conduct meditation. According to Rebecca, one of her devotees would drive her up every Sunday morning early and drive her back after lunch. There would be an hour of meditation but there would be no talks, no question and answer sessions, no words.

Whereas once he might have felt agitated, impatient, apprehensive or excited about this dramatic change in her availability, instead he felt only relief. Would he behave foolishly, as he had at the retreat? No, this time it would be different. Martin had prepared him for this. The next step, he had said. Be ready to take the next step. Would it be confronting? He had no idea. By now, all he knew was to expect the unexpected.

~

The house in Strathfield was a large stone Federation villa with an old English privet hedge in front. A sign on the front door directed visitors to a path that ran around the side of the house and a walled garden at the rear. It was clear that the original land had been sub-divided decades before so that a series of red-brick townhouses could be built next door. All that remained of the once impressive grounds was a wide courtyard surrounded on three sides by a high brick wall that enclosed what must have been a terrace of huge flagstones, now cracked and worn. An old frangipani tree grew in one corner, and a dilapidated garden shed stood in the other. A few big terracotta pots were dotted about, newly planted with the brassy yellow of marigolds. A birdbath cut from tin and painted in rust-red and bright blue stood incongruously under the frangi-pani tree.

The courtyard had been swept clean, and near the back door a table set up with a white cloth, a vase of flowers and some incense. In front of this table was her peetham, a large padded stool as big as a coffee table, which he recognised from her public programs in the past. There were rows of plastic chairs arrayed in the middle of the courtyard, and a gathering of around eighty people had assembled, among whom was Rebecca. She saw Rick enter, and waved.

It was odd, waiting for her to appear, as if they were waiting for an emissary from Venus. An attendant rang a small bell and announced she would soon be with them, and he found he was holding his breath. And yet when she emerged from the back door of the villa, a diminutive figure in a plain white cotton sari with her blue-black hair drawn back in a bun on the nape of her neck, her presence seemed utterly natural, as if she, and they, had always been there, and indeed some of them laughed, involuntarily, as if they were all participating in some delightful joke.

She paused beside the peetham to smile at them. With her right hand held to her heart in her customary greeting, she looked around the courtyard, meeting the gaze of many of them, though not all. Then, matter-of-factly, she settled herself cross-legged on the peetham and rested her palms on her knees. An attendant leaned over to whisper in her ear and she raised a hand to point in the direction of the house.

How natural, how graceful her every gesture. Every small thing, he thought: *every small thing.* It was her gift to make of every small thing a benediction. And with that thought his body went loose and he felt as if he might cry out: At last I have found perfection! He had gone through life thinking he would never know it, and here it was, so plain, so unadorned.

Turning back now to face the assembly, she joined her palms together in the prayer position and raised her hands above her head in a salute. To them. He could not begin to describe his feelings at the moment of that salute. So natural, so joyous, so down-to-earth. Had he ever felt more at home in his life, here in this old courtyard he had never before set eyes on? What fortune had brought him here? How strange and yet how not strange. How homely and unremarkable. It was as if everything else in his life at that moment was strange and alienated, warped and unnatural, jarring, pushed out of shape and, above all, banal. This alone was the bliss of nature, inherent in all matter, revealed now and made manifest in her form.

She lowered her arms and composed them in her lap. For a long minute she looked around the courtyard, gazing at each one of them with her tender, radiant smile. Then, tucking the hem of her sari in under her feet, she closed her eyes to indicate the beginning of meditation. In her deep, resonant voice she murmured the syllable *OM* three times so that it wafted on the air of their enclosure like a benign tremor.

For an hour they meditated, an hour that might have passed in a matter of minutes. After what seemed an absurdly short time a bell rang and he opened his eyes. Sri Mata continued to sit there in silence, looking around from face to face, smiling. Then, abruptly, she rose and in an instant had disappeared into the gloomy interior of the villa, the white folds of her sari illuminating the dark hallway.

Rebecca announced that refreshments would be served, and the word 'refreshment' struck him as comically inapt. They had already been refreshed beyond measure.

He had no desire to linger, to risk dissipating the moment in small-talk, but nor did he feel in any state to drive a car, and feared he would run a red light. Instead, he went for a walk, strolling for several blocks in that unremarkable suburb, stared at by children, barked at by dogs, restored to himself in some incalculable way.

When he got home Zoe took one look at him and raised an eyebrow. 'Well, you look relaxed.'

He put his arms around her but said nothing, too full to speak.

Evidently, then, in Martin's terms, he was still a child, still clinging to the hem of the teacher, too dependent on the physical form. Surely if his practice had matured, and by now it ought to have (hadn't he been diligent, apart from that one lapse?), then he would not need this, this primitive subjection to another human being. What did it signify? That old ally, his intellect, was on its guard; as usual, it held many questions in reserve. It must protect him from any softening in the head. Was he at the mercy of some cycle of regression?

Over the weeks that followed he began to experience a subtle change in his outlook. For one thing, he found he was becoming less judgemental. There was the occasion on which he had to listen, yet again, to friends talk obsessively about the renovation of their cottage in the Dordogne, and for once he listened without irritability. The property was not a cottage but a 'sheepfold' and accessible only by a rocky track of two kilometres. It was, they intoned, the perfect retreat (as if, he remarked later to Zoe, the Australian continent was too noisy for them). He, who was impractical and had never so much as driven a nail, even managed to ask them a few questions. Was there drinkable water? Were the tanks they planned to install local or imported? How were their French lessons going?

'You were very congenial tonight,' said Zoe as they drove home. 'Since when did you develop an interest in water tanks?'

He shrugged. 'If it makes them happy . . .' To the rest of their friends and acquaintances it would make far more sense than his own eccentric path. Who was he to pronounce on anything? The more time he spent with Sri Mata, the more aware he became of how little he knew, really *knew*, as opposed to all the knowledge he had acquired so easily since boyhood. At its core this peculiar new state of unknowing was generous; he might even describe it as, well, loving.

On the fifth Sunday he decided to sit to the side of her peetham, because he liked occasionally to open his eyes and glimpse her in profile: the coiled bun of her blue-black hair; the curve of her nose; the composure of her rounded shoulders; the white cotton of her shawl ruffled by a mild breeze. This, he told himself, was the image he would call to mind at the moment of his death.

For now, he marvelled at the perfect poise with which she sat, straight-backed and with no visible movement, for an hour. Except that now and then she would observe, or in some way sense, that one of the meditators had nodded off; then she would pick up a small pebble from a handful she kept in a brass bowl beside her and throw it, with unerring aim, at the forehead of the lucky miscreant. These stones became treasured items among the devotees, though it had not as yet happened to him. Nor did he yearn for any token. To be there in her presence was enough.

He found that each Sunday morning he drove to these meditation events with questions in his head, and on each occasion these questions evaporated in her presence – either that or an answer came to him during the meditation, though always in a form that he could not put into words, and that could only be described as the deepening of a spiritual intuition that grew in and was nurtured by her presence. If afterwards he could recall these questions, they ceased to seem important, to have lost their charge, as if the meditation process was a liquid solution in which such cerebral irritants were dissolved. It reminded him of Martin's idea of the laboratory of the self; in his Sunday-morning state he was a beaker of fluid that filtered out the dross, and Sri Mata was the flame. Which is not to say that there weren't times when he wasn't restless, when thoughts from work didn't intrude, or anxieties, about Luke especially, but he focused on his breath and returned to his mantra. In her presence it seemed all too easy. He was a child at the breast. And in time he became complacent; everything, he told himself, is fine as it is.

But then, one morning, she ambushed him. He felt himself being drawn up into a vortex as if at any minute he might leave his body and not return. Death was only an instant away; he could drop the sheath of the body without fear or regret, for it was not death as he had until then imagined it; rather, it was like boarding a train, and she was there, in the carriage, inviting him to sit beside her.

I could let go, he thought, *let go now of everything*. Ah, but no, no, it was not possible, and he felt a hot wave of panic shimmy up his spine. *No, I'm not ready for this*, he heard himself say, silently. *Not now. Not yet. I am not a monk. I have my wife and son to look after. Would you have me abandon them?* He opened his eyes and stared at her, motionless on the peetham. Her eyes were closed, her stillness uncanny.

One Sunday, after she had risen and turned towards the door of the villa, she hesitated, turned back to the peetham and stooped to the brass bowl to pick out a pebble. Then she looked at him and held out her hand.

Taken aback, he glanced around. What was the meaning of this gesture? The meditation was at an end and he had not fallen asleep. Moreover, he had never seen her do this, offer a pebble to a devotee *after* meditation. Nor was he sure at first that the pebble was intended for him, but her gaze was so direct, and prolonged, that there could be no doubt, and as he reached out to take it, brushing her cool fingers lightly, she said, in her deep-throated and heavily accented English, 'For your friend.' And before he could in any way respond, she had turned away and was walking in her quick, matter-of-fact stride towards the house.

He stood there, in shock. He hadn't the faintest idea what she was talking about. What was for his friend? Well, the pebble, of course, but what did that small stone signify? And what friend? He headed for his walk around the streets of Strathfield, his usual stroll after meditation, fingering the stone in his pocket, rubbing it between thumb and forefinger, turning it over and over until at last it came to him. *Martin*. Martin Coleby. She meant Martin. How did he know this? He just knew.

But Martin was in New Zealand – at least, he had said he would be remaining there for several months, and perhaps indefinitely. Was he meant to post the stone to him in the mail? Perhaps that was it, not that he had a forwarding address, but it should not be difficult to discover the location of Martin's centre in Auckland. And when the stone arrived Martin would know what it meant.

He returned to his car and was not far into the journey home when it occurred to him that Martin might be in Sydney. Perhaps he had returned and she was directing Rick to renew contact, to resume their dialogues and the teaching Martin had been so generously willing to offer him. By the time he reached Parramatta Road he had resolved to ring Martin the next day, and then corrected that thought. Martin would have given up the rental of his little terrace house and the old number would be disconnected. He drove on, past the turn-off in Camperdown, but the pebble in his pocket was like a hot coal that burned into his thoughts. Finally a voice arose in his head – or, to be more precise, reverberated in his chest, like a struck gong. It said, 'Go now. Go to Martin's place.'

He doubled back to the turn-off and drove through the labyrinth that is the back streets of Newtown. It was just on noon when he parked outside Martin's house and knocked on the front door. Silence. He knocked again, louder this time. No-one home. On impulse he tried the door. It was unlocked. He pushed it open and glanced into the front room. There, slumped on the floor in front of the couch, was Martin. His eyes were glazed in a dark stare, his shoulders were hunched; he had both arms clutched around his chest and his breathing was hoarse and shallow.

In his account to others of the events that followed Rick was mindful of not addressing the most remarkable aspect of his improbable intervention. He let it rest with whomever he was speaking to, left them to make of it whatever they chose. In that first moment he had knelt beside Martin, who by now was almost rigid, but he felt that Martin recognised him. 'It's Rick,' he said, uselessly, and fumbled for his phone.

In the ambulance he sat opposite the paramedic as they hurtled their way along Missenden Road to the Royal Prince Alfred. The medic was a woman in her mid-thirties with cropped black hair and muscular forearms. When she had arrived at the flat he had helped her raise Martin's t-shirt up around his neck so that she could apply the nodes of the ECG machine. Twelve nodes: he had counted them. She had asked Martin a series of questions but he had just stared at her, appearing to have lost the power of speech.

Rick had said almost nothing, but after they settled Martin in the ambulance, still upright, still in some feverish zone of his own, he had looked at her and, pointing to his own chest, mouthed the words, 'Heart attack?' At which she had given an almost imperceptible shake of her head and murmured, 'Don't think so.' Already she had rung ahead to the emergency unit, and before long they were at its doors and Martin was assisted into a wheelchair. The triage nurse signalled for him to be pushed into a resuscitation bay and Rick followed behind, into one of those curtained cells lined with machines. They lifted Martin onto the surgical bed and he winced with pain and looked deathly pale. A nurse began to set up an ECG and a young Indian doctor appeared, bleary-eyed with fatigue.

Rick felt in the way. There was only so much room in the cubicle and he was taking up too much of it. He asked the nurse what would happen next and she told him, brusquely, that Martin would be given tests, including blood tests, and it would be several hours before he could be moved to a ward. Was there anything, Rick asked, that he could do?

'Are you family?' she asked.

'No.'

'Well, best to advise them.'

It sounded ominous.

He walked out through the doors of the emergency bay, out into the sun, and hailed a taxi on Missenden Road. He would return to Martin's house, which he had absentmindedly left unlocked, not that there was anything worth stealing, and he would look for Martin's mobile, or an address book that might give clues as to family.

Once inside that dark space, the first thing he noticed was that the kitchen was almost bare. It told him that Martin could not have been back long, had not had time to settle in, or even to clean up, for the cockroaches had run rampant, their black dots of excrement scattered like malignant seeds.

In the bedroom he searched through Martin's things. There was an empty suitcase, some clothes hanging in a cupboard, a makeshift altar set up on a stool with a red silk cloth the size of a table napkin, a framed photograph of Martin's teacher and a glass mug filled with water and a single red geranium. On the floor was a thin futon mattress and beside it a small address book.

He seized on this with relief and looked under 'C'. The first name listed was a Susan Coleby and next to it a number with a Blue Mountains prefix. He rang the number but no-one answered.

He pocketed the address book and took the photograph of Martin's guru, with the intention of placing it beside Martin's hospital bed.

Then he rang Zoe and told her he would be late.

In the foyer of the hospital he re-dialled Susan Coleby's number. This time a woman answered.

For almost two hours he sat by Martin's bed in the emergency department, where they were waiting for the results of blood tests to establish whether Martin had had a heart attack. On present indications they thought not. Rick asked if he could wait until Martin's sister arrived and they said yes, and brought him a chair.

Martin was propped up in a sitting position with pillows on all sides, unable to lie down because the pain in his chest was excruciating and could only be relieved if he sat upright. In his own way he acknowledged Rick's presence, but, though conscious, he appeared to inhabit some internal space into which no-one could reach, a point of concentration, or pain, that could not or would not admit distraction.

It was just after six in the evening when Susan Coleby rang to say she was only minutes away. By this time a bed had been found for Martin in a general ward and Rick was sitting beside it. He said he would wait there until she arrived.

When Susan entered, white-faced and breathless, Martin was asleep, still propped upright in the only position that gave him ease. She stared for a moment at the pale figure in the bed, and moved to drape the stiff hospital sheet around his shoulders. Then she turned to Rick, and asked what he knew, and he told her the little information he had been given. Martin had not suffered a heart attack; he was afflicted with a severe form of pericarditis, a condition in which the membrane sac around the heart became inflamed and filled with fluid so that it rubbed abrasively against the heart muscle. 'It makes a creaking sound,' he said. 'That's how they diagnose it. That and the ECG and the fact that he can't lie down.'

'I've never heard of it.'

'They say it's most probably caused by a virus. They think he's had it for a while and neglected it. Probably thought it was pleurisy, or bronchitis.'

'Typical.' She was angry, and sank into a chair on the other side of the bed. '*Typical*,' she said again, and gave a deep sigh. 'Have they given you a prognosis?'

'They've given me very little because I'm not family. If you go to the nurse's station and tell them who you are they might find you a doctor.'

Susan was gone for some time. Everything in this place, he thought, was agonisingly slow. He was tired, and his back ached from sitting on hard plastic chairs. For five hours he had been a visitor in a human refuge of daunting wounds. In the brightly lit dungeon of the emergency room he had sat beside the dozing Martin and observed this strange otherworld of crisis, its strict hierarchies, its methodical protocols. The medical staff looked weary, as if they had been up all night, and he overheard a nurse saying it had been a tough weekend. Only the paramedics looked fresh: they were positively jaunty, strutting around in their fluorescent-striped uniforms like pirates who were looking forward to their next raid. But the disturbing thing had been the young man in the bed next to Martin's. Only a thin curtain separated them and Rick had eavesdropped on the conversation being conducted on the other side.

It soon became clear that the young man, a student, had razored his wrists. You've done this before, said the nurse, curtly. Yes, he replied. Do you have any razors on you now, any sharp instruments? Yes, he said, he had three razors in his wallet. Rick heard her call an orderly and tell him to remove the wallet from the boy's jacket. Rick listened with a taut, sick feeling, listened to the boy, who was softly spoken and polite. Thank you very much, he kept saying. Sorry about this. Thank you. No, he didn't hear voices. Yes, he had seen the uni counsellor. And the nurse, so matter-in-fact, sharp even. Your jacket's covered in blood, she said, you'll have to soak it in cold water when you get home. Then she walked off.

When, some time, later she came to check on him, the boy asked if his friend could come in from the waiting room and sit with him. Yes, she said. The voice of another young man was soon heard, and for the next forty-five minutes the stricken youth described in great detail a problem he had been having with a software program he was developing, and his friend listened and made sympathetic noises until Rick had an impulse to fling back the flimsy blue curtain and shout at them both in exasperation. Instead, he sat quietly and meditated on the boy. He was glad Martin was asleep.

Where was Susan? He was hungry; he'd had enough. He stood and looked out the window at the busy road below, and heard her voice behind him. 'It took them a while to find a doctor,' she said. 'It's hectic out there.' They were optimistic, she began. The tests showed a chronic condition of inflammation and excess of fluid around the heart, now in an acute stage. Martin had developed an arrhythmia and had trouble breathing. He was running a high temperature. He would need strong doses of anti-inflammatory drugs and complete rest for up to three months, possibly longer. She sighed. 'He hasn't been the same since he had the tumour removed,' she said. 'It was a rare one. Most people die of it, but not Martin.'

'How long will they keep him here?'

'On present indications, two weeks.'

'Then what?'

'He will live with me. After he's discharged.'

Rick was relieved. His mind had played out the options for Martin's convalescence and they were few. And Susan inspired confidence. He had already decided he liked her, liked her blunt way of speaking. She was a short, wiry woman in her early fifties with a strong physical resemblance to Martin and the same natural reserve.

On two occasions over the next fortnight they had coffee in the hospital café and he learned that Susan was divorced, with two adult children who lived interstate. She was the bursar at a high school in the Blue Mountains, where, luckily, as she put it, she had long-service leave owing and would take it in order to care for her brother. He said he imagined it would be onerous for her to be a full-time carer without assistance, and asked if arrangements could not be made for a private nurse to come in and occasionally relieve her. He said he would be happy to contribute to the cost.

'Thank you,' she said, 'but we will manage.'

He liked that 'we'. Perhaps she had inherited her stoicism from the Major.

Most evenings he visited Martin on his way home from work and, oddly, he looked forward to these visits. Martin was in a four-bed ward with three much older men, one of whom coughed incessantly, but it didn't matter for he was enclosed in a deep exhaustion and not inclined to speak. He had lost weight, was pale and skeletal, his eyes both dark and dulled. The medication made him nauseous; on several occasions his blood pressure plummeted to dangerous levels and he fainted, though never when Rick was there. Rick did not linger on these visits but would sit beside him for fifteen minutes and meditate.

One evening, as he sat with his eyes closed, he recalled with a sudden jolt how he had once sat by his brother's bed, and it was as if a familiar current had surged through his veins. History repeats itself, he thought, and said it to himself again: history repeats itself. But with repetition the words lost their charge. No, it did not; it did not repeat itself. It could not, because he was different now, and this was different, and he thought of the pebble Sri Mata had given him. He had made no mention of this to Martin, imagining that in his current state he would not have cared how it was that Rick came to knock on his door that Sunday morning. Perhaps he had not even registered the uncanny coincidence of Rick's being there. Nor had Susan. As she knew nothing of his history with

Martin, she had not thought to ask about his presence.

But there were some things that Martin did seem able to acknowledge. On Rick's first visit he had glanced in the direction of his guru's photograph. One of the nurses had moved it out of the way, to a shelf on the wall, and Martin had looked over to it, then back to Rick, and smiled ruefully.

Susan was still unable to discover how Martin had been able to return to his old rental, or why; he had always maintained contact with her but mostly with quirky messages that said little about his domestic arrangements. Like most men, she said, he never spoke of such things, assuming they were of no interest.

Rick asked her how she felt about the life her brother had chosen.

She shrugged. 'He's very like our father,' she said. 'Single-minded. They're both warrior types, if you know what I mean.'

He did.

~

One Saturday in early spring he drove up to Susan's house in Katoomba. It was a white weatherboard bungalow from the Federation era, set on the high side of the street with wooden steps that led up to an unruly native garden. Susan ushered him along a dark hallway to a bright, enclosed sunroom that ran along the back of the house. Here Martin was propped up in a cane chair.

They shook hands and he seemed pleased that Rick had come but it was a strange, muted afternoon for it was an effort still for Martin to speak – either that or he was disinclined. Susan made coffee and sat watchfully beside Rick; she seemed protective, concerned that Martin not be fatigued by visitors. Rick took the hint and mostly directed his conversation to her. From time to time Martin would nod at something they said but then he would lay his head against the rim of the high-backed chair and doze. His exhaustion was palpable.

As Rick was leaving, Susan walked him to the front door. He could see that she was weary. Martin's appetite was poor, she said. He slept a great deal during the day but was restless at night. Once she had been woken in the night by a thump, and when she rose to check on him, found he had fallen out of bed and was sitting on the floor trying to meditate in the lotus position, his left leg twisted awkwardly. She had struggled to help him back into bed and he had grown angry and ordered her to leave the room. She had dark circles under her eyes.

He asked Susan if she had managed to discover why Martin had returned so unexpectedly to Sydney. Yes, she said, he had sublet his house to another man who was supposed to take over his classes, but the man had been summoned home to Singapore on the death of his father. Martin had flown in for just a few days to settle the lease. She didn't ask Rick why he had appeared at Martin's door that Sunday morning when he believed Martin still to be in New Zealand. If he had not turned up when he did, Martin might not have survived the next twenty-four hours. Rick had been the agent of a small miracle and no-one wanted to know.

On the second Saturday, Martin again dozed for much of Rick's visit. But on the third Saturday he was more animated and ate a thin slice of Susan's cake. His appetite had improved, she said, though not by much. Rick wanted to show him the pebble Sri Mata had given him, and ask Martin what he made of it, but something told him it was not the right time. They spoke of the birds in the garden, Martin in halting phrases. And this was to become a ritual, week by week, this sitting and observing the birds. A pair of gang-gang cockatoos might descend to feed noisily in the trees, or currawongs come scavenging on the lawn with their brazen strut and bright yellow eye. Occasionally they would hear a lyrebird – at least, they thought it was a lyrebird, but since it often mimicked the calls of other birds it was impossible to be sure.

On those early visits, Susan would join them. One afternoon, when a magpie came pecking in the grass, she said, 'Did you know that only the adult magpie is allowed to sing?'

Rick had looked at her blankly.

'I mean,' she continued, 'the young males are not permitted to sing in the company of the adults. They have to go away somewhere on their own and practise. If they don't, their throats fail to develop in the way that they need to so that they can sing when they mature.'

'Sounds like a lonely apprenticeship,' he offered.

'Well, if they can't sing as adults, they can't mate.'

'At least they sing,' he said, in one of those polite non-sequiturs she drew from him, 'unlike the wattle-birds that squawk.'

Martin had turned his head towards them and said, through chafed lips, 'I like that squawk.'

Susan had looked at Rick. 'He would,' she said. 'Always the difficult cases, always the lame ducks . . .'

She often spoke in this way, nervously, and he wished she would leave them alone. He felt that she didn't trust him not to burden Martin with his own anxieties. 'My brother has made a sacrifice of himself,' she had said to him one afternoon in the hospital coffee-shop, and he sensed her determination that no-one would now sap Martin's strength.

He could not tell whether Martin was indeed recovering, or even what it was that he was recovering from. The inflammation around his heart had subsided and the pain in his chest was gone. But the fatigue remained and he seemed withdrawn. Wherever he was, thought Rick, he was where he needed to be, and he took a strange comfort in Martin's silence. In Sydney Park they had talked so much, and at times so urgently, that it could not go on indefinitely, and in this weekly hour when they said very little to one another he was prepared to settle for a more subtle intimacy.

At the end of the fourth week, Zoe expressed a desire to accompany him on his next visit to Martin. It took him by surprise. At first he was pleased, and then anxious that Martin might find her visit intrusive. She was a stranger to him, and though she had never expressed any hostility towards Martin, she remained sceptical – not that Rick had ever mentioned her teasing remarks.

On the Saturday morning he was ill at ease and just a little over-anxious to please. Sure, they could have lunch at that restaurant in Leura and drop in on her friend Cassie. But really he didn't want to do any of that, was impatient with the very idea of it. His visits to Martin were a ritual, and like any ritual should be unvaried and without interruption. On several occasions he had invited Zoe to come with him on Sunday mornings and meditate with Sri Mata and she had rolled her eyes, or said, 'Give it away, Rick. That's your thing, not mine,' or words to that effect. Why now did she want to be part of this? Was she checking up on him?

By the time they reached Katoomba he was on edge. He had endured a ridiculously expensive lunch, and Cassie's husband had been boorish: hearty and effusive one minute, rude the next, full of an unfocused anger that men of a certain age tended to exude. When they arrived at Susan's house they found her in the front garden, pruning the low branches of a clump of young ribbon gums, and she waved her shears at them and said she would be in soon to make tea. Rick led Zoe through the dark hallway to the sunroom, hoping Martin would be awake, and he was. He looked up as they entered and smiled.

'My wife, Zoe,' said Rick, sounding, he thought, pompous and unnecessarily formal.

Zoe put out her hand to shake Martin's and he studied it for a moment. Then he took it in both of his, and kissed it. It was a gesture so touching, so graceful and above all so natural that Rick felt his irritability melt away. It was not the practised kiss of male gallantry but a form of humble salute, and Zoe, he saw, had tears in her eyes. Her gaze locked onto Martin's until he gestured for her to sit down, at which point, slightly fazed, she looked around for a chair and sat demurely opposite him.

For the next hour Martin spoke with her as if he had never been ill, was not now convalescent, had no difficulty breathing and was receiving an old friend. They spoke of the hospital (Zoe had once worked there), of New Zealand, of the garden and of the birdlife of the mountains. Rick was reminded that his wife had been a social worker and that she knew how to speak to someone who was, or had been, unwell; she didn't talk too much, didn't ask too many questions, wasn't afraid of long pauses.

On the drive home they said almost nothing to one another. There was no need. But as they pulled up outside the house, Zoe turned to him. 'Do you think Martin will recover?'

'Well, the doctors say there is no reason why he shouldn't.'

'What will he do then?'

'I haven't asked him. Susan says he's determined to return to Auckland. That's what his guru instructed him to do so that's what he'll do. For a monk, obedience is everything.'

She smiled. 'No chance of you ever becoming a monk, then.'

'Never on the cards.' He laughed, but felt a pang. It was a heroic life, of a kind, and he didn't have the . . . the what? What did it take? He didn't know, and the very fact of not knowing made it opaque to him. And the loneliness, he thought, must be acute, unless somehow you were able to live as the consort of an invisible lover, whatever that meant – though he had some apprehension of what it might mean, if only in the way of looking down the wrong end of a telescope at a speck on the far horizon.

'Rick?'

He realised that he was sitting, distracted, with his hand still on the ignition key. He removed it and leaned across to kiss his wife on the cheek. 'I'm glad you came today,' he said.

~

On the sixth Saturday Susan met him at her front door in a state of agitation. Her pregnant daughter in Rockhampton had gone into premature labour, there were complications and she needed to fly north.

His offer of before lay unspoken between them. 'I can arrange for Martin to have a nurse,' he said. 'Live-in.'

'Can you afford this?' she asked bluntly, as if he might be some confidence man given to rash promises he couldn't fulfil. But then, he reflected, she knew almost nothing about him.

'Yes,' he said. In the overall scheme of things it was not a significant amount of money, and she, Sri Mata, had entrusted him with Martin, so how could he not?

'He's bloody-minded. He'll say he can look after himself.'

But in the event he didn't, which perhaps indicated how weak he still felt. He accepted the proposition with surprising detachment, as if it had not come from Rick but from someone else. And this pleased Rick: he was released from any position of patronage, or role of do-gooder. They were just pieces on a chessboard. Life was living them both and they were its servants.

That night, on advice from Zoe, he rang a private nursing agency. Arrangements were made and a young man, Raoul Martinez, arrived at Susan's house early the next morning. It was a Sunday, and on the Monday Rick took a day off and drove up to see that things were in order.

Immediately he entered the house he felt more at ease, released from Susan's anxious gate-keeping. Raoul was thickset, and Rick could see that he would have no trouble lifting Martin if he fell. Raoul too had shaved his head, and he and Martin looked like monks together. Rick remarked on this and Raoul laughed and said, 'Not me, I'm married. And besides,' he added, 'I like my food. No fasting, señor. Every day a feast day.' There was something fleshy and expansive about Raoul, but above all he was cheerful.

Rick thought he ought to begin by making it clear that it was he and not Susan who was Raoul's employer and that he would expect regular reports on Martin's care.

Raoul held his arms out wide and laughed. 'Of course,' he said, 'of course.'

He had a Latin charm about him and was not anyone's idea of a nurse. While Martin was sleeping he made Rick coffee and told him that his parents had emigrated from Chile when he was a child. As a young man he had trained as a paediatric nurse but the death of a ten-year-old girl had affected him badly; the parents had blamed him, had turned on him in their grief, and after that he had given it away. Now he worked on a casual basis for the agency and was taking private art classes. He had brought with him his paints and an easel, and had set them up in the sunroom, though not, he explained, with oils, since the fumes could be toxic. He said that his patient liked to watch him work; and that although Martin offered no comment, he appeared to be following every stroke of the brush with rapt attention.

Rick was satisfied: Raoul was a gift.

Each Saturday he drove up to the edge of the great escarpment, to the little town with its steep High Street, its grand old hotel, its famous lookout and its air of wintry desperation. Perched on a plateau a thousand metres above sea level, it looked out over the deep ravine of the Megalong Valley, and there was one day when a low mist filled the valley and the town looked as if it were floating on a cloud.

In the past he had thought of Katoomba as gloomy but now he began to look forward to arriving at Susan's cottage. He would drive up, wanting to talk to Martin about what was happening in his meditation but knowing he would restrain himself when he arrived. And perhaps because of this he had begun of late to talk instead to her, Sri Mata; had begun to conduct long internal dialogues with the diamond in his chest. And in some oblique way she answered him, so that he would come out of these silent raves having intuited the essence of what at that moment he needed to know.

One day it occurred to him that Martin's silence might have to do with forcing his acolyte into this very process of internalising, of communicating with the source. Or was this mere vanity, the idea that whatever Martin did might in any way be for his, Rick's, benefit? The answer was irrelevant because the process was liberating. I have become like some kind of evangelical, he told himself, the kind that is forever talking to Jesus.

This drive from the city soon became a time of recollection. Incidents would come to him that had lain buried in his unconscious for decades, and of these the most vivid was a moment of panic that had ambushed him as a boy of six. It was a school day and he had jumped off a train because it was about to take him beyond his home station. He had never been further along the line, and who knew where it led, and how would he return home? He had been daydreaming and had rushed to the door of his carriage, which in the old trains could be wrenched open, and had leaped from the moving train onto the last few metres of platform. Luckily, he had been in the last carriage and the train was not yet clear of the station. The stationmaster had seen him jump and ran to him while he sat there on the concrete surface, unhurt but for his right knee, badly grazed. And now, he reflected, he was on some other train, only this time he was staying put.

It was during this period that something in him shifted and he began to feel as if he and Martin were leading the one life. If he had said as much, he knew it would sound facile since it was not he who was suffering, not he who spoke through strained lips, whose heart raced out of kilter, who still could not shower unaided. Often, said Raoul, Martin would stumble, as if his feet had little or no traction on the floor, no anchorage in gravity.

As for Rick, he had never felt more grounded, and yet he could only register that this was how things were, that he was one half of Martin's dilemma.

Now and then in his meditation he would see that he was irrevocably bound to Martin by an invisible cable; it appeared in his mind's eye as a long rope in the form of a double helix, and while he might go hours without thinking of Martin, that cable swayed between them, a vibration that animated both their bodies. He did not speak of this to anyone since it was too peculiar a state of being when spoken of, even as, in his everyday experience of it, it could not have been more mundane.

On the Saturday before Susan was due to return, on impulse he took the pebble Sri Mata had given him out of the drawer in his desk and put it in his pocket. The time had come; Martin was visibly brighter and he would present it to him as a gift. Over the past ten weeks they had said very little to one another, nor felt the need. It was not a common symptom of pericarditis, even in the most dire cases, for the patient to lose speech, yet Martin had been bound into long periods of silence. But that was fine. Rick had felt not the least slight in this, indeed had intuited that silence was an essential condition of Martin's recovery. It had suited them both just to sit and look out onto the garden, where he was able now to identify each tree, the black sassafras as well as the drooping she-oak, the cedar wattle alongside the brazen banksia.

When he arrived he settled into his chair in the sunroom and took the pebble out of his pocket. He held it out to Martin, who looked at it, nodded silently, but didn't reach for it.

Rick leaned across, took hold of Martin's right hand and very deliberately pressed the pebble into his palm.

Then, feeling pleased with himself, like a child who fancies he has a good story to tell, he explained how he came by it.

'Why did she send this to you?' Rick asked.

Martin gave his crooked smile. 'She didn't,' he said, with a grimace. 'It's for you. It's for you, Rick. She's *your* teacher, not mine. Any message from her is for you, not me.'

'But she said it was for you.'

'If I heard you correctly, she said it was for "your friend". *You* made the assumption it was for me.'

'It seemed obvious. At the time.'

'Yes. But maybe there was a little more going on there.'

'More?'

Martin was silent, and looked out to the garden where a wind was whipping up the she-oaks so that they gave off their mysterious hum. Finally he said, 'Maybe she wants you to think about who your "friend" is.'

'Meaning?'

'Meaning not *just* me.'

'Not just you?'

'There are others.'

Who were these others? Rick would have liked to ask but he didn't. This, he knew, was for him to find out. First he would look after Martin, and then those others might present themselves. Would he recognise them when they did? Yes, he would. *She* would see to it.

Martin was looking at him indulgently, like he was a favourite pupil but a slow learner. Then he held out his right hand with the pebble nestled in his palm, and it was clear that he wanted Rick to take the pebble from him.

Just then Raoul appeared in the doorway. 'I've made chilli,' he said. 'I make the best. Would you like to eat with us, Rick?'

'Thanks, but better not.' He would leave them to it. What an odd pair they were, the ascetic and the sensualist. And their third party, him, who was neither, just a fixer in the world, the very person that as a youth he had determined not to be.

He rose from his chair, leaned down to Martin, took the pebble and slipped it into his pocket. They shook hands as they always did when he was about to leave. How dry Martin's skin was, papery and taut, and often it felt hot, as if he were burning. Rick stifled an impulse to kiss the crown of his head, grey stubble that failed to conceal the livid suture that ran like a battle wound along the side of his skull.

Nine lives, he had once said. I have nine lives.

When Rick turned to follow Raoul into the hallway, Martin called after him. 'Rick?'

He looked back.

'I don't believe I've thanked you.'

He laughed, and shook his head. Of course Martin hadn't thanked him. It was unnecessary, and they both knew why.

Raoul saw him to the front door. 'You could always stay overnight,' he said. 'I forget to tell you. Before she left, Mrs Coleby said it would be okay.'

'Thanks, but no.' It had never occurred to him. He would not impose on Martin in that way; it would be entirely the wrong kind of intimacy. But the proposal gave birth to an impulse. It was a long weekend; Zoe was at a conference in Brisbane and Luke at a sleepover. There was no rush to get home. The last time he had spent a night in the Blue Mountains had been over two decades ago, and on the drive to Katoomba he had passed near the resort where as a young man he had been part of that crazy corporate abseiling jag. He could not see the hotel from the road but many times had registered the sign beside the freeway, and the turn-off to where it lay among dense bush on the rim of the Jamison Valley. Here he had failed some kind of test, had hung against the cliff-face like a stuck pendulum.

He decided to spend the night there.

It was just after four when he pulled into the grand circular driveway lined with dwarf she-oaks. The car park was almost full, and a black limousine idled outside the main entrance with a white ribbon attached to its bonnet.

'You're in luck,' said the clerk at the desk. 'We've got a wedding tonight and there's only one room left.'

Since he had no luggage, he pocketed his room keys and returned to the front garden. He had decided to walk to the look-out. He remembered the path and had time to catch the last of the evening light. It was only a short distance through stands of ti-tree and banksias, and within minutes he was on the small rock plat-form that jutted out over the cliff edge. And it was all just as he remembered it.

He stood with his arms braced on the steel fence and looked down into the purple depths below, canyons of eucalypt and moun-tain ash.

By now the golden stone along the cliffs was deepening into a burnished flame-coloured red; the grandeur of it was exhilarating. And yet, just two weeks before, a student had fallen to his death from this same lookout, the horror of his fate compounded by the possibility that he might have jumped. And that man, he thought, might once have been me.

Below him in the valley some rock-climbers were completing their ascent of the eastern cliff-face. Locked on to the rock like giant stick-insects; they moved with excruciating slowness; the intensity of their focus could be felt even at a distance. The narrow rope that connected them was barely visible but the late sun glinted off their white helmets with such a dazzling flash that for a moment they appeared to him as a party of luminous pilgrims, scaling the face of an unknown god.

For a long time he continued to stand there, gazing out across the deepening hues of the escarpment, until he became aware that a shadow had begun to creep over the valley. Soon it would be dark, and he must turn back. Halfway along the track, he reached into his pocket and felt for the pebble. He had been certain that it was intended for Martin, but no, Martin insisted it was for him. So he was none the wiser; just when he thought he had a fix on things, the smallest and most inert of objects could throw him off balance. There was more to come, and the riddle was not yet unravelled.

When he emerged from the narrow track the grand dining room was lit up, its chandeliers ablaze. French doors opened onto the terrace and he could see waiters darting among chairs swathed in white satin bows and tables set with flowers and purple helium balloons.

Because he was the only houseguest not attached to the wedding they offered him an early meal in the old red-velvet bar, small and womb-like. There he sat in a quiet corner and drank himself into a daze. The muted sound of revellers wafted in from the dining room until at last the band struck up a brassy fanfare, followed by a round of excited applause.

Now he was tired. He walked to the east wing, down a long corridor of red carpet patterned in dark blue diamonds. His room was at the very end and looked out onto the smoky blue depths of a canyon.

When he entered the room he felt a thin shaft of terror strike him between the shoulder blades, felt he had opened the door into a void and teetered now on the brink. With one arm he braced himself against the wall, and as swiftly as the dizziness had come over him it subsided.

Slowly he undressed, and stood for a long time under a blissfully hot shower so that the billow of steam enveloped him and the water washed away his fear. Now he would like to meditate, but he had drunk too much. He lay on the bed and rang Luke to check that he was okay. Then he rang Zoe and they talked for over an hour.

'What on earth are you doing there?' she asked. 'Something to do with abseiling,' he said, and realised he had never told her about his pendulum experience. 'I'll explain when I see you,' he added; it was too intimate to go into over the wire. 'It's alright,' he said, 'I'm in a good place. Tell me about the conference.'

He thought that afterward he would fall asleep instantly, but instead he drifted pleasantly on the threshold of oblivion. When at last he did sleep he dreamed that he was in the midst of a wedding. It was midday and the wedding guests wore bright clothes and stood about in a field of dry wheat. The sun was high overhead and gave off a searing white light, and as he walked among the sunstruck crowd it came to him: *I am the bridegroom.*

Well, then, he must hurry and take his place, and he made his way to the front, and stood there with his back to the others. He looked down and saw that his feet were bare, and his pockets weighted with pebbles. He could not see his bride but knew that she lingered on the path behind him, an ethereal presence, a column of light, a promise. He stood still, he waited on her arrival, he could not see her but he knew that she approached . . .